A DECK STACKED FOR MURDER

A CAFE ARCANA MYSTERY

BOOK 1

ALIZA LEVINE

For Lisa—my dear, dear friend.

*You were the Queen of Swords, but you were also the Empress and,
most of all, Strength.*

*I'm so glad we found each other that November day at Eisley library.
I wouldn't be the same me without you.*

1

Just after six in the morning, Ava Goldberg rumbled down the gravel road from her late grandfather's farmhouse into the little town of Shiloh, Nebraska. A mishmash of thoughts rumbled through her mind as well. She couldn't have asked for better weather on the opening day of her new cafe, but the card she'd snatched out of the mailbox ten minutes prior to mounting her bicycle still had her reeling.

A slight chill still hung in the early June air, the dew beading the tall grass of the ditches. Cornfields lined the horizon on her left, and a pale pink sunrise glowed behind the quaint little buildings as they came into view. As she made her way down the bumpy Main Street cobblestones, surveying the line of shop windows she had yet to visit, Ava took in the shimmer of the plaza fountain. Its cool waters usually glimmered with piles of coins tossed in by idealistic townsfolk looking to snag a wish, but this morning she could see all the way to the mosaicked bottom. If only she felt as unruffled as that cool blue water.

Ava jerked her bike to a stop with a squeeze of the handbrakes. Why was she still *thinking* about that card? Today was what she'd waited for, the first day of her new life, the reason she'd emptied her savings and moved to Shiloh: Cafe Arcana was finally opening. The day she'd been counting down to had arrived, and here she was, letting a thoughtless card from her thoughtless mother ruin the day. She shouldn't have checked the mail on her way out.

Get a grip, Ava. She hopped off her bicycle and gave a sharp heel to the kickstand. Threading her bike lock around a lamppost, which still sported the red, white, and blue buntings of last weekend's Memorial Day parade, she stood for a moment on the edge of the sidewalk. From her back jeans pocket, Ava pulled out the unopened, now crumpled card. The words were still there on the envelope, the handwriting menacingly perfect.

Mrs. Ava Shapiro

Ugh. She wanted to vomit. The card was from her mother —the handwriting and return address left no doubt. But why Sara Goldberg had addressed a card to her very much divorced daughter, who had very much legally changed her last name back, was a different story. Ripping open the card and scanning the brief note of congratulations and good luck her mother had signed on behalf of both parents, Ava hardly noticed the actual words she'd written. This same woman had declared that Ava was making a mistake in finalizing her divorce and was throwing her life away by moving to Shiloh. If it weren't for the blatant affront of the address, Ava might have thought her mother had reconsidered and really *did* wish her good luck—she'd seemed more supportive in the recent handful of phone calls they'd had. But addressing the card to *Mrs. Ava Shapiro*? If that's how Sara Goldberg was going to play the game, she could keep her *mazel tovs* and stick them up her—

"Morning, Ava!"

A cheery voice jolted Ava out of her thoughts. She shielded her eyes, sunglasses and all, to peer at the jovial figure who she recognized by now as Tim Meyer, the owner of the town's art gallery and her shop's next-door neighbor, bustling down the sidewalk toward her. She managed a rigid smile. The hearty greetings, constant grinning, and friendly waves were something she hadn't yet gotten used to since moving to Shiloh, and it wasn't what she needed this morning. The transition from Illinois to Nebraska hadn't exactly been a culture shock, but from what she had seen so far, these small-town folks operated on a whole other level of friendly—one she honestly wasn't sure she liked—compared to the big city residents of Chicago. It was bad enough having her parents' temple friends murmur platitudes, let alone a whole town of well-meaning do-gooders. The last thing she wanted was for people to try setting her up with young, eligible farmers. So far, she was doing a good job of lying low. She'd have to stick to it.

"Morning." Ava hoped her curt nod appeared friendly, but not inviting. She stuffed the card back into her jeans pocket.

"Opening day, right?" Tim flashed her a wide grin. He slowed to a stop and gave Ava a hearty clap on the back. She tried not to grimace.

"Right," Ava said. She prayed he wasn't looking for a stop-and-chat.

Tim ran a hand through his wiry, swooped-back hair, his grin unwavering. "It's gonna go great. We've never had a coffee shop in town. Trust me, they'll be beating down your door."

"I hope so." Ava offered him a weak smile. Her grandfather

had always talked about how *nice* the people in Shiloh were. Their genuine kindness was a little disarming.

"Well, I won't keep you. I'm sure you've got lots to do," Tim said. He winked, already starting back toward his gallery. "If you need anything, let me know. I'm just next door."

"Thanks," Ava called after him. The enthusiastic tone of her own voice made her cringe.

With Tim safely in his gallery, Ava let out her breath, relieved at not having to think up fodder for yet another vague but chummy conversation. How had her grandparents done it —all this *socializing*? Back in the early '80s, before Ava and her brother were born, her paternal grandfather, Melvin Goldberg, had taken a job as professor of Judaic Studies at the university of Nebraska-Lincoln. Although the Jewish community in the surrounding towns was sparse, Ava's grandparents —or, as she called them, her zaidy and bubbe—had settled down in Shiloh and fallen in love with it, opting to live out the rest of their old age in cornfield-laced simplicity. Ava's grandmother had died when Ava was young, leaving few memories of her bubbe. But nearly all the memories Ava had of Zaidy Melvin were from Shiloh: bicycling through Larkspur State Park in summer, rambling through the pastures bursting with orange and red in fall, the whole extended family packed around the seder table inside the old farmhouse he'd made his home.

Ava's mother claimed Melvin had stayed in Shiloh even after Bubbe Lucille's death because he didn't want the old biddies at his home synagogue in the Chicago suburbs trying to set him up with one of their so-called matches, but Ava had never believed that. Zaidy Mel had known the magic of the prairie, and he'd passed his love on to her, along with his farmhouse. And now here she was, back in town, and setting up shop—literally.

Cafe Arcana had taken a hefty chunk of her already dwindling divorce settlement, but it was the labor of love Ava had poured herself into nearly as soon as the judge banged his gavel. God knew she wasn't getting help from her parents—not with her mother so staunchly set against the endeavor. But with the judge's ruling had come one of her own: If she wanted to put the jagged pieces of her life back together, she would have to get out of Chicago. And so, she had come here—to Shiloh—with a single U-Haul bumping along down I-80 behind her dingy little Honda Civic.

Ava's hand found her pocket again. Her fingers slid past the offending envelope and came to rest on a cool, familiar smoothness. She'd been ten when Zaidy Mel had given her the hunk of polished lapis lazuli she now carried with her everywhere she went. She'd entered the living room to find him working on a mosaic, a representation of the breastplates the *Cohanim*, the ancient Israelite high priests, would have worn. As she knelt beside him on the floor, sifting through the twelve stones that stood for the twelve tribes of Israel, a stone of radiant blue flecked with electrifying gold enthralled her. Lapis lazuli, her grandfather had called it. Known to their ancestors as *sappir*—sapphire—and representative of the tribe of Issachar. He'd pressed it into her palm, probably thinking it would end up stashed away in an attic next to her Barbie dolls and plastic purses. But Ava had held on to the stone, always gathering a sort of strength from it, and now she carried it with her always, a constant reminder of Zaidy Mel.

Letting the hunk of lapis lazuli slip from her fingers and settle back down into her pocket, Ava gave her storefront a quick once-over before she headed inside. The rustic handi-work of her shop's sign brought the entire storefront together in a delicate air of delicious mystery that was perfect for a tarot cafe. Sandwiched between Tim's gallery and a chic Instagram-worthy wine bar, and only a block away from the Shiloh town plaza where the mosaicked fountain looked like something out of a magazine, Cafe Arcana's location was prime real estate. And somehow, the rent for the place had been doable. According to local lore, the building that housed Arcana was the site of a grisly murder back in the 1960s, making most native residents hesitant to set up shop in the place. But none of that bothered Ava. Her own history was far from rosy, and she was in Shiloh to make a new start for herself. She may as well help the building get a new start, too. And god, it was beautiful. She'd just have to be sure her mother never caught wind of the stories, or a misaddressed card would be the least of Ava's worries.

Ava swung the heavy wooden door open and slipped inside, relishing the inviting jingle of the doorbell she'd placed on top. It took a moment for her eyes to adjust to the cozy dimness of the cafe. She was proud of the work she'd done with the decor, staying true to the rustic feel of the exposed brick walls by adding in a touch of darkness to keep any country cottage vibes at bay. God knew there were enough of those stores on Shiloh's main street. Cafe Arcana was to be Ava's new start—not the manifestation of a college girl's Pinterest board.

The counter in front of the espresso bar was built of polished cherry wood, which matched the moldings at the base of the walls. The east wall, the only one that wasn't brick, was papered in a deliciously dark fleur-de-lis pattern, contrasting with the naked lightbulbs that dangled over the espresso bar and gave the entire place a modern feel. In the back corner stood a wood-burning stove, a tapestried rug placed before it and cozy, tall-backed armchairs circled around. Stately bookcases, their shelves full of delicate vintage tomes, lined the back wall, waiting for the winter's day when passersby would come off the street, select a book, and curl up in front of the stove with a hot cup of joe. Yes, she'd spent a small fortune, but Arcana was hers in a way that her previous life never had been. Ava sniffed. *Mazel tov to me.*

Ava ripped the envelope from her mother out of her pocket and, tearing the entire card into satisfying shreds, stuffed it into the garbage can. The cafe would open at eight o'clock, and Riley, her sole employee, was to arrive at seven. Although two weeks of training hadn't made the teenager a coffee master, Ava was confident they could pull things off. Today had to go *well*— especially given that she'd chosen the date of Arcana's grand opening to distract herself from what the day had meant in previous years. She wasn't just papering over the cracks; she was rebuilding from the ground up. And what better day on which to start it all than her now defunct anniversary? No longer would this date be a commemoration of her failed marriage, a reminder of a double betrayal by two people who— *no.* She wouldn't think about that. She'd spent long enough thinking about *only* that. No, from here on out, this date would commemorate a *new* anniversary. A new chapter—and a successful one. Cafe Arcana had to be *perfect.*

But for that, she'd need another cup of coffee. Ava pressed a portafilter beneath the grinder, breathed in the heavenly aroma of freshly ground beans, and deftly tamped down the shot. As she slid the portafilter into the espresso machine, the doorbell jingled.

"Hey," Riley said, flashing a quick two-fingered salute at Ava. She dropped her book bag in a heap on one of the nearby tables and stood blinking from behind a wisp of blue tinted hair. "I'm not late, right?"

Ava glanced at the clock on the far wall. "Nope. Right on time."

The espresso machine gurgled as dark, silky coffee streamed into Ava's shot glass. As soon as the shot dripped to a stop, Ava added a dash of hot milk to it, locking in the full-bodied flavor she loved. Some liked the taste of espresso as it oxidized, but for her, the velvety richness of the freshly brewed shot was best. She sipped her espresso, leaning back against the counter and closing her eyes in bliss. Now, *that* was perfection.

"Uh..." Riley's voice cut into her reverie. "What's all this torn up paper?"

Ava's eyes flew open. Riley was standing over the garbage can, one nail-bitten hand hovering dangerously close to the shreds of Ava's mother's card.

"Nothing." Ava slammed her shot glass onto the counter and all but shoved Riley out of the way. She grabbed an empty bag of espresso beans off the counter and chucked it into the trash. "Just an ad. You know, those newspaper inserts. Hate them."

"Right." Riley raised an eyebrow. Crossing her arms, she stood gazing at Ava. "Anyway, what should I start with?"

Thank god. That card was the last thing Ava wanted to discuss this morning. She downed the rest of her espresso, flashing Riley a tight smile. "That's the spirit! Let's start by weighing out the beans for the day. I want to make sure we have enough ready to go in case we get any long lines." She hoped there *would* be long lines.

"We'll do the Colombian as our medium roast," Ava called over her shoulder as she grabbed the chalkboard easel she kept in the back supply room. "And for dark, let's go with the Yirgacheffe. I'll let you pick the flavor, how's that?"

Riley slapped a scale on the counter. "Cinnamon."

"Great. Cinnamon it is!"

Riley looked bored now, the expression in her eyes unchanging. Without a word, she strode to the back cupboard and began pulling bags of beans down onto the counter. Ava finally let her insides unclench in relief. What was it with the Gen Z kids, anyway—too much Billie Eilish? Riley might be moody, but she was also diligent—and knew when to stop asking questions. Ava couldn't complain. From here on out, her life would be her own and everything would go down as smoothly as that freshly brewed shot of espresso.

At least, she *hoped* that's what the cards held in store.

2

———————

Almost an hour later, Ava and Riley had finished their preparations; they'd weighed the beans, wiped the tables, straightened the chairs, rearranged the bookshelves, and plated the three dozen cookies Ava had baked the night before. Her attempts to source a baker had so far come up short, and she hoped no one would chip a tooth on her own subpar baking efforts. Ava's mother's card had *almost* faded from mind, but she still couldn't shake her nerves. She needed reassurance, something small to hold in her mind throughout the day. An intention perhaps.

The percolator stopped its puttering. Ava slid the final urn out from under the machine, flipped the top closed, and carried the steaming metal container to its stand at the counter. With only one more pot of coffee to brew, there was time for a quick tarot spread; hopefully, it'd give a brief glimmer of wisdom she could take with her into the day.

Rummaging through her handbag, Ava fished out a small velvety sachet and slid into a chair at one of the round wooden tables that littered the room. She could feel Riley's eyes on her back, but she pretended not to notice. The girl had seemed rather taken with the cards as she and Ava set up shop the past couple of weeks, even asking once or twice to skim through Ava's deck, but right now, Ava wanted to concentrate. Untying the satin cord that held the sachet closed, she extracted a worn deck of cards and began to shuffle them. The familiar feel of the cards in her hands, the softness of the edges as her fingers flipped through them, was comforting. Ava cut the deck three times and placed each pile one on top of the other. She closed her eyes and drew a deep breath, gathering in her focus. It was just her and the cards, her and... herself. Ava drew the top card and flipped it over. She laid the card down, stared wide-eyed, and let out a low whistle.

Death.

Well, that's starting off with a bang.

Ava gave a small chuckle, shaking her head in confused curiosity. Her fingers smoothed the surface of the card, as though its energy would seep into her skin and tell her what it meant to say. A skeleton in armor sat atop a white steed, stepping over and through a field strewn with corpses. Below him was a young woman, begging the skeleton to spare her life. But, as everyone alive knows, death is simply a part of the cycle, and no one is immune.

Had Ava been a novice reader, she might have thought the Death card signified impending, well, death. Either for herself —god forbid—or, taken more metaphorically, for her shop. Not quite the message you'd want to get on opening day. But having studied the cards for almost two decades, Ava knew the chances of this card signifying actual loss of life were rare. More likely, she reasoned, the "passing on" nature of the card pointed toward the death of her marriage and her recent "rebirth" as a single, independent woman. *The cycle of life in motion.* However, if she'd turned over The Fool card, it might have been more logical, since it represented new beginnings. But that could—

A rap sounded on the shop window. Ava glanced up, a bit startled, her expression softening at the beaming face of the pixie-like woman waving through the glass. The door swung open, and in strolled Rose Robinson, Ava's childhood friend from her summers spent in Shiloh. Rose carried a round-eyed, golden-haired baby strapped to her chest.

"Yikes," Rose said, pulling the door shut behind her with a huff. Her round, porcelain cheeks held a flush of color. "Nearly broke my ankle out there. Someone's going to trip and break their neck one of these days if the city doesn't do something about those stupid cobblestones."

Ava glanced out the window. Red and brown stones worn smooth with time and set in powder gray concrete provided a frame of nostalgia to the street. "They're so pretty, though."

Rose was right—the streets looked rather uneven—but it added to the rustic charm of the town.

"Speaking of pretty," Rose cut in, finally taking in the cozy array of colorful books and the flash of shiny machinery behind the counter. With each energetic whip of her head, her flaxen curls bounced. "*Look* at this place. It's gorgeous!"

"Thanks," Ava said. She gave her a friend a small smile. "I think the lights really bring it all together."

As Ava turned back to the table where her stack of tarot cards still waited, she nearly collided with Riley, who'd come wordlessly from behind the counter to survey the card Ava had left face up. The girl's brown eyes studied the skeleton in fascination.

Rose, too, walked over to observe. "Yikes. Death? You might want to keep that under wraps, especially right now, considering that letter to the editor and all..." She let the sentence trail off.

"Letter to *what* editor?" Ava narrowed her eyes.

Rose's face had gone pink. She shifted uncomfortably, jostling Ellie. "Well, you know I get the Shiloh Gazette delivered, right? It came this morning, so I was reading it with my breakfast and..."

Ava crossed her arms over her chest. Riley was also waiting, her dark eyes wide with curiosity. "For god's sake, Rose, just say whatever it is."

"Fine. There's an article—well, a letter to the editor, actually—that doesn't exactly paint Cafe Arcana in a pleasant light. And I just thought you should know."

"What do you mean by a 'not pleasant light'? It's just now opening day—no one's even been here! Who wrote it?"

Rose sighed, kept her voice low. She bounced Ellie again, whose lower lip was sticking out threateningly far. "So, that's the thing. Donna Schroeder wrote it—she's the Methodist pastor's wife—and it's all about how our town was founded on family values and that giving business to an out-of-towner involved with the occult and demonic practices is going to lead to—"

"Excuse me, *what*? Demonic practices?" Ava nearly laughed aloud.

Rose's gaze flickered to the front window that lined the street. "You're promoting Arcana as a tarot cafe. You've got a tarot sign in the window. To her, that's 'demonic'."

"Good god," Ava groaned.

"I know. Her being the pastor's wife and all, I can imagine

some congregants will count her opinion as law. But who knows? Maybe the buzz will be a good thing. I wouldn't panic yet."

Ava heard the word "yet" and cringed inside. She had known from the get-go that most Shiloh residents were church-goers, and if Christians were anything like their Jewish counter-parts, anything related to divination would fall into the same taboo category. Still, her grandfather, a lover of all things mystical and a learned Kabbalist, had taught her to read the cards. Offering readings at her own cafe seemed a beautiful tribute to the man she missed so much.

"Well, whatever," Ava said, setting her jaw and glancing up at the clock. She swept the deck of cards off the table, slipped them into their sachet, and placed them back in her purse. "Riley, will you take this to the supply room and set the last pot of coffee to brew?"

The girl nodded, traipsed down the hall, and disappeared into the back room.

"Anyway," Rose said, speaking softly, out of earshot of Riley. "Is that seriously Riley Novak? I haven't seen her since the kids' ballet classes I taught in high school." Rose looked incredulous.

Ava wasn't sure why Rose sounded surprised—Riley had been a great help so far. She shrugged. "Yes. In fact, she was the only person in this entire town to apply. Not the most outgoing, but..."

"Honestly, people are probably just nervous about the tarot sign. They'll figure out that it's just for fun soon enough."

"Right." Ava pressed her lips together, resisting the urge to offer a rebuttal. Although she, too, found the cards "fun", that wasn't all they were. They'd been a helpful, enlightening tool for centuries for numerous cultures. But Rose, the physical therapist who knew all about how to strengthen weak adductors and could teach a master class on the amazing benefits of Pilates for hip mobility, was categorically not a believer in things mystical. But dismissing it as fun was at least better than calling it demonic. Ava would pick her battles.

"So are your parents coming out?" Rose shifted Ellie in her harness, jostled her up and down gently.

"Ha. Touchy subject." Ava wasn't opening that can of worms today—not after that horrible card. She knew Rose meant well, but she also wished her friend hadn't asked. Ava's parents, too disapproving of her choice to move to Shiloh instead of continuing to soldier on within a marriage that was clearly a disaster, would *not* be coming to support her.

"Seriously? They're still upset at you for doing your own thing?"

"Mom is," Ava admitted, watching as Riley slid an urn beneath the brewer and set it gurgling. "She loved Noah."

Rose wrinkled her nose in thought. "You ever think he might come back around?"

Ava scoffed. "Noah? Rose, we're divorced."

"I know," Rose said, looking embarrassed. "I just mean... what if he was really sorry?"

"He is sorry—sorry he got caught!" Ava gave a bitter laugh. Oh, Rose. Ever the romantic. Just because she'd gotten lucky enough to marry her high school sweetheart and live happily ever after, didn't mean that's how it always worked. Ava didn't bother to mention the Instagram post she'd seen of Noah and Lexie, the world's worst best friend, strolling along Lake Michigan just two days before.

"Okay, okay. Touché." Rose's cheeks grew pink.

Their laughter was cut off by the tinkle of the doorbell. The door opened, and an auburn-haired woman breezed in, followed by a gust of muggy summer air and a cloud of spicy perfume. Without saying a word, her narrow green eyes raked over the bookshelves, the stove in the corner, the minimalistic lighting overhead. After a moment, she nodded her approval and let the door swing shut behind her. Riley, returning from the back, stopped short at the sight of the woman. A hint of curiosity lit the girl's face for an instant before her expression fell into one of boredom again. Ava felt Rose tense beside her.

Small towns, Ava mused. She'd have to get used to the fact that everyone knew everyone else.

"Hi," Ava said, making her way to greet her first visitor. She snuck a glance at her watch. Five to eight. *Close enough and a good sign.* "Ava Goldberg."

"Audrey Wilson." The woman gave Ava's hand a cold, firm shake that matched her demeanor. Removing her sunglasses, she flashed a dazzling grin at Ava. Her teeth were perfect and white, but they somehow reminded Ava of fangs. "You're new in town, right?"

"Yeah," Ava replied, her face reddening despite the forced smile she was attempting to maintain. She knew small towns and newcomers didn't always mix. She ran a nervous hand through her thick, chestnut hair. "I used to come here during the summers when I was a kid. My grandfather lived here. So I'm not exactly a newcomer."

"How nice." The woman was smiling, but it was too dazzling, too plastered on. Her eyes roamed the shop again, and Ava had the sudden feeling that more than her shop was under scrutiny. "Anyway, I'm co-chairing the Shiloh Days committee this year, and we're hosting an event tonight. I know it's late notice, but I thought you might be interested in stopping by. You know, get to know some folks in town, that sort of thing."

Behind her, Rose coughed. "You sure you're not just planning to haze her, Audrey?"

Audrey's green eyes snapped, but her expression remained serene. Even as Rose approached the two women, with baby Ellie still fussing, Audrey kept her smooth, red-lipped smile.

"I'm not sure what you mean by that, but no—we're excited to finally have a coffee shop in town. I figured with Mrs. Schroeder's little letter in the gazette this week, it might be a good chance to clear up some differences. We'd love to have you at the event, Ava."

When Ava glanced back at Rose, who said no more, she saw Riley leaning on the counter, brazenly eavesdropping. It was the first time Ava had seen her look interested in... well, anything.

"Well, that's certainly an idea," Ava said, turning back to Audrey. "It'd be nice to meet some other vendors. The event's here in town, I'm assuming?"

Audrey flashed her teeth again and gave a small toss of her head. Her long auburn tresses rippled like storm clouds. "Yes, at La Fontana—just down the street. Eight o'clock."

As Audrey produced a memo pad and scribbled down her number in prim, loopy handwriting, Ava saw Rose set her jaw. Riley was still watching in amusement from across the counter. What was their problem? Audrey's invitation seemed genuine, and Ava wasn't about to shoot down an opportunity to get her foot in the little town's door. It was hard enough being the newcomer, and the sanctimonious Donna Schroeder had just made it worse. Ava couldn't afford to be turning down invites.

"I'll see you tonight," Audrey said, her heels clattering on the hardwood floor as she turned to leave the shop. "It was nice meeting you!"

"You too," Ava called faintly after her. The door clicked shut.

"Well, that was weird," Riley said, breaking the silence that had fallen over the shop. She gave a little snicker. "I've never seen her that nice."

Rose snorted. "Take it from someone who went to high school with her—she knows how to turn on the charm when she wants something."

Through the window, Ava watched Audrey's back grow smaller and smaller as she headed down the block. She turned to Rose. "You just had to come out with that hazing line, didn't you?"

"Trust me," Rose said, jiggling Ellie once more as she fussed. "Take her up on as many invites as you want, but you've got to watch out for Audrey."

"Seriously," Riley agreed. She shook her head at Ava. "You're, like, the coldest person to enter this town in my lifetime, and *Audrey Wilson* is who you pick to trust?"

Ava flinched. "Well, that wasn't exactly a compliment."

Riley shrugged. She hiked herself up onto the counter. "I'm just saying. The Wilsons aren't exactly known for their generosity. My stepdad calls 'em filthy rich."

Ava cast a disapproving glance at Riley, folding her arms across her chest. "Well, I guess I don't care whether she comes from a stand-up family. Getting involved with Shiloh Days could really help with getting Arcana on people's radars."

Finally fed up with being jiggled around, Ellie gave a mournful wail and wrenched violently in her harness. Rose took it as her cue to leave, opening the front door and glancing back at Ava.

"You're probably right. She may be just fine with you," she said, trying to get Ellie to accept her pacifier. "Anyway, Joel will be at the dinner, so you can stick by him if you need."

"But why? What's *wrong* with Audrey? You guys act like she's wanted for murder or something." Ava's voice held a soft chuckle.

Rose dismissed the comment with a roll of her eyes. "I've got to get going. Joel lost the grocery list I sent with him again, so I've got to swing by the store quick after I drop Ellie off. I've got a couple of PT clients this morning, but Joel and I will both stop in today, alright?"

With both Rose and Audrey gone, Ava turned to Riley and clapped her hands once. "Okay, you. It's showtime."

She couldn't help but wonder how her enthusiasm for her shop and new life translated as her being "cold" in the eyes of this teenager. But, for now, all that mattered was being ready for customers.

IT WASN'T long before the aroma of freshly brewed coffee began to waft out into the street, luring a handful of passersby into the shop as they strolled down Main Street, running their daily errands. So far, none of the customers had seemed very interested in chatting—an observation Ava was both relieved and sorry for. Her first customer, a frazzled mom with two preschoolers in tow, had slapped a few bills on the counter as she scooped up her latte and tore off after her kids who'd somehow made it halfway down the street. Next, a sporty looking older woman in a velvet sweatsuit and Michael Kors handbag had cast a longing look at the snickerdoodles in the pastry case, finally opting for a plain coffee with skim before striding back on her way again.

Over the following hour, only a handful of other customers trickled in. Police chief Matt Greathouse stopped in on his way to work, grunting that he'd take any alternative to the watered-down heartburn potion they heated up at the station, and someone named Chris Mitchell—from the law firm down the street—picked up a small carrying tray of lattes for everyone at his office. Ava could only cross her fingers that the gesture would lead to his coworkers coming in as well. She wasn't expecting a line out the door on opening day, but the straggle of hesitant visitors was, admittedly, disappointing. However, it wasn't until a wobbly old man came tripping down the side-walk and stopped, cane in hand, to peer skeptically at the tarot sign in the window before shaking his head and disappearing the way he'd come that Ava felt her heart sink.

Was this how it was going to be then? Had Donna Schroeder's letter really struck so much of a chord with the people of Shiloh? Ava's eyes narrowed, following the stooped old man as he made his way back up the street.

Okay, she thought, a flicker of determination sparking to life. *Challenge accepted.* She wasn't going to let some woman she'd never met ruin her business before she'd even got it going. She'd just have to outmaneuver Donna's doings in what-ever way she could, which meant—Ava swallowed hard—*small talk.*

Ava summoned the perkiest, most midwestern self she could. No way was she going to be considered 'cold' by anyone else. Greeting each customer with a smile that hopefully didn't look as fake as it felt, she did her best to take a mental snapshot of each face—which wasn't hard given the relative scarcity of faces coming through the door. If she could recognize her regulars from day one, along with the details of their orders, it was sure to make a good impression. All her favorite coffee shops in college had been the ones where the barista knew the regulars by name and had their order going as soon as they set a hand on the doorknob.

Rose arrived again at eleven, volunteering her services as a "planted guest" until Joel arrived, which, she explained, meant she'd attract customers by lounging in one of the comfy brocaded armchairs near the window with a mug in one hand and a book in the other. That way, she said, passersby peering in would not see the place empty.

"That sounds more like an excuse to just sit around drinking coffee," Ava remarked, pressing a mug of cinnamon coffee into Rose's hands. "But I'll take what I can get."

To her credit, Rose did an altogether fabulous job of making small talk with the customers who stopped by. Being more of a people person than Riley, Rose knew nearly every single person who stepped inside the shop, a definite advantage when it came to making small talk. Ava would have to observe, to learn how to emulate a small towner in its natural habitat. From what she could tell, small nuances made all the difference. Asking what the other had done for Memorial Day weekend, cocking one's head to the side while nodding sagely, laughing along at jokes about the impending tornado weather plastered all over the news. The constant flow of pleasant conversation, polite smiles, and two-fingered waves were a language all their own. Ava could've sworn Rose had even begun dropping her g's: *doin', lookin', goin'.*

Although the idea of small talk pained her, Ava knew it was key, and if memorizing the names of the Shiloh regulars would help sales, she'd hop right to it. She was already bending over backwards trying to be what Rose referred to as "Nebraska nice". Hell, she hadn't even commented on the streaky handprint of grease that Ricky Birch, the guy who owned the auto body shop down the street, left on her front window. If he'd been a teenager, she might have half expected it, but Birch was an ambling, sour-faced, sixty-ish man who should know better.

What she *did* comment on, though, much to Riley's amusement and Rose's dismay, were the matching t-shirts donned by a cutesy couple who came waltzing in off the street, holding hands. The pair were in their early twenties and couldn't resist gazing at one another, their cheeks the kind of pink and their eyes the kind of alive seen only in the not-yet-jaded phase of youth. They'd clearly never lost a job yet, never come home to find a spouse cheating on them.

"You guys pick those out together?" Ava asked, raising an eyebrow as she slid their lattes across the counter to them.

The man handed Ava his credit card, while the girl grinned. "Yeah, we ordered 'em off Etsy. Aren't they cute?"

"That's one word for it." Ava handed the girl the receipt. Then, under her breath, she muttered, "Co-dependent is another."

The girl blinked, wrapped both hands around her latte cup. If Ava's words had registered, the girl chose not to comment, instead linking her arm through her boyfriend's and prancing out of the shop the way they'd come.

Next to Ava, Riley was peering at her curiously. Their eyes met, and the girl snapped her attention back to the espresso she was sweeping into a small mound on the countertop.

"I heard that," Rose said, perched in the armchair across the room. She cast Ava a disapproving glance. "Those shirts were obviously hideous, and I know it's irritating—but is it *really* worth losing business over?"

Ava shrugged. Rose had a point, but she didn't care. "If it means not having to see those nasty matching shirts again, then sure."

At eleven thirty, Joel Robinson swaggered in, joining the small talk Rose was making with Arthur Whitlock, long-standing Shiloh mailman, who'd just wandered in moments prior. When the doorbell jingled again, a tall, lanky man, hands shoved deep inside his crumpled work pants, entered the store. He held the door for Mr. Whitlock, who was now on his way out. As Rose turned, her face lit up.

"Owen! So nice to see you!" Rose made her way across the room to give the man a side hug. Joel shook his hand as Rose motioned to Ava from across the room. "Ava, this is Owen O'Kelly. He's a good one to know. Owns the hardware store here in town—O'Kelly's."

The man grinned sheepishly and ran a tanned hand through his tousled honey-brown hair. "Aw, shucks. You flatter me."

At the mention of Owen's name, Riley's gaze lifted. Ava thought she saw a faint flush of pink creep into the girl's cheeks, but no sooner had Riley lifted her head than she'd hid back behind the espresso machine again, steaming a pitcher of milk. Ava moved out from behind the counter to shake Owen's hand. He had a loud, booming voice when he introduced himself, which somehow contrasted with his laid-back posture.

"I guess Rose beat me to it, but—Owen O'Kelly." The man flashed another sheepish grin, holding Ava's gaze for a second.

His palms were rough as he shook her hand, his knuckles solid. "You're new in Shiloh, I take it? Our resident occultist?"

Internally, Ava flinched, but she tried to keep her face unruffled. The guy had shown up in her store, after all. "Yeah, officially moved here from Chicago about a month ago. I'm Ava Goldberg."

"Goldberg..." Owen thought for a moment. "I remember a Melvin Goldberg used to live in that tiny farmhouse on the west edge of town. Any relation?"

"My grandfather," Ava said, a bit surprised this stranger would have known Zaidy Mel. Then again, from what she could remember, Mel had always been pretty involved in the town. It had been his way of staying connected. "I used to come in the summers to visit. That's how I know Rose, and I guess why I moved back here, too. Kind of fell in love with it."

Recognition dawned on Owen's face. "You're that little girl that always used to be running around with Rosie here, aren't you? Swimming in Larkspur Lake and getting yelled at?"

Almost simultaneously, Ava and Rose burst out laughing. Ava didn't remember many other kids in town from those days and had never stayed in touch with anyone but Rose, but the very memory of the two of them cavorting around Shiloh in their bare feet was enough to send her into grateful laughter. She supposed they'd be doing that again, but with shoes on this time, and a baby to boot.

"That'd be her," Joel said, shaking his head with a chuckle. "I wasn't in with them back then, but I've heard all about it."

"Yep." Rose smiled at Ava as she smoothed her baby's wispy hair. "A lot's different, of course, but she's back. Here to stay by the looks of it." She threw a proud glance around the cafe.

"Well done," Owen said, nodding as he, too, took in the rustic little space. "It's a beauty."

"Yeah, well," Ava shrugged. She'd never been one for compliments. "I'm giving it my best shot. On the bright side, it can't work out much worse than the last thing I undertook—marriage."

Rose clucked her tongue. Joel looked uncomfortable. The words had just kind of slipped out, but once they'd been said, Ava had to admit she felt a tiny glimmer of satisfaction. Maybe she wasn't good at small talk yet—but at least she kept things interesting.

"Well, I wish you the best. May even toss a coin in that fountain out there for you," Owen said, his green eyes glinting with amusement. "And apropos of nothing, could I get some coffee?"

This sent Rose and Joel to laughing, the conversation back on solid ground. Ava went to pour Owen's coffee—dark roast, as she had easily pegged him since he first stepped in the door. She could hear Rose's tinkling laughter, the low hum of Owen's and Joel's voices as they chatted.

"Here you go," Ava called to Owen, sliding his cup across the counter.

He paid for the drink, dropping two crisp dollar bills into the tip jar and shooting a wink in Riley's direction. Nodding his thanks to the both of them, Owen then tipped his head in greeting toward the small group of women who'd wandered in off the street. When Ava next turned, after busying herself with the new customers, he was gone, and Rose and Joel were waving goodbye from the doorway, already having been gone from work too long.

If Ava were honest, the amount of straggling foot traffic to the shop was disappointing. It wasn't the opening day she'd imagined while lying in bed the night before, trying to focus on the energy she hoped to manifest in her little shop. The urns of brewed coffee went stale faster than customers could drink them, there was never more than one table occupied at a time, and Ava and Riley did a whole lot of standing around, avoiding eye contact. By noon, only two dozen cookies had sold, and Ava thought she heard one woman remark that she'd almost broken a tooth biting into a snickerdoodle. Ava sighed. She was no good in the kitchen. She'd have to figure something else out.

As she stood leaning against the counter, arms crossed and waiting for some passerby in need of an afternoon pick-me-up to wander in, Ava thought back to the Death card she'd drawn that morning. She'd been sure it was pointing to the transformation she'd been working so hard to bring about. But after the slow morning and bored faces of the people in the window as they glanced at her shop and continued on, she wasn't so sure. Was another kind of death in store? One that involved the sinking of her business before it could even pick up speed?

No. The thought came with such determined force that Ava nearly said it aloud. The only death in store was the death of her old life, of allowing others to call the shots. *No more.* She would take back her own power, no matter the cost.

3

———

It was three minutes to eight when Ava entered La Fontana that evening. Although she'd arrived early, she'd waited in the dark, parked car until there were only a few minutes left to kill. The last thing she wanted was to get stuck making small talk. As Ava approached the hostess stand, the smell of fajitas wafted around her.

The perky pony-tailed hostess greeted her with a smile. "Hi! Here for the Shiloh Days committee dinner?"

Ava nodded, glancing around the restaurant for any sign of a familiar face.

"They're in the party room," the hostess replied, ushering Ava toward the hallway at the back of the room. She beamed. "Follow that to the end, then take a left. You can't miss it."

Ava thanked the hostess, setting off in the direction she'd indicated. The door to the party room was ajar, with a sign on it that read *Shiloh Days Committee*. Inside, the room hummed with friendly chatter as guests milled about from wall to wall. A few faces seemed familiar, but most belonged to people Ava had never seen before in her life. She vaguely remembered having attended Shiloh Days events as a child, but she'd had no idea it was this big of a deal. Clearly, the people of Shiloh took their festival days seriously.

Scanning the crowd, Ava was suddenly hyper aware of the fact that she was standing alone. The rest of the guests were scattered around the room in clusters, the merry tinkle of laughter ringing out through the room. Where was Joel? As the owner of Shiloh's New Heights fitness club, Joel never missed an opportunity to promote his business, and Rose had said he'd be attending the dinner—right? A swish of crisp, satiny suit pants and a wave of perfume startled Ava out of her thoughts. Audrey Wilson, wrapped in a delicate silk top and perched on a pair of pointed red heels, had floated to her side as though out of thin air. Her auburn hair was swept up into a French twist, the perfect picture of chic.

"Ava," Audrey said, her voice even more velvety than Ava had remembered. "So glad you could make it."

Ava was horrified to find she had the sudden urge to curtsy. "Thanks for inviting me."

"Here, come meet Ed and Elaine Walsh. They own the wine bar downtown—Looking Glass. Unless you've already met?"

"Not yet," Ava said, following Audrey as she turned to lead her into the clusters of guests. She drew herself up taller, hoping the adage about faking it until you make it was really true. If Donna Schroeder was, for whatever reason, attending this dinner, she wanted to look polite and collected. Not demonic.

With exquisite grace, Audrey slipped seamlessly into a group of guests with Ava on her arm. Ava marveled at Audrey's skill. They may as well have been a part of the conversation the entire time.

"Ed, Elaine. This is Ava Goldberg. You've heard about her new cafe that opened today, right? Organa?"

"Arcana," Ava corrected, her tone perhaps a little too sharp. She shook hands with Mr. and Mrs. Walsh, trying her best to emulate Audrey's pleasant, closed-mouth smile. "It's nice to meet you both."

Elaine Walsh reached out a prim, perfectly manicured hand. Her sharp blue eyes, fringed by stark lashes, met Ava's as she smiled through pursed lips. "It's lovely to meet you. I've always said—haven't I, Ed?—that the only thing missing from Shiloh is a coffee shop."

"You certainly have, dear," her husband said, beaming at his wife.

"Well, I'm glad," Ava said. "I'm pretty excited myself."

"Yes," Audrey continued. "And if the sign in the window doesn't lie, she'll read your fortune as well."

Ava tried hard to keep her expression unruffled. She hadn't been planning to lead with that. Instead, she managed a small laugh and a wave of her hand.

Elaine Walsh flicked her eyes to the side, as though searching for an exit from the conversation. It was clear she'd seen the letter in that week's gazette.

Beside her, her husband frowned, his huge eyebrows furrowing beneath his shiny bald head. "What's that?"

"Oh, it's all in fun, Ed," Audrey soothed, patting his arm and offering Ava a wink, like they were in cahoots. "It's not real, you know."

Ava swallowed hard. She wasn't sure which was worse, the accusations that she frolicked with the devil or the complete disregard of her practice as legitimate. Ava had heard every opinion under the sun regarding tarot, and people were free to believe what they wanted. But to dismiss a genuine part of her business right in front of her like it was some kind of inside joke? It was belittling. The relieved looks on Ed and Elaine's faces told Ava she was better off not jumping in to defend her craft.

"Well, just so long as I can get in, get my coffee, and get out," Ed offered. "Right?"

"I only read the cards for people who want me to," Ava assured him. She chanced a glance at Audrey, but the woman was already looking across the room, waving to someone who'd just entered.

"You three will have to excuse me." Audrey gave Ava's arm a quick squeeze. "Juanita Martinez just arrived, and I should say hello." With that, Audrey was off, her thin hips shimmying as she disappeared into the crowd.

Elaine Walsh turned toward Ava. "Now. When I saw your name in the paper, I said to Ed, that girl must be related to the Goldbergs who used to live out west of town. Is that right?"

Ava felt something in her chest loosen. Elaine had seen Donna's letter, but she was still engaging. That was a good sign. Plus, it was always a comfort when someone had known her Zaidy Mel.

"Yes, my grandparents," Ava said. "I grew up in Chicago— my family still lives there—but I used to come in the summers to stay with my grandfather. I figured this would be the perfect home for Cafe Arcana. And also for me personally—I'd like to experience that close-knit, small town family kind of feel. That's harder to come by in Chicago."

"How lovely," Mrs. Walsh crooned. She beamed at Ava. "We *are* a family sort of place, I suppose. Most folks here have been in Shiloh, or at least Nebraska, for generations, which I think helps create that sense of homey-ness. Ed's family has been right here in Cass County since the 1800s! That's even deeper roots than the *Wilsons* have."

"That reminds me," Mr. Walsh said, turning to his wife. "Speaking of the Wilsons, Audrey mentioned to me the other day that Lucas is back in town—starting a landscaping business, I guess."

"Well, that's a development," Mrs. Walsh replied, her lined eyes going wide. She pursed her lips. "I never thought I'd see the day. He must be realizing that Warren's health isn't coming back."

"Sorry," Ava interrupted, figuring that if she had to be a part of this conversation, she might as well know who was being talked about. "Who's this?"

"Oh, that's right." Mrs. Walsh seemed to suddenly remember that Ava was still there. "You *wouldn't* know, would you? Warren Wilson, Audrey's father, has been in poor health for quite a while now, so they've moved him into the assisted living center here in town. That was just about a month ago, I believe."

"Yes, in April," her husband confirmed.

"Anyway, it's been very hard on Audrey, and where has her brother, Lucas, been during all this? God only knows, but not in Shiloh, that's for sure. I know he and Audrey don't always see eye to eye—and heaven knows she and I don't either—but you'd think he'd have the decency to come home and help care for his aging parent. After all, he's Warren's only biological child." Mrs. Walsh finished her announcement with yet another triumphant pursing of her lips.

"Wait—aren't Lucas and Audrey siblings?" Ava figured she must have missed something.

"Step-siblings," Mrs. Walsh corrected. "Warren and Leta married when both of their kids from previous marriages were quite young. Audrey never knew much of her own father—he passed away—and Warren adopted her. If you ask me, she's a Wilson through and through, but Lucas seems to think differently."

Mr. Wilson cleared his throat. "Well, Elaine, the boy's back in town. Looks like he's finally going to take some responsibility, so let's credit him that."

Mrs. Walsh raised her thin, silvery eyebrows. "I'd say it's about time. We'll see if he shows his face this weekend at the barbecue."

"Speaking of," Mr. Walsh continued, turning back to Ava. "You heard about the community barbecue on Saturday? At Sanderson Park?"

Ava shook her head. "I'm not very up on community events yet, I hate to admit."

"Well, no better place to make connections than a barbecue," Mrs. Walsh pointed out, her lined eyes squinting into smiling half-moons. "It starts at one on Saturday. And no need to bring anything—they've got plenty of volunteers already."

"Great, that sounds like fun. I'll see what I have going on." Ava flashed a polite smile, knowing full well her social calendar for the week was completely empty.

She was about to add in a word of thanks to Mr. Walsh for having thought to invite her when she stopped short. Not more than five yards away, a woman stood against the wall, staring at Ava with icy blue eyes. Their eyes met, and the woman held Ava's gaze even as she raised a glass of water to her wrinkly lipsticked mouth.

Elaine Walsh glanced toward Ava's stare, pursing her lips

once more. When she spoke, the airiness of her voice contrasted with the flustered expression she wore. "That's Donna Schroeder. No doubt you've heard about that letter she wrote to the gazette, but I promise you, she means no harm."

"I heard about it, all right," Ava remarked, turning to face Elaine. "But I'm not sure there's any *other* way she could have meant it, except to harm my business."

Elaine looked helplessly to her husband.

"Well, now," Ed drawled, looping his thumbs through his belt loops. "She gets a bee in her bonnet, Donna does."

Ava wished she could take whatever bee was in Donna's bonnet up with the woman. But as she glanced around at the happy, chatting people milling about the tables, she forced her jaw to unclench. This wasn't the place. Small town Midwesterners valued politeness—it wouldn't do to make a scene. But perhaps a personal introduction...

"Oh, I don't think—" Elaine began, stopping mid-sentence as Ava shook her shoulder free of Elaine's gentle patting.

Ava tried to keep any sign of a scowl from her face as she approached Donna. With a slight look of surprise, the woman pulled the cardigan she'd draped over her shoulders tighter, as though it were armor that might protect her from the battle she herself had started. She gave a slight toss of her short, permed head and pressed her feathered pink lips together.

"May I help you?" Donna peered at Ava over her glasses.

"Yes, I wanted to introduce myself," Ava said, feeling the heat of adrenaline creeping into her ears. Her palms were sweaty. This woman had no right, no right at all, to write that letter. *Focus, Ava.* All she needed to do was calmly dispel Donna's concerns, and she'd be off on a better footing with both Donna and the community. "I'm Ava Goldberg. We haven't met, but you wrote a letter to the Shiloh Gazette editor this week, condemning my business. I wanted to see if I could ease your mind about some things."

Donna laughed, her voice as feathery as her lipstick. "Well, to begin with, *condemn* is a rather harsh word. I believe I called on the good people of Shiloh to examine their consciences."

"Right, the implication being that if they're people of good conscience, they won't visit my shop." Ava had to fight to keep her voice level. This woman was really trying her.

Donna shrugged. "I'm simply asking my community to remember the values they were raised on. I'm not in control of how you choose to interpret my words."

Ava's pulse pounded in her temple now. She grit her teeth as she tried to speak without raising her voice. "Come by the shop sometime this week, try out a free coffee, browse through the books. You'll see there's nothing—"

"No, thank you," Donna cut in, her voice infuriatingly prim.

"Then just take it back," Ava blurted out. "Write another letter."

"No. Now, if you'll excuse me, my husband is signaling for me to join him. It was lovely to meet you."

With that, Donna fluttered away, her long skirt swishing at her calves. Ava stared after her, gaping at the sheer disrespect of what had just happened. And here she'd thought these small town folks were supposed to be polite. *As if.*

Fuming, Ava fought to get her breath under control. She was in public. She was at a committee event, surrounded by people on whom it was *crucial* she make a good impression. *Keep it together, Ava.* She couldn't let Donna Schroeder get to her—that was exactly what the woman wanted. She had no doubt that if she even opened her mouth to speak so much as a sentence against Donna, the woman would be all over it in an instant...

Suddenly, a dull thump rang out on the speakers overhead. All heads turned toward the front of the room, where a podium stood. Audrey Wilson was behind it, tapping daintily on the microphone. She cleared her throat.

"Good evening," Audrey said in her velvety voice. "Most of you know me, but if you don't, I'm Audrey Wilson, co-chair of this year's Shiloh Days committee. We're so glad you all could make it this evening."

A round of polite applause erupted across the room. Her shakes subsiding, Ava scanned the crowd again. Donna Schroeder had gone to join her husband, who was chatting with another middle-aged couple. On the far side of the room stood Tim Meyer from the gallery. Joel was crossing the room to join him, having just arrived. He met Ava's gaze, and Ava gave him a quick wave, glad for the friendly face. As Ava's eyes continued to dart from face to face, she was startled to see another pair of eyes smiling back at her from across the room. Owen O'Kelly stood on the other side of the podium, behind one of the long tables that waitstaff were now scooting in and out to set with flatware. He gave Ava a nod, and the corner of his handsome mouth pulled up into a small smile. Curtly, she nodded back, then turned her attention back to Audrey at the podium.

"We'll begin with dinner, after which we'll start our presentation. Our main goal for the evening is for us all to have some time together, but there is business to discuss as always. We'll try to keep things short so you can all enjoy your evening. So—without further ado..."

Audrey smiled her red-lipped smile once more, even

showing a brief flash of dazzling white teeth before replacing the microphone into its holder and nodding to the waitstaff. Several servers, including the hostess who'd greeted Ava, bustled into the room with carts.

Seating had been assigned, and Ava found her place card at the same table as the Walshes, who were delighted to see her again. Ava was sure it was not a coincidence that Audrey had introduced her to Ed and Elaine, considering that she'd most likely been the one to place her near them at dinner. And the personalized name card? Even when Ava had only confirmed with her that morning? Ava had to hand it to her. Inconsiderate or not, this Audrey lady was on top of things. Ava was thanking her lucky stars she hadn't ended up anywhere near the Schroeders.

The food at La Fontana was delicious. Ava made a mental note to come back with Rose on their next dinner date. The thought of Rose and the way she and Riley had rolled their eyes at Audrey that morning still nagged at Ava, but she pushed the thought aside. Rose had always been the dramatic kind—loving hard, hating hard, and glad to have you along for the ride. At the moment, Ava had figured that Rose and Riley were just being dramatic, letting themselves get caught up in the small town dynamics they'd grown up with. Now, after Audrey's dismissive comment about her shop, Ava wondered if there wasn't something more to it. Then again, if Audrey were the trouble-maker that Rose implied, she would have seated Ava with the Methodist pastor and his wife.

As the dinner wound down, the clinking of forks on plates growing dimmer, a clean-cut, good-looking man whom Ava was sure had visited Arcana that morning took the podium. She fought hard to recall his name but came up blank. Flashing a perfect set of straight white teeth that matched the crisp polo he wore, he exuded an air of control, and the buzz of conversation faded.

"Good evening," the man said into the microphone. He clicked a button on the remote he held in his hand. A projection screen rolled down behind him. "I'd like to thank La Fontana for having us, first off. If we could get a round of applause? That's it."

The man looked rather pleased with himself. Ava saw Audrey shift uncomfortably in her seat across the room.

He continued: "You all know me, but I'll introduce myself anyway: I'm Chris Mitchell. I'm a partner at Finkenbaum Law Office—along with Audrey, of course—and I serve on the parish board at St. Patrick's. I'm really pleased to be co-chairing the Shiloh Days committee this year. Now, as Audrey said, we've got some business to go over."

That's right, Ava thought. *Chris Mitchell—from the law firm.* She really needed to do better at remembering her customers' names.

Chris clicked his remote again, and the title slide of a presentation appeared on the screen.

"We need to decide on dates for this year's Shiloh Days," he said. "And a theme. Last year we went with Oregon Trail, which is going to be hard to beat, so we need your best ideas."

A murmur once again buzzed amongst the guests. Ava found her eyes wandering the room. The semi-formal atmosphere of the evening had already begun to dissipate, the guests now lounging in their chairs, trading ideas back and forth. From across the room, she caught Joel's eye again. He winked.

"You'll see you've got some slips of paper in the middle of

your tables, as well as pens." Chris gestured to the tables with gracious authority. "If you could take a few minutes to think up your most smashing, most exciting, most talk-of-the-town ideas for the 2024 Shiloh Days, we'll gather your ideas and hold an informal vote."

There was a flurry of movement and laughter as the guests all began reaching for their pens and papers. Chris held up his hand once more to get their attention. He cleared his throat into the microphone. "I forgot to mention—please only write one idea. I promised my wife I'd be home by eleven."

The room erupted into laughter, and the commotion began again. Chris Mitchell stepped down from his spot at the podium and took his seat next to Audrey Wilson, scooting his chair ever so slightly away from her. She remained seated and aloof, arms crossed over her chest, eyes surveying the room.

As she reached in front of Mr. and Mrs. Walsh to grab a pen, Ava heard Mrs. Walsh mutter to her husband, "I bet Chris promised his wife he'd stay away from the casinos last weekend, too."

Mr. Walsh shushed her, shooting her a glance that said to mind her own business. Ava didn't disagree with him. As much as she was fond of Shiloh, she was glad she hadn't had to go through her divorce in such a small town. People had talked enough in Chicago—she couldn't imagine what it would've been like in a town like Shiloh. Then again, from Donna's letter and the way the Walshes had reacted to Audrey's quip about Ava's "fortune telling", it was looking like Ava might be the subject of gossip sooner than she cared to be.

Ava tapped the end of her pen against the table, trying to think of an idea. She snuck a peek over at what Mrs. Walsh was scribbling onto her paper. Mrs. Walsh caught her looking and eagerly held up her scrap of paper.

"I've been telling Ed for years—haven't I, dear?—that we need to do a Little House on the Prairie theme. I can't believe it's never been done!" Her eyes widened in gleeful enthusiasm.

"Oh, that's a good one. I wouldn't have thought of that!" Ava said, offering a polite smile. The idea of dressing up in a skirt and bonnet was her personal idea of hell, but she wasn't about to say that to Mrs. Walsh. No, smile and nod was the name of the game when you were a newcomer. That was becoming ever clearer.

"Ed, what did you write?" Mrs. Walsh elbowed her husband, craning her neck to see what he'd written.

A movement across the room caught Ava's eye. As she turned to look, she caught only a glimpse of Audrey Wilson disappearing soundlessly out through a side door. Chris Mitchell was deep in animated conversation with the man sitting next to him, likely discussing the ideas they'd written. Audrey's purse was still on the table in front of her chair, which meant she must have only slipped out to use the bathroom. Ava glanced down at her empty paper, slipped it into her pocket. Come to think of it, she wouldn't mind a bathroom break either —or at least a stroll down the hall. The enchiladas served at dinner had been delicious but heavy, and the thought of stretching her legs seemed suddenly glorious.

"Excuse me," Ava murmured to the Walshes, pushing back from the table.

She set her purse on her empty chair to signal she was coming back, but slipped her phone into the pocket of her leather jacket. Then, trying to make as little noise as possible, Ava slipped out the door and into the hallway. She wasn't sure where the bathroom was, but already the hallway was much cooler than the stuffy room full of people had been. Ava made her way down the hall, relishing the quiet as the sounds of conversation from the main dining room faded. No one else wandered about whom she could ask for directions. But the bathroom had to be around somewhere. The place wasn't *that* big.

Up ahead, Ava could see a glass exit door where the hallway branched left. Most likely the restrooms were near there, maybe down that side hall. As she neared the end of the hallway, she hesitated—no sign. She was about to turn around when she heard a woman's voice, tense and tight, around that left turn. A voice strained but still velvety, like one of those old movie star vixens. *Definitely Audrey.* Had she gone there to make a phone call?

The conversation had piqued Ava's curiosity, especially given the tense tone but...

Her mother had always taught her not to eavesdrop—but then again, there were plenty of things her mother had taught her that Ava had chucked to the wayside. Besides, maybe the restroom was down that way.

The voice got louder as Ava neared, though it still sounded restrained and harsh. Just as Ava was about to round the corner, another voice cut Audrey off. A man's. Ava stopped short of the end of the hallway; she really didn't want an awkward encounter with Audrey. The man's voice was gruff, with the same country-sounding twang so many of the town's older residents seemed to have. This voice, too, sounded familiar.

"Oh, you can try, but people here in town will see right through that," the man said, giving a harsh laugh.

"I wouldn't be so sure," Audrey replied in the same tight voice. "I have it on good authority that—"

"That what? Another one of them hifalutin folks comin' from Lincoln or Omaha will back you up? I swear on my grave, lady, there was no way for me to know the engine would—"

Audrey laughed coldly. "Well, then you're not fit to be doing business in this town, Mr. Birch."

Mr. Birch. *That's* who the man was. Ricky Birch from the auto shop, who'd left that streak of grease on Arcana's shop window. Ava knew she should just turn and leave, but she hesitated, intrigued.

"Who do you think this town is going to believe, Mr. Birch? You, the slimy mechanic who goes around cheating honest people—or me, whose family practically runs this town?"

Ava grimaced. *Yikes.* This didn't sound like a conversation she wanted to butt in on.

"Oh, that's rich, ma'am. I've owned that shop for decades. These people know the work I do, and they also know how your family likes to throw their weight around—"

Audrey cut him off. "Mr. Birch, I'd stop right there if I were you. You mark my words: I will run your shop into the ground."

"No, *you* stop right there," Ricky jumped in, his voice roaring this time. Gone were their efforts at keeping quiet. "You say one single word about me or my shop, and it's game over. And you don't want to go there."

Audrey must have smiled then, because her voice sounded eerily pleasant. "Oh, but I do."

"I know some people, Miz Wilson. I know some awfully good people."

"Perfect," Audrey said, her voice cloying. "A good lawyer will come in handy."

Ava turned, creeping as quickly as she could back down the hallway toward the dining room. Whatever that had been, she'd be staying out of it. She had enough drama on her plate with Donna Schroeder and that stupid letter. This thing between Ricky and Audrey would have to stay between them.

As she neared the double doors to the dining room, her eye caught the sign "Restroom" at the other end of the hall. She sighed. Sometimes she missed the most obvious of signs.

4

Ava arrived at Arcana early the next morning, still somewhat shaken by the conversation she'd witnessed between Ricky Birch and Audrey Wilson. After Ava had slipped back into her seat at the table in the dining room, Audrey had returned several minutes later, looking as cool and collected as always, save for a small tinge of color in her sculpted cheeks. Ricky Birch had never returned, and as far as Ava could tell, no one mentioned it.

I guess that's just how it goes in small towns. Ava was sure that everyone else in Shiloh, like anywhere else in the world, had their own set of problems, their own drama. Having been so young during the summer weeks she'd spent in Shiloh with her grandfather, she just hadn't noticed it before. She'd have to consult her tarot deck as soon as she got home that evening to see if there was anything she should know about the situation. But for now, she was determined to push the ordeal from her mind. She had more important things to focus on—like making her new cafe a success. God knew after yesterday it would need every ounce of strength she still had.

As she stepped inside the door of her shop, Ava halted in surprise. Riley was already there, tying an apron around her waist and rubbing her eyes.

"Good god!" Ava placed a hand on her chest. "You scared the hell out of me! And I thought *I* was here early."

"Sorry," Riley grunted, managing a sleepy half smile. She pushed her wispy blue hair, which looked even more rumpled than usual, out of her eyes.

Ava set her purse down behind the counter, took her apron off its hook on the back wall. "Well, I can't complain. At least you're here on time, right?"

Riley nodded, and the two of them set to work brewing coffee. At eight o'clock, Ava unlocked the shop door and set the chalkboard outside on the sidewalk. The flavor of the day was crème brûlée. Like the day before, there was hardly a rush of customers waiting to get inside the shop, and Ava wandered between the cash register and empty tables, wiping down surfaces she'd wiped just ten minutes before. Shooting a glance at the still empty pastry case, Ava made a mental note to find somewhere she could order sweet breads or scones. The lack of sweet treats on offer wasn't helping business, that was for sure.

Suddenly, a deafening shriek pierced the air from outside. Across the room, Riley's head snapped up, wide eyes flashing to Ava's. *What the...?* Rushing to the front shop windows, Ava peered out into the street. Riley, too, pressed her face to the glass. At first, they saw only the same handful of cars that Ava had seen coming in an hour earlier, still parked across the street. But the shriek came again, and this time a blur of movement from across the other side of the intersection caught Ava's eye. Without stopping to think, she flew out the front door, with Riley close on her heels.

Other shop owners were coming out to stand in the sidewalk, shielding their eyes from the morning sun as they tried to figure out what on earth was going on. There was another bloodcurdling shriek, and then: "Help! Somebody!"

Every head on the street whipped toward the Main Street plaza, right across the street to the west from Cafe Arcana. At first, Ava didn't recognize the frantic older woman who was stumbling toward her down the sidewalk, arms flailing through the air, permed hair frazzled from running. But as the woman grew closer, still shrieking, Riley's stance grew rigid, her face pale. "Is that Donna Schroeder? The Methodist minister's wife?"

"It's—she's—oh *dear*," Mrs. Schroeder gasped. Her eyes were wild, crazed. "Somebody call the police!"

By this time, Ava had broken into a run and the others on the street were rushing toward Donna, too. Arthur Whitlock, no doubt on his way out of the post office to make his early morning mail rounds, got there first. He put an arm around the shaken woman's shoulders.

"Are you hurt, Donna? What's wrong?"

"She's dead," Mrs. Schroeder wailed, collapsing into shuddering gasps of breath. Her shoulders shook.

Ava came to a screeching halt at the edge of the crowd that had now gathered around Mrs. Schroeder. She saw Riley's eyes widen in shock, her gaze flitting to Ava's, and then around at the crowd.

Mr. Whitlock sucked in his breath. Still gripping Mrs. Schroeder's shoulders, he glanced around, as though hoping he hadn't heard correctly. His voice was sharp when he replied. "Who? *Who* is dead? And where?"

Mrs. Schroeder pointed a shaking finger toward the plaza

just behind them. And then, her eyes narrowing into tiny slits, brought her finger to point to Ava.

"I told you all," Mrs. Schroeder announced, her voice shrill in the silence of the crowd. "You mess around with devils and witches, and *this* is what happens. God's punishment."

"Bullshit," Riley muttered.

"Shh," someone next to Mrs. Schroeder murmured as Mr. Whitlock took off in a run toward the plaza.

Ava said nothing. Someone was—*dead?* This was hardly the time to make the situation about herself, despite how wildly unfair Donna Schroeder's accusations were. Instead, she caught Riley's eye. The girl's gaze was sharp, angry. Scared. Behind Ava, someone was on the line with 911.

As Mr. Whitlock came to a stop in the middle of the square, Ava craned her neck to see over the crowd. She gasped as her gaze fell on the fountain. There, sprawled over the side, lay a body. Although she was too far away to make out who it was, the crooked angle of the figure's unmoving legs could mean nothing good. Along with Riley and the rest of the crowd, Ava rushed forward, not even sure of what she could do.

Mr. Whitlock knelt next to the body, flipped it over, and began slapping frantically at the person's cheeks. "Audrey? Audrey, can you hear me? Audrey!"

Ava's heart sped up. As Mr. Whitlock placed two fingers against the unmoving figure's neck, Ava caught a glimpse of the dripping, bluish-tinted face, the soaking auburn hair now plastered to its forehead. It was Audrey Wilson.

"My god," Mr. Whitlock breathed.

A voice boomed from behind the group of onlookers. "Everybody move—Shiloh police!"

The group parted to let the officer through. As he barreled

toward the fountain, he flashed his badge at them, though there was no need. Everyone in Shiloh knew Chief Matt Greathouse. As the chief hauled Audrey out of the fountain, Mr. Whitlock murmured something to him that Ava couldn't hear. Greathouse nodded, laid Audrey down on the cobblestones, and began chest compressions. From the back of the crowd, Donna Schroeder howled.

After a few moments, the chief stopped. He felt once again for a pulse. Then, standing up, he barked something into his radio. A panicked buzz had broken out amongst the small crowd still gathered at the corner of the plaza.

Greathouse turned to face them, clearing his throat for attention. Once all eyes were on him, he spoke. "Folks, I'm afraid I have sad news. Audrey Wilson is no longer with us."

There were several gasps from the crowd. It still didn't seem *real*. Audrey Wilson? Hadn't Ava just seen her last night, less than twelve hours before? She'd been alive and kicking, strutting her stuff like she had no other care in the world. She'd even held her own against—oh. Oh, no. Ava's whole body stiffened. Suddenly, the argument she'd overheard the night before took on a whole new meaning. Without thinking, her hand went to her pocket, her fingers closing around the stone she always kept there, no matter where she went.

"We don't have many details at this time," Chief Greathouse continued, his voice booming. "But I'm going to need you to all clear out so we can get the square cordoned off—except for you, Mrs. Schroeder. And Arthur, if you'll stay to clarify a few things, I'd really appreciate it. If you're a business owner on Main Street, sit tight. I'll be coming to speak with you shortly."

As Ava and Riley made their way back to Cafe Arcana, still too in shock to utter a single word, Ava's stomach roiled. Audrey

Wilson—this woman who'd been so alive and in charge less than a day before—was dead. Ava moved her hand once again to her pocket, tried to focus her attention on the weight and smoothness of the lapis lazuli in an effort to still her swirling thoughts. She couldn't get the argument she'd witnessed the night before out of her mind. Was it related? Ava didn't know. She'd have to wait until Greathouse stopped by to tell him what she'd seen.

CHIEF GREATHOUSE SANK HEAVILY into one of Arcana's straight-backed wooden chairs. It had been an hour since the discovery of Audrey Wilson's body in the plaza fountain, and it seemed to Ava like she'd been pacing the cafe the entire time. Riley had been even quieter than usual, scrubbing already clean counters and tabletops as though to keep herself moving. The police had set up a perimeter around the plaza, and though they said there was no reason yet to suspect foul play, downtown Shiloh was abuzz with nosy residents coming to stand on the corner and crane their necks, hoping to catch a glimpse of the drama. With how slow business had been, Ava should have been happy about the extra foot traffic inside her shop, but she couldn't shake the unease of the morning.

To Ava's surprise, her suggestion to Chief Greathouse to discuss what she had or hadn't seen over mugs of steaming coffee had been well received. She and Riley both sat across from him, waiting, glad for the comfort of the mugs in their hands and the Closed sign hanging temporarily in the door.

"Alright," the chief grunted, flinging his memo pad down in front of him onto the table. "Let's get this over with."

Ava couldn't have agreed more, though she was trying not to shake. Riley looked more relaxed than Ava felt, though her face, too, was dark.

"Were either of you acquainted with Audrey Wilson?" Chief Greathouse asked. He looked tired already, and it was still mid-morning.

Ava and Riley glanced at one another, then Ava spoke first.

"I'd met her, yes," she said.

"Elaborate, please."

"Well," Ava began, taking a sip of her coffee. She tried to think back. All that came to mind was the argument she'd overheard between Audrey and Ricky Birch the night before. "She came in here yesterday. Riley and I were both here getting ready for opening day, along with a friend of mine. Audrey came in, introduced herself, invited me to the Shiloh Days dinner last night, and left. That's when I met her."

"And did you attend said dinner?"

"Yes, I did. And actually—"

Chief Greathouse cut her off. "And the friend that was here when Audrey came in? Who was that?"

"Rose Robinson."

"Huh." Chief Greathouse grunted something and started scribbling in his pad. Then, setting his pen down, he folded his hands and turned his attention to Riley. "How about you? You knew Audrey Wilson?"

"Not really," Riley said. Then, after a beat, she wrinkled her nose. "I mean, not since she led my Girl Scouts troop in second grade."

"Why the face?" Greathouse raised an eyebrow.

Riley shrugged. "You know the Wilsons. Audrey was most definitely a Wilson."

To this, Greathouse said nothing, but the cough he gave made clear to Ava that he most certainly did know the Wilsons.

"Can I say something?" Ava was losing patience. Could they not just get this show on the road, give the police chief what he'd come for, and get on with trying to distract themselves from the whole thing?

Greathouse sighed. "I'm listening."

"So, I know this whole thing is probably just a freak tragic accident, but I went to the Shiloh Days committee dinner last night and—"

"So you said. Good for you." The chief didn't even glance up from his notepad.

Ava felt her ears growing red. "Do you want to take my statement or not, sir?"

At this, Chief Greathouse looked up. Seeing the irritation on her face, he chuckled, set his pad down. "Knock yourself out, kid."

It was a herculean effort to keep her eyes from rolling, but Ava ignored the jab. "I went to the committee dinner last night, and I happened to overhear a pretty heated argument between Audrey Wilson and Ricky Birch—the guy from the auto shop."

"I know who Ricky Birch is," Chief Greathouse barked, looking at Ava intently. She'd piqued his interest. "What was the argument about?"

"Well, I'm not actually sure," Ava admitted. "Ricky said something about an engine, and how he couldn't have known, and then Audrey said she would drive his business into the ground. Ricky said he knew some people."

Chief Greathouse scratched his chin. Outside, passersby lingered at the window as they made their way too slowly down the sidewalk, clearly trying to catch a peek at the investigation. Finally, he said: "Did you intervene at all?"

"No. They didn't know I was there."

"And why was that?" he questioned.

"Well, they were around the corner of a hallway, and I was looking for the restroom and—"

"So you didn't see them?"

"Well, ah, no," Ava stammered. "It sounded pretty intense. I didn't want to make things worse by barging in on them mid-argument." She hated admitting to eavesdropping, but there was no getting around that this sounded just like that.

"Are you certain it was Audrey Wilson and Ricky Birch?" Chief Greathouse furrowed a skeptical brow in Ava's direction, leaned back in his chair.

"I'm certain," Ava said. She set her mug down on the table in emphasis.

Chief Greathouse heaved a sigh. "Well, that complicates things."

Ava shifted in her seat. Her first thought that morning had been that Audrey had simply had too much to drink at the dinner after her argument with Ricky and had somehow tripped and fallen, ending up in the fountain. It seemed odd, but weirder things had happened. Those cobblestones were a hazard. But something in the chief's solemn demeanor made her uneasy. She knew it wasn't any of her business—and maybe wasn't even legal for her to be told—but she had to ask.

"You don't think..." Ava began. She wasn't sure how to phrase what she was thinking. "You don't think it was anything more than an accident, do you?"

Chief Greathouse raised his eyebrows. "That's police business, ma'am. I wouldn't tell you either way."

Suddenly, the front door flung open. As the knob smacked backwards into the adjacent wall, Riley started as though she'd heard a gunshot, and all three heads turned. A young man stalked through the doorway, shaggy auburn hair curling around his ears, clinging to his sweaty neck. He ran a hand through said sweaty hair, surveyed the room through narrowed, scornful eyes on his sharply angled face.

"Cute little shop you got here," he remarked. "Too nice for this dump of a town."

"I'm sorry," Ava said, halfway rising from the table. "We're closed right now. Try back in half an hour—we should be open again by then." She shot Greathouse a pointed look.

Greathouse, however, was looking straight at the man now running a lazy finger across the cherry wood countertops. The police chief's eyes were wary, and when he spoke, his words were slow and even, like someone approaching an animal they didn't want to startle. "Lucas, I said I'd talk to you at the station after lunch. Is there something you need?"

Lucas. The name sounded familiar, but Ava couldn't remember where she'd heard it. Beside her, Riley looked on with a downward tilt of her chin and narrowed eyes.

"There sure is," Lucas drawled. He leaned backwards against the counter, crossing his arms over his thin chest. "It'd be great if you could do your job, Greathouse, instead of treating me like a criminal." His fiery tone contrasted with an unnervingly placid face.

Greathouse grit his teeth. "I'll repeat: I'll talk to you at the station, Lucas. No one is treating you like a criminal."

"Oh, yeah? Well, that's funny, because when Dan Harding called to tell me someone had finally offed my sister, he wasted no time demanding I come down to the station to 'answer a few questions'."

Lucas Wilson. *Of course.* Mr. and Mrs. Walsh had mentioned him the previous night. How he was, apparently, back in Shiloh to start a business and help care for his aging father.

"We're covering all our bases," Greathouse said, his posture rigid. "I'm very sorry for your loss, but I'm not saying any more until this afternoon."

Lucas snorted, taking a step toward the table where Greathouse, Ava, and Riley sat. Even in his anger, he moved as though slithering. He smiled a tight-lipped smile. "Well, *I'm* not sorry."

Greathouse sighed. "Alright, Lucas. We get it. You've got a lot going on. Now, this is the last time I'll ask you: Please get out while I finish taking these ladies' statements. If you don't vacate the premises, I'm going to call Officer Harding to come remove you."

The smile on Lucas's face widened into a sneer. He threw his head back and laughed, slapped one hand on the table. "Geez! You're so uptight, Greathouse. Fine. I'm going. But you're in for an earful this afternoon, I'm telling you that."

"No problem," Greathouse said, his eyes following Lucas as the man moved toward the door. Only when Lucas disappeared outside, the entire building seeming to shake with the slam of the door behind him, did Greathouse turn his attention back to Ava and Riley. He looked almost apologetic.

"Well," Ava said. The cafe was silent, save for the faint hum of chattering voices drifting in from Main Street.

Riley let out a snicker, followed by a low whistle. "Wow. Bro is on one."

Greathouse cleared his throat, attempting to regain his professional composure. He looked from Ava to Riley, then back again. "Now. As I was about to say before that unfortunate interruption, we have yet to determine a cause of death for Ms. Wilson. If—and that's a big if—it turns out I need to speak with you again, I'll get in touch. As for right now, I'd suggest lying low. There are—clearly—certain people it's best not to tangle with."

All three rose from the table. The air between them had changed; it was as if the scene they all had witnessed with Lucas had given them an unspoken rapport of sorts. Instead of the shortness he'd shown them before, Greathouse now seemed worried. He carried his mug to the counter, heaving another sigh. As Greathouse turned toward the door, Riley trailed along behind him.

"Chief," Riley piped in suddenly. She looked Greathouse straight in the eye. "You're pretty sure it was an accident, right?"

Greathouse held her gaze, his mustache drooping. "Time will tell, kid."

With that, Chief Greathouse turned and lumbered out of the coffee shop, pulling the heavy wooden door shut behind him. Ava and Riley watched through the window as he lumbered down the sidewalk toward the corner. Instead of turning north toward the station, though, he continued straight, past the plaza where Audrey's body had been found, and on down Main Street.

"He's not going to the station," Riley observed, taking the words right out of Ava's mouth.

"More interviews?" Ava wondered aloud.

They sat in silence a moment longer, then Ava snapped her fingers. "Isn't Ricky Birch's garage up that way?"

"It sure is," Riley said, her eyes growing wide. "You think

he's headed there? I mean, that's where *I'd* go next if I suspected foul play, given that argument you overheard. That, or Lucas Wilson's place."

"Yeah, but Greathouse said he's got something set up with Lucas already," Ava pointed out.

"Well, whatever. Something is definitely up."

Riley set her chin as though that settled the matter and wandered back behind the counter. Ava remained at the window a moment longer, gazing out at the empty street. A few people milled about, stopping to chat for a moment on the sidewalk, plugging meters as they ran their errands, but it was a forced sort of normalcy, as though the town were trying to eke out a few more normal minutes before all hell broke loose. It was the calm before the storm. *Or*, Ava thought with a wry smile, *the eerie silence before the funnel cloud descends.*

5

———

It was nearly dark when Ava pulled up outside Rose and Joel's tiny one-story house. She'd shooed Riley out of Arcana at six on the dot, telling the girl to go straight home. Although Audrey's death appeared to have been an accident, Ava was taking no chances. Now, as she sat in the car outside the Robinson home, she fought to keep her spirits high. Whether the leaden feeling that had settled itself in her gut had begun with the discovery of Audrey Wilson's lifeless body or had crept up as she ran the sales receipts at Arcana after closing, she wasn't sure. Even with the extra foot traffic from rubberneckers looking for an excuse to swing by the plaza, Arcana's second day numbers certainly weren't any better than the first. *Well, that's what friends are for—to cheer each other up.* She hoped Rose wouldn't mind her dropping by unannounced.

The porch light was off, but she could see the lamps on in the living room, casting an orangey glow from behind the kitchen curtains. Ava strode up the porch steps, pressed a firm finger to the doorbell. She heard a chime ring inside. Then, the pad of footsteps approaching and a pause. Rose must have looked through the peephole, because her face seemed relieved when she opened the door, wordlessly gesturing Ava inside. A very dazed looking Ellie, perched on Rose's hip, gave a noncommittal wave of her chubby hand as Ava followed them inside. Rose pulled the door shut behind them, led them to the living room.

"Sorry I haven't texted you back," Rose began. She didn't look sorry—just tired. Given the drained looks on both her and Ellie's faces, it had been a long day.

"It's fine," Ava said, waving a hand and sinking down onto the plush sofa. Rose and Joel's house was small, but it gave off the same homey vibes that Rose always had. "I'm just shaken up, I guess."

"I know. Audrey's drowning... I think the whole town's on edge." Rose set Ellie on the floor to play. "Is Riley freaking out?"

"Not really. She didn't say much after Chief Greathouse stopped by to interview us. I, on the other hand, still feel so upset. Like, something feels off to me."

Rose didn't answer right away, just sat down in the armchair across from Ava, one dainty leg crossed over the other. Her mouth was pinched, and she seemed to be debating whether to open it. Finally, she caved. "Well, I didn't want to have this conversation without Joel here, but..." She glanced toward the door as though she half hoped her husband might come striding in before she had to continue.

Ava's stomach clenched. This was weird. She'd expected Rose to reassure her, come out with some theory that would explain what could have happened to Audrey: *Oh, she'd always had heart palpitations.* Or, *we never thought her alcoholism had gotten so bad...* This was a different reaction entirely.

"Where is Joel? Is he okay?" Ava was becoming more alarmed by the minute.

"He went to work out, relieve some stress. He's as okay as he can be, considering."

"Considering what?"

Rose blew out her breath. "Well, considering the fact that Chief Greathouse seems to suspect him of having something to do with Audrey's death."

Ava lurched forward in her chair. "What?! That's insane. Riley and I just spoke to Greathouse today, and he said they still thought it could've been an accident!"

Even as she spoke, the same feeling of dread settled in the pit of her stomach. A classy, composed woman like Audrey Wilson passing out drunk and falling face first in a fountain? She hadn't wanted to admit it, but it seemed unlikely. The Death card flashed through Ava's mind.

Rose shrugged. "They don't know either way. The autopsy results aren't back yet. But I guess the station received a tip..." Her voice broke off, her rosebud mouth quivering.

Now, *this* was alarming. "A tip? About Audrey?"

"Yes. The person said... They said..."

The sound of keys jangled in the front door. The door swung open, and Joel walked in, face strained, his tank top stuck to him with sweat. As his gaze landed on Ava and Rose sitting frozen in the living room, his face crumpled. Without even speaking, Joel dropped his gym bag in a heap and stalked off to the kitchen. This time, Rose really did burst into sobs.

Ava shifted uncomfortably. She wished she were the kind of person to reach over and run a comforting hand along her friend's back, but the thought alone made her shrink. Instead, she leaned over and hooked her hands under Ellie's armpits, heaving the still-dazed baby onto her own lap. She perched the little girl gingerly on her knee, hoping the girl wouldn't cry at having switched hands.

"Rose," Ava began, unsure if she should press. She was treading on dangerous turf. "Do you mean someone identified Joel as a witness?"

As if on cue, Joel reappeared in the living room with a glass of water in his hand. He took a long gulp, his Adam's apple moving up and down, and sat down across from the two women. Normally, Ava was sure Rose would have told him to get his sweaty self off the furniture, but her friend didn't even seem to notice. Instead, she wiped the back of one hand across her eyes and looked expectantly at Joel to answer Ava's question.

Joel ran an anxious hand through his hair, flicking drops of sweat into his eyes. "Chief Greathouse was here around noon, saying he got an anonymous email from someone—apparently someone here in town. The long and short of it is, that person claims I was having an affair with Audrey and that she threatened to tell Rose."

The feeling of dread that Ava had been trying to push down all day rose in her chest. She'd been here before. The affair, the cover-up. But murder? Thank god, her situation hadn't led to anything like that. Suddenly, infidelity took a backseat to murder. But what was Joel saying?

"So..." Ava glanced at Rose, whose eyes traced patterns on the tapestry rug on the floor, and then back at Joel. "They're saying you went and killed Audrey?"

Joel nodded, not meeting Ava's eyes. "Something like that,

yeah. No charges pressed, since they can't even say definitively that it was murder. But the chief was in here grilling me earlier, so I guess that's where his mind is."

"Hold up," Ava said, still trying to make sense of things. "First off, wouldn't you have been home at the time Audrey died? Surely Rose can vouch for you."

Joel rubbed the back of his neck and closed his eyes. "That's the thing. I went for my run at 4:30 this morning—like I do every day—which doesn't do much for me in terms of an alibi. She probably died sometime around then."

Ava's stomach tightened. "Okay, well, regardless—I can't believe *this* is the direction Greathouse is leaning. It's ridiculous! I heard Audrey and Ricky Birch going at it in the hallway last night at the committee dinner. It was bad—Ricky threatened Audrey, sounded like he was going to send someone after her."

Rose turned sharply to Ava. "Are you kidding me? And Greathouse knows that? You told him?"

"Of course, I told him!" Ava exclaimed, exasperated. "And anyway, Audrey's brother, Lucas, came storming into Arcana today while Riley and I were talking with the chief. He seemed almost glad his sister was dead, but you're telling me that Greathouse has chosen to home in on *Joel* as a suspect?"

Joel rubbed his temples. "Apparently. None of this makes any sense."

"Joel," Ava said, her voice hesitant. She wasn't sure she wanted to say the words, but she had to know. She had to ask. "Is any of it true?"

Joel looked shocked. "Are you kidding me, Ava? Do you really think I murdered someone?"

"That's not what I meant. I know you wouldn't *kill* someone. But I asked if *any* of it was true—not just about the murder..."

Rose was fidgeting, her fingers twisting in her lap. Although Ava kept her gaze fixed on Joel, she could tell that Rose wanted nothing more than to run out of the room, shut the whole thing down.

"No," Joel said, his eyes sparking. "It's absolutely not true. Rose and I have been through this a million times today, and I don't know what else to say. Audrey and I dated in high school, and yeah, she'd been coming on to me the last few months, but I swear to god—"

"What do you mean she'd been coming on to you?" Rose's voice was sharp, summoned from somewhere that didn't show on her porcelain face. "You never told me about that."

"Why would I tell you?" Joel threw up his hands. "To make you worry? I shot down her advances, and nothing was going to happen. There was no reason to tell anyone."

"Well, apparently there was, because someone else knew about it, and now look!"

"Listen. I don't know what that person thinks they saw, but I promise you, nothing happened between me and Audrey Wilson. And I sure as heck didn't kill her."

"I know you didn't kill her." Rose had gone quiet. She studied the rug again. "But I'm not so sure about the affair."

Joel's face fell. He got up from his chair, began stalking the room, water glass still in his hand. His eyes were wild, desperate. From her perch on Ava's lap, Ellie whined, reaching her hands out to Joel. It was the comfort he needed. He walked over and took the baby from Ava, settling her onto his broad chest.

"Rose, you have to believe me." Joel rubbed Ellie's back.

"Never once since our senior year of high school have I so much as shaken *hands* with Audrey Wilson. You know her family made it clear that I wasn't of the kind of stock they wanted for their daughter."

"Oh, and that's the only reason why? And then you ended up with me, since I'm from the same kind of low-class family as you?" Rose was on her feet now, too, her face reddening.

"No! You know that's not what I meant. I'm just saying—it ended then, and never once did I look back. I found you. I didn't want Audrey."

Ava, still sitting straight-backed on the sofa, felt like an intruder. She shouldn't be hearing this kind of conversation. God knew she'd had her share of similar ones, and they weren't something she'd have been happy about another person outside her marriage witnessing.

Rose stared at Joel. Then, the tension on her face smoothing into something even scarier than anger, she pointed to the sofa. "Get your stuff. You're sleeping out here tonight."

"Rose, do you actually think there was something between—"

Rose held up a hand to stop him. "I don't know what I think, Joel. You didn't tell me about her coming on to you, so what else haven't you told me? I need time to process. But to do that, I need space, which means you're sleeping on the sofa the next couple of nights until we figure this thing out."

Ava grabbed her bag from the floor, getting to her feet. She'd come here to make sense of the day's events, not pull at the loose ends of a marriage that seemed scarily on the verge of unraveling. Her presence was not what the Robinsons needed right now. And god knew her own experience had steeled her against this kind of thing. She wouldn't be of any comfort to anyone right now.

"I'm going home," Ava murmured, touching Rose's shoulder. "My phone's on if you need me."

As she stepped around the coffee table and let herself out into the night, she realized it was raining. The coolness of the mist on her skin as she made her way down the porch steps and into her car was comforting, a release from the darkness of the day. Audrey Wilson's sudden death, the worryingly low sales she was bringing in at Arcana, the allegations against Joel... Nothing about this was the fresh start she'd had in mind when she moved to Shiloh. Ava rested her head on the steering wheel a moment before pulling out of the Robinsons' driveway and making her way home. Her chest felt heavy, and she wished for a moment that she remembered how to cry. But then, in the silence, she heard the patter of the rain on the roof of the car. Tears coming to save the day.

THE HOUSE WAS quiet when Ava arrived home. It was still bizarre, walking into what she'd known as her grandfather's kitchen only to be met with silence, but after the chaos of the day, she welcomed it. Ava hung her jacket on the back of a kitchen chair and sank down at the table, desperate to shake off the gloom that had crept its way ever closer since the morning.

What was *happening*? It was bad enough that opening day had gone so poorly, that Donna Schroeder's letter to the editor had apparently resonated with half the town. But now someone was *dead*, and her best friend's husband was being dragged into the mess. Ava rose to fill a glass of water from the tap. As she drank, she relished the cool water, willing herself to swallow the lump that had taken up permanent residence in her throat.

Her phone buzzed. She glanced at it, groaned.

"Hi Mom," Ava said, trying to keep the dread out of her voice. She hadn't spoken to her mother since she'd received the card addressed to *Mrs.* Ava *Shapiro*, and she wasn't sure she had the strength.

"Oh, thank god," Mrs. Goldberg all but wailed into the phone. "We've been seeing the news. We thought you were dead. Oh, Ava, I told you that place was full of hooligans. Come on home, we've still got your room—"

"Mom. Calm down. What do you mean you've been seeing the news? You don't get Shiloh news in Chicago." Ava rubbed her eyes, leaning against the kitchen counter. She recognized that tone in her mother's voice, and she was way too exhausted for this kind of stuff.

"We joined all the Shiloh Facebook groups, your father and I—the second you moved there—and we see every wedding, every traffic stop, every funeral, every *body* in a fountain that happens along in that town, Ava. I know you've just started your shop, honey, and–and–and doing that stuff with the Magic cards—"

"Tarot cards." Ava was never sure if her mother truly couldn't remember the name, or if it was a chosen forgetfulness.

"Well, whatever," Mrs. Goldberg went on. Ava could almost picture her giving a dismissive wave of her hand. "But it's not safe there, Ava. It's too far from civilization."

"We have a very competent police chief," Ava replied, shocked by the words as they came out of her mouth.

Greathouse? Competent? "And anyway, I'm sure it was an accident. Audrey Wilson was a very prominent woman in town. I'm sure no one wished her harm."

Mrs. Goldberg clucked her tongue. "That's not what they're saying in the news, Ava. They're saying that this poor Ms. Wilson was involved with another man in town—married, mind you—and after she decided to come clean to the wife, the man killed her. They've received an anonymous tip. The autopsy reports will come back soon and then they can slap the charges on him. But until then, he's a killer running free..."

"Well, speaking of accidents that weren't really accidents," Ava began, rubbing her forehead. She couldn't believe she was about to bring this up. "I got your card in the mail. *Mrs. Ava Shapiro*, Mom? Really?"

Mrs. Goldberg was silent for a beat. "Did I write that? Oh, goodness, I must have forgotten. I didn't even *realize*—"

"I don't believe you." Ava sank down to the floor with her back against the bottom row of kitchen cupboards. She wasn't even sure what she meant to achieve by confronting her mother, but hey, her mom had been the one to start it. Two could play this game.

Her mother scoffed. "Don't be ridiculous, Ava. It *was* your last name for four years."

"Yeah, and because of that, you should know how much it mattered to me, getting rid of that last name."

"I won't apologize for something I didn't do on purpose." Mrs. Goldberg's tone was defiant.

"Big surprise."

"Don't take that tone with me," Mrs. Goldberg said. "I am your mother. I loved you. I raised you. I kept a roof—"

"I know, I know. You and dad kept a roof over my head, and

of *course* I'm thankful, but none of this has anything to do with that."

"Oh, really? If you ask me, it seems an awful lot like you wanted to get as far away from Noah as you could—so you wouldn't have to reckon with forgiveness."

Ava snorted. "Oh, come on. I'd be stupid to forgive him. Forgiveness is not even on the table."

"Well, that's a selfish attitude," Mrs. Goldberg remarked, her voice thin. "If it were me, and it was your father who had—"

"Stop. It's not you, and it wasn't Dad. It's not your decision."

Ava briefly considered asking her mother if she'd ever considered the possibility that maybe her daughter had moved to get a little peace from her need to play dictator, but she bit back the words. That was an explosion she didn't want, not tonight.

Mrs. Goldberg tried another tack. "We're just worried about you, Ava. When we see these things on the news, these–these bodies—"

"There was *one* body." Ava was well acquainted with the soothing tone her mother's voice had taken on. It was a trap.

"Will you just consider coming back home? Noah's been wishing he could go there to see you."

Ava's throat tightened. No. He wouldn't *dare*. Besides, he was out living it up with Lexie and company—knowledge she couldn't admit to her mother, who would view Ava's keeping tabs on her ex as promising. "You told him absolutely not, I hope."

"I told him you'd call if and when you're ready." Mrs. Goldberg's voice was wheedling.

Something inside Ava snapped. Blood rushed to her face.

She stood up and set her glass in the sink with a clatter. What part of *divorced* did her mother not understand? It was legal, over, finished, a done deal. Sure, Noah had seemed like the perfect, promising, handsome young Jewish man Ava's mother had dreamed of for her daughter—and for a while he had been. Until he wasn't. And somehow, Sara Goldberg wasn't catching on.

"It's done, Mom. I'm not getting back with Noah," Ava said. And here this call was supposed to have been about her mother's concern over the news of Audrey Wilson's death. Somehow, it always came back to this. Well, she should have known better than to bring up the name issue.

"Okay." Mrs. Goldberg was quiet a moment. "Just promise me you're okay, honey."

Ava sighed. Her mother was, ultimately, caring, and she couldn't fault her for that. "I'm fine, Mom. I've got Rose. I'm getting involved in the town. My shop is keeping me pretty busy." None of which was exactly the truth, but she wasn't about to add to her mother's reasons to coax her to move back to Chicago.

"Well," Mrs. Goldberg said, sniffling a bit. "I'm glad to hear all that. You keep us posted, though, honey—okay? And we'll be keeping an eye on the news."

Ava ended the call and stood in the dim light of the kitchen. She'd gotten away with it this time, but it was only a matter of time before her mother put two and two together: the allegedly murderous lover she'd heard about was none other than Joel Robinson, little Rosie Jacobson's husband. Ava pushed the thought away. As tragic as the events of the day had been, she'd spent too long turning them over and over in her mind, and none of it made any sense. She needed to clear her mind, snap out of the funk she'd let herself sink into. A bike ride would do the trick.

THE SUMMER NIGHT air was clean and comforting as Ava coasted down the hill, letting her feet rest on the pedals as she picked up speed. As a child, she'd loved the feel of the crisp, earthy Nebraska wind whipping through her long hair, the satisfying crunch of gravel beneath her tires, the grittiness of dust in her mouth, and she loved it no less now. This evening ride was what she needed; the messy remnants of the day had already dissipated. Just another quick circle around the edge of town, and she'd have cleared her mind and tired her muscles out enough for sleep.

The lights of Shiloh had dimmed, and the lampposts lining main street twinkled in a hazy, glowing row. The sounds of laughter, of muffled music and pulsing beats drifted in from the town's lone bar, a decades-old fixture near the underpass leading to the highway. Ava hadn't been there, but she pictured it as the beating heart of a Shiloh weeknight, a toughened organ fed by the same locals that it, in turn, fed. A communal watering hole, a church for the ones who found their relief in the metallic rasp of a karaoke mic, the sweat of an ice-cold beer on a worn wooden table. Ava had always thought those were the ones who really lived.

She rounded the curve on the southwest edge of town, coming up near the cemetery on her left. She'd never understood the superstition of holding one's breath when passing a cemetery. Were the bodies buried there not really dead? If so, it had always seemed to Ava that if one were to breathe them in, some of their still-vibrant life force might somehow fortify the breather, making it all the more reason to breathe the spirits in. As she pedaled past, the tombstones jutting up like dark, beautiful talons caressing the sky, Ava drew a deep breath in, letting the air fill her lungs. Her grandparents were buried here—and they were a part of her present, and now inextricably linked to her in breath. She laughed to herself in the dark. Her mother would have deemed the notion horrifying.

Reaching the corner, Ava stopped. Somewhere at the far end of the street was the undeniable flashing of blue and red lights. She narrowed her eyes, trying to peer through the darkness to determine the lights' approximate whereabouts. Not quite to Adams Street, the northwest corner of town, which put them about at...

No. Ava felt her heart rate quicken. In a flash, her heels were back on the pedals, her legs racing as she leaned into the stinging wind and flew up the street. Surely she was wrong. She'd just been at Rose and Joel's how long before—an hour? Two hours? Still, as she neared the Robinson home and the lights loomed brighter, her stomach twisted itself into an increasingly hopeless knot.

She skidded to a stop at the intersection and an icy wave of fear washed through her. There, in front of Rose and Joel's driveway, were two police cars, their lights flashing eerily in the darkness. A single police officer stood leaning against the driver's side of one of the cars, wide-brimmed hat pulled low on his forehead, muttering into a radio. Ava heard only the faint rumble of a deep voice, followed by a few quick blips and a second of static. As she got closer, walking her bicycle next to her, she could make out the officer's face in the dark.

"Officer Harding," Ava called, her voice cutting into the eerie stillness, punctuated by the flashing lights.

The man looked up from the radio. "Ma'am, I'm going to have to ask you to leave the premises."

"Right," Ava said, trying hard to hide her sinking sense of despair. "It's just—well, I'm close with the Robinsons, and I'm worried. Is everything okay?"

Officer Harding studied Ava for a moment, as though debating whether he could trust her. "I'm limited as to what I can say, but the chief's inside serving a search warrant."

"Search warrant?" Ava's voice trembled.

"I really can't say any more, ma'am," Officer Harding replied, shaking his head. "Now, I suggest you go on home—"

"Ava!"

A frantic voice from the porch cut into Harding's reply, as both he and Ava turned to see Rose tripping down the front steps toward them with baby Ellie in her arms. Her curly blond hair streamed out behind her, and even in the darkness, Ava could see the panic in her pixie-like face. She stopped short in front of Ava and the officer, clutching Ellie to her chest.

"What's going on?" Ava demanded. "Greathouse has a search warrant? For what?"

"The coroner says Audrey was murdered," Rose said, her voice strangled. "And apparently they found a note in Audrey's pocket—"

"What? What kind of note?" Ava's eyes flitted between Rose and Officer Harding. "What's that got to do with Joel?"

"He wrote it," Rose choked out. "Or, at least, they think he did."

"Well, what's it say? And what are they looking for?"

"Evidence, Ava," Rose hissed. "The murder weapon, love

letters, photographs stashed away. Who knows? And I don't know what the note said."

The screen door of the house creaked open, and Chief Greathouse stepped out onto the porch, a couple other officers whom Ava didn't recognize close behind him. Ava was too far away to see the chief's face, but his steps were heavy. Catching sight of Ava and Rose huddled together at the end of the driveway with Officer Harding standing a few feet away, Greathouse grunted something to the other officers and they made their way to the squad car. The chief turned and lumbered down the steps, making his way toward Ava and Rose.

"Ms. Goldberg, you need to leave." Greathouse sounded tired.

"Not yet," Ava said, her voice firm. "What grounds do you have for a search warrant?"

Greathouse sighed, rubbed his temples. "I'm not giving you details right now. We've got a homicide on our hands, and that's all I'll say."

"And you think Joel is the person responsible?"

Beside her, Ava felt Rose stiffen, heard her murmur something to Ellie, who was beginning to fuss.

Greathouse nodded, his expression grim. "We received a tip that alleges Joel and Audrey had a little fling going on" —he shot a wary glance at Rose— "and when Joel ended it, Audrey threatened to tell Rose all about the affair. Joel couldn't have that, so he arranged to meet her at the plaza, and he... Well, he took care of the problem."

"Officer Greathouse, with all due respect," Rose broke in, her voice shaking. She switched Ellie to the other hip. "Do you actually believe that my husband would murder a woman in cold blood?"

"I've seen stranger things come to pass, Rose," Greathouse replied, his face dark. "It's the only thing that makes sense, as much as it pains me to say it."

"Well, I don't believe it," Ava declared. "Affair or no affair, I don't believe Joel Robinson would ever murder someone."

"Unfortunately, it's not up to you," Chief Greathouse said, rounding on Ava. Their eyes met, and she held his gaze in defiance. "You're new in town, so maybe you need a pointer. We don't have murders in Shiloh. We live simple, peaceful lives in this town, unlike what you might have been used to in the city. So, when something like this does happen, it rocks our community. You better believe the entire police force is going to be working around the clock to follow any and every lead we can find—even when those leads aren't to your liking."

"I'm glad to hear you've checked out Ricky Birch then," Ava said, the heat rising in her face. Rose shot her a warning look. What was she doing, talking back to a cop?

"We're checking all leads, Ms. Goldberg," Greathouse replied coolly. He tipped his hat, then turned to Officer Harding. "Nothing to report inside, Dan. Let's hit the road. Ms. Goldberg, I expect you to go on home, too."

Officer Harding cast an apologetic look toward Ava and Rose before ducking into the driver's side of the car. Greathouse heaved himself into the passenger's side, setting the car rocking. The car doors slammed in the stillness of the night. As they rolled out of the driveway, the flashing lights blinked off, and soon they were nothing more than a pair of hazy taillights in the distance.

"I've got to put this one to bed," Rose murmured, rubbing

Ellie's back. The baby had nestled against her chest, her eyelids drooping.

"Is Joel...?"

"Inside."

"Okay. But Rose—" She looked her friend dead in the eye, already knowing she'd be seeing those flashing blue and red lights in her dreams that night. "Joel didn't do it. But I'm going to find out who did."

6

————

It was ten past one the next afternoon when Ava brought her bicycle to a stop along the curb of Sanderson Park. The upbeat twang of country music drifted in from somewhere as Ava breathed in. The tantalizing smell of barbecue and charcoal floated through the town, along with the occasional snap of sidewalk poppers and crackle of lady fingers. Were those even legal this long before the fourth of July? Ava doubted the people of Shiloh—police included—really cared. And certainly the police had more on their plate right now, anyway.

Ava started up the sidewalk, pushing her sunglasses up the bridge of her already sweaty nose. After last night, she'd had her doubts about coming to today's barbecue. It didn't seem right to spend the afternoon drinking and laughing with other people in town while Rose and Joel were home, trying to sort through the allegations Greathouse had dumped at their feet. But Rose had been adamant in her texts that morning, insisting that Ava use the opportunity to connect with the community. The news of the search warrant was contained, the two women reasoned, and the whole thing would blow over soon enough. Life needed to carry on.

As she approached the sheltered area under which several rows of peeling picnic tables stood covered with food, Ava's eyes scanned the crowd. It was a good turnout; everywhere she looked, the park was full of people in jean shorts, red Solo cups in hand, milling about and laughing. That was something she'd noticed about these rural folk—they laughed no matter what, their eyes crinkling up at the edges. It didn't matter what joke you told, they would chuckle and slap their knees like it were the funniest thing in the world, too polite to ever tell you otherwise. Ava doubted she had that much politeness in her. It was no wonder these people seemed to think she was unfriendly.

"Hey."

Ava's chest loosened in relief at the sound of Riley's voice. Although, as she looked around at the group on the other side of the picnic tables, she spotted many more familiar faces than she'd expected. She honestly wasn't sure if that helped or made things worse. She gave a small, awkward wave to Riley, pushed up her sunglasses again.

"I didn't know you were coming," Riley said, looking Ava up and down with an expression that was somehow impressed. She pushed a paper plate into Ava's hands. "Here. Scott just took a fresh round of Fairburys off the grill. Get one before everybody else takes 'em."

Ava barely managed to hide a grimace; she'd suffered through those as a child with her grandparents on such civic occasions. Those cherry red beef hotdogs were the *worst*. Instead, she slipped into the small line that had formed in front of the tables. "Who's Scott?"

"My stepdad," Riley replied. She glanced around the

crowds, her dark eyes flitting through the clusters of people. "He's helping grill." Riley headed off in that direction as Ava stayed by the buffet table.

The center picnic table, covered with red, white, and blue checkered plastic table roll, boasted an impressive array of potluck dishes. Syrupy baked beans, salads stuffed with Jell-O and marshmallows, platters of crunchy chopped veggies, all manner of chips and dips. Ava grabbed a starchy white bun, pleased with the mental image of the horrified expression her mother would have worn had she seen the stuff Shiloh folks considered salad. She took a large helping of something green and bouncy, which looked suspiciously as though it contained chunks of Snickers, and finished her plate off with some kind of apple tart, its edges baked to a glorious, golden perfection. Somehow, it looked too pretty to belong with the rest of the food—like a homecoming queen dropped into the middle of a marching band camp.

"Here," Riley said again, coming up next to Ava and dropping a perfectly charred hotdog onto her plate with a pair of tongs. "I'm gonna go grab a Coke. You want one? Or something else—Bud Light?"

"Water?" Ava had been hoping for a beer, but Bud Light was further than she could bring herself to go. Riley nodded and tromped away.

"Are you Ava Goldberg?"

Ava looked up from the bite of macaroni salad she'd scooped off her plate. A freckled, dark-haired woman, who was also very pregnant, had appeared out of nowhere. By her side was the same man who'd helped Audrey host the committee event just two days before. Chris Something? It was crazy how long ago it all seemed.

"That's me," Ava said, setting her fork down and reaching out to shake first the woman's hand, then the man's. The woman had a friendly sort of girl-next-door smile. Both she and Chris looked to be around the same age as Ava, but the woman's eyes showed faint traces of crow's feet, like someone who had spent a little too long in the sun during their teenage years. Somehow, though, the lines made her appear more friendly, as though she were perpetually smiling.

"It's so nice to meet you," the woman said, eyes shining. "Katie Mitchell. I haven't been able to make it into your cafe yet, but Chris tells me it's exactly what Shiloh's been needing."

The man next to her—Chris *Mitchell*—chuckled, flashing a dazzling grin at Ava. "I meant it. Regardless of what Donna Schroeder says in the paper, you've got a gem of a place there."

"Well, thank you," Ava said, blushing. She'd never been good at taking compliments, and she didn't want to discuss Donna. "Things are starting out slow, but I'm hopeful they'll continue to pick up."

Katie's expression was sympathetic. She nodded her head. "I'd imagine things took a hit with everything that's been going on. It's just so sad about Audrey—and scary."

"Well, you know what Melanie told me she heard from Donna at prayer group the other night," Chris cut in, giving Ava a sly grin. He continued, raising his voice in a clear imitation of the pastor's wife. "'Harm is bound to befall a town once you let demonic practices into the community.'"

"I still can't believe she said that," Katie said, rolling her eyes. "That's the most ridiculous thing I've ever heard."

Ava thought back to the crooked finger Donna Schroeder had pointed at her, that look of pure malice, after discovering Audrey's body in the fountain. She nearly shuddered just thinking about it. Discouraging people in town from giving Cafe Arcana their business was bad enough, but to blame someone's death on the existence of a coffee shop was, frankly, stupid.

Chris raised his hands in innocence. "Hey, I'm just the messenger. But look on the bright side, the only people who believe her are ones you probably don't want coming around, anyway."

"I guess..."

"Anyway," Katie broke in, done discussing Donna. "I heard someone say Audrey's death was *murder,* but I just can't imagine it. Not in Shiloh."

"I don't know..." Chris shook his head like it pained him to say it. "We've been seeing a lot more crime here these past few years. Stores being robbed, cars stolen out of driveways. St. Patrick's was broken into several times. More folks passing through off the interstate, I guess."

Ava didn't know what to say, so she simply nodded in agreement. It was a grim thing to admit, but having grown up familiar with Chicago public transit, it took a lot to shock her. There were plenty of folks in the big cities—hell, probably even in Lincoln and Omaha, who'd kill (pardon the pun) for crime rates as low as one murder every several years.

"Seems like not only crime is bad," Katie added, rubbing her belly protectively. "There's just so much going on in the world—and the inflation, these housing prices... My god, is it just us? How can anyone afford it?"

Just then, Riley reappeared with a bottle of water, which she tucked under Ava's arm. Noticing Chris and Katie, she flashed a shy smile. "Hey."

"Nice to see you, Riley," Katie said, beaming at the girl. Even her eyes seemed to smile. "I hear you're working at Arcana, right?"

Riley nodded. "Scott told me I needed to get a summer job."

"Well, I bet you two are having a ball," Katie continued, resting her hands on her shelf of a belly. "Ava was just telling us that business has been a little slow, but I told her it's probably only temporary. You know, people being a little hesitant about venturing out when there's—allegedly—a killer on the loose..."

Riley's eyebrows raised as she glanced at Ava. "You mean Audrey? I thought the chief was still pretty sure it was an accident..."

Ava took a huge bite of her hotdog, hoping to buy herself time from having to answer. This barbecue was supposed to have been a distraction—the last thing she wanted was for the conversation to turn toward potential suspects.

"There's no official word yet," Chris said, his face solemn. "Just speculation around town. I've heard there's no way Audrey could've died by tripping and falling, given the angle they found her in."

"Yikes." Riley grimaced.

Katie rubbed her belly again. "It's just too bad, isn't it? If it *was* murder, I really hope they catch whoever did it."

"I heard Greathouse was looking at a couple people," Chris put in, taking a sip of his Bud Light. "Maybe he'll wait until after the funeral to release more details. You know, out of respect for the family."

Ava took an enormous bite of the green goopy salad to avoid the subject. *Yep. Snickers.* Her gaze traveled across the park, taking in the sea of Huskers caps and aviators. Aside from Arthur Whitlock, the mailman, and a couple other folks she figured she recognized from the cafe, there weren't many people she'd met. She realized Riley hadn't even introduced her to her parents, who were apparently present. She'd make sure to meet them before heading out, just to say hello. It would be the polite thing to do.

"Hey there."

Jolted out of her thoughts, Ava turned to see Owen O'Kelly approaching the group. *Thank god. A distraction.* He, too, held a Bud Light, and a well-worn Huskers cap was pulled down low on his brow. His perpetually tousled hair curled around the edges of the cap, complementing the jovial smile he wore. He shook Chris and Katie's hands, then reached for Ava's.

"Good to see you out and about," he said to Ava, dimples flashing. "And Katie, you're due in not too long, right?"

"July 4," Katie said. "We may have ourselves a little firecracker!"

"I already put my vote in for Yankee Doodle as a name," Chris chuckled. "Either that, or Sam. Someday he can be an Uncle Sam."

Katie rolled her eyes and gave her husband a playful swat. "You can all rest assured that I have vetoed both."

Everyone laughed. Ava's stomach unclenched as she began to relax. With Owen's arrival, the conversation had moved into more neutral, less awkward territory.

Owen took a swig of his beer. "You guys hear what Greathouse is saying about Audrey?"

Oh, come on. It was all Ava could do not to shoot a death glare at Owen. *This damn guy.* She kept her face neutral, unscrewed her water bottle top with one hand.

"We were just talking about that." Chris's expression turned serious. "You got news?"

"Well, I don't know what all you guys have heard," Owen

said, rocking back and forth on his heels. His dimples were gone, hidden by sandy brown stubble. "But my cousin who lives across the street from Joel and Rose Robinson said there were police there last night. Flashing lights and everything."

His eyes moved pointedly to Ava as if to convey that said cousin had also seen the town newbie dropping by for a visit. Luckily, Chris and Katie didn't seem to notice, and Ava broke eye contact without so much as a ripple in her expression. If he thought she was going to comment about the situation, he'd thought wrong.

Katie frowned. "Well, that seems odd..."

Riley, who had until now observed the conversation in silence, piped in, her voice skeptical. "How do you know the police being at the Robinsons' is related to Audrey's murder?"

"That's a good point," Owen admitted. "Lisa—my cousin—didn't leave her house, so I guess it's only speculation. You're right."

"Don't you think you ought to avoid speculation until you know for sure? That's a pretty serious thing to speculate about, murder." Ava's voice came out frostier than she expected.

Owen raised both his hands and shrugged his shoulders. He looked straight at Ava, as though daring her to tell him what he already knew: that she knew more than she was letting on. "Hey, I'm not accusing anyone. Just telling you what I heard."

"Right, right," Katie cut in with a soothing voice, trying to defuse the situation. "We know, Owen. Ava's right, though. We should probably stay out of it for the time being. Don't want anything to get misconstrued or start any rumors."

"Of course not," Chris said, as though that settled the matter. He glanced at his watch. "Shoot. Honey, it's almost two. I'm still hoping to get to the gym this afternoon, if possible."

"Two already?" Katie made a show of being shocked. "Well, I guess we'd better be heading out…"

Chris and Katie excused themselves, slipping into the throng of barbecue guests. Riley, announcing that she wanted another Coke, also disappeared. If Ava hadn't been so annoyed at the direction the conversation had gone, she would have found the Mitchells' expert escape almost comical. It was as though they'd practiced it, timing their lines and reactions down to the second. A glorious Midwestern trait, Ava thought. Practiced, polite, and under the radar. These small-town folks especially had the art of inoffensiveness down to a science. The only trouble was, they'd saved themselves and left her alone with the rumor starter.

"Did you try that yet?" Owen pointed to the apple tart on Ava's plate.

As the tart was still clearly intact, Ava took Owen's question as a peace offering. He was attempting to smooth things over. As long as he didn't bring Joel up again, she'd go along with it. "Not yet. Are they good?"

"I dunno, you tell me." He watched as she cut the tart with the side of her fork and took a bite.

Ava's eyes lit up. She was a sucker for a good dessert. "Oh, that's divine. You definitely need to grab one before they're gone."

Owen chuckled. "I saved some back for myself at home."

"You… I'm sorry, did you make these?" Ava knew her voice was probably offensively incredulous, but she couldn't help it. Looking at Owen, with his sweat-stained baseball cap and five o'clock shadow, she'd never have pegged him as a man who liked to bake—and *could* bake.

He shrugged, his green eyes twinkling. It was clear he was

relishing the surprise in Ava's expression. "Just a little hobby I have."

Suddenly, a thought came to Ava. "You know what? I've been looking for a place to get fresh baked goods for Arcana—"

Owen gave a curt shake of his head, cutting her off mid-sentence. "I said hobby."

"Yeah, but these are fabulous," Ava said. "You have genuine talent. You could absolutely sell these."

"I appreciate that," Owen said, flashing her a smile that seemed somehow practiced. "But I've got a hardware store to run."

"Of course." Ava took another bite of the tart, letting her eyes flick to the rest of the crowd. She hoped the disappointment didn't show on her face. Where was Riley when she needed her?

Owen swigged from his beer, watching her from above the can. She pretended not to notice, hoped he wouldn't bring up his cousin again. The only evidence they had against Joel was a note—which anyone could have written, honestly—and that pesky anonymous tip, which meant their case was pretty flimsy, as far as Ava was concerned. She didn't want to go around talking about it and add fuel to the fire.

"So, you done any tarot readings in the new cafe?"

Ava, still searching the park for any sign of Riley to come and save her, looked at Owen in surprise. "Nope."

Owen adjusted his ball cap, then crossed his arms over his broad chest. "Huh. Well, I'll have to put in a good word around town."

This time, it was Ava's turn for a stiff, practiced smile. "Thanks, that'd be great. Listen, I've got to get going, so I'm going to find Riley and introduce myself to her parents before I head out. It was nice seeing you."

She turned to traipse back across the lawn, but Owen touched a light hand to her forearm. "I'm heading out, too. Mind if I walk with you?"

Ava considered telling him she did mind, but decided against it. Owen was most likely going to admit that he knew she'd been at the Robinsons' the night before, but so be it. They'd all have to confront the problem eventually, and now could be as good a time as any to shut the rumors down before they snowballed any further. She flashed him a weak smile. "No problem."

At that moment—and just a moment too late—Riley came sauntering back across the grass, hands stuffed deep in the pockets of her denim shorts.

"You leaving?" she asked Ava.

"Yeah, although I wanted to say hello to your parents."

Riley stiffened, giving a quick shake of her head. "That's alright. You can just go."

"Really? I haven't met them yet."

Riley's cheeks flushed.

Owen, whose green eyes had drifted once again across the lawn, cleared his throat. He smiled. "Don't worry about it, Goldberg. You'll catch them next time."

"Okay..." Ava looked at both Owen and Riley suspiciously.

Owen jangled his keys in his pocket, clapped Riley on the back. "Good to see you. Tell Scott I said hey, and if he wants to stop in this week for those cables, he's more than welcome."

Depositing her empty plate in a nearby trash bag slung over a folding chair, Ava gave Riley's shoulder a quick, awkward squeeze. She'd never hugged the girl before, but figured it would be the nice, small-town thing to do. Owen chucked his beer can in the recycling bin, and together, they turned to head back toward the street.

"THAT WAS WEIRD JUST NOW, with Riley," Ava remarked as they left, the roar of laughter and the hum of twangy guitars fading behind them.

"Ah," Owen said, as though he'd known she was going to comment. He shrugged. "Tami and Scott... They have a little too much to drink sometimes. Most folks in town are used to it, but Riley probably wants to save you the experience. You being her employer and all."

"Please. Does she think I've never seen anyone drunk before?" Ava laughed.

Owen furrowed his brow. "It's kind of different. Anyway, where'd you park?"

"Here." Ava pointed to her bicycle, parked next to a mailbox with a tacky cover that flapped in the breeze.

"Oh, you biked," Owen said in surprise. "Nice. Well, I won't keep you long, but I wanted to make sure you're okay."

"I'm fine," Ava said coolly. She slipped on her sunglasses. "Why wouldn't I be?"

Owen ran a hand through his tousled honey blond hair. He looked embarrassed. "Well, you know. I just wonder how you're holding up with this whole murder thing. You just moved here, and already... this."

Ava raised her eyebrows. "Thanks for the courtesy call, but if I let myself get shaken up every time a crime occurred in Chicago, I'd never leave the house. It's tragic about Audrey, but I'm sure they'll find who did it, and justice will be served."

In her mind, she smirked. *I'll find out who did it. And you can bet your ass it won't be Joel Robinson.*

"You think Joel did it?" Owen was gazing at her, his green eyes serious.

"Pardon?"

"Come on, Goldberg. You can drop the facade. I know you know, and we can discuss it like adults. My cousin said you were out there at the Robinsons' last night, and I just want to be clear that I don't think Joel did it."

"Of course, Joel didn't murder anyone," Ava snapped. She gave her kickstand a sharp kick.

"Why are you so hostile?" Owen asked, looking slightly hurt. He crossed his arms once again over his chest and leaned back to look at her.

"I'm not hostile," Ava retorted, wheeling her bike down the driveway to the street. "I just don't want to give any weight to the rumors. And I don't know why you would have said anything to the Walshes to *start* a rumor."

He shrugged off the accusation. "Well, unfortunately, it sounds like Chief Greathouse is giving them weight. You were there last night. You ought to know."

Ava let out an exasperated breath, stopped walking. "Yes. I was. I do know. But Greathouse doesn't have a leg to stand on with that silly tip he received. Anyone could've made that up."

"Agreed," Owen said, nodding. "To be honest, I'm a little surprised Greathouse is going along with it. My guess is he's feeling a little panicked and went with the first lead that sprang up. I heard you overheard some kind of argument between Audrey and Ricky Birch at the committee dinner?"

Just how had he heard that? Owen was quite the gossip, it seemed.

"Yep," Ava said, slinging a leg over her bicycle. She knew she was being rude, but she hoped Owen would finally take the hint and get on his way.

"Interesting." Owen seemed lost in thought for a moment, then snapped back to attention. He pulled his wallet from out of his jeans pocket and extracted a business card, which he handed to Ava. "Well, listen, if you think of anything else that might exonerate Joel and want to bounce ideas off someone before going to Greathouse, let me know. That's my card."

Ava looked down at the business card and back to Owen. "Thanks. I'll keep it in mind."

Owen smiled, his dimples glowing. "Sounds good."

Giving Ava a parting wave, he readjusted his cap and turned. Ava stood a moment, watching him as he moved away down the sidewalk, his broad back growing smaller. She could still see the brightness of Owen's grin, the shyness of his dimples, and she hated it. *Nope. Not going to think about it.* It was time to put the mental brakes on. She knew all too well the sweetness a man who looked like that could talk. She'd been there, done that. And she was not doing it again.

The merry ruckus of the party, with guests no doubt getting drunker by the minute, floated down from the park behind her as Ava rode off down the street toward home. It occurred to her she hadn't asked anyone else how they were taking the news. Take Owen, for example. For all she knew, he'd gone to high school—even elementary school—with Audrey Wilson, had chucked dodge balls at her at recess, or stood next to her in the choir. They could've ridden on the homecoming float together, swapped Little Debbie snacks at lunch.

Perhaps she'd underestimated just how much Audrey Wilson's death had affected the lifelong residents of Shiloh, Nebraska. After all, she'd been horrified to read in the news several years before that a boy who'd sat next to her in high school chemistry had died in a car accident—and she hadn't spoken to him for a decade. How much more shocking must the same news be when the death was of a person you saw every day? Ran into at the grocery store? And then when it was murder? No wonder they wanted to talk about it. Word was bolting through town. Ava knew it wouldn't be long before everyone in Shiloh knew Joel Robinson was the chief's primary suspect in Audrey Wilson's murder. Sliding Owen's business card into her back pocket, Ava hopped on her bike and spun out of the driveway. She would have to move fast if she wanted to get to the bottom of things before Joel's reputation had been damaged beyond repair.

7

———

The tiny town of Shiloh was still half asleep when Ava arrived at Arcana the next morning. Most businesses in town were closed on Sundays, but, out of respect for the Jewish Sabbath which fell on Saturday, Ava had decided to switch things up. Although she didn't consider herself very religious, didn't keep the Sabbath by taping the refrigerator light down and turning off her cell phone every Saturday like her family on her mother's side, she liked the idea of refraining from work on Saturday. Besides, by being one of the few businesses open on Sunday, she'd have a better shot at snagging some of the chill, lazy Sunday crowd in search of an open shop to sit in.

And, Ava thought as she hopped off her bike and entered the shop, *Maybe I'll finally be able to get back to some shred of normalcy.*

As expected, with everyone off at church, business at Arcana was even slower than usual. Riley was back in her armchair, having graduated from her phone to one of the books Ava kept in the back wall bookcases. Ava found herself sprawled at a table, scrolling mindlessly through Instagram. One tropical vacation here, another Starbucks photo there. Everything looked the same. She gave the feed one last flick of the finger and was about to close out of the app when she stopped short, disgusted.

There it was, another tropical vacation, but this time of someone she knew. Apparently, Ava's now-safe-to-say-former friend, Lexie, had decided it would be a good look to head to Costa Rica with a couple other friends—one of them being Noah Shapiro. Unable to help herself, Ava flicked through the pictures on the post. Lexie, Noah, and company lined up on the beach, fresh coconuts in hand. Lexie, Noah, and company posing beneath a waterfall. Only Lexie and Noah, shoulder to shoulder in the glowing light of the setting Caribbean sun. Their sun-bronzed arms touching.

The doorbell jingled, and Ava snapped her head up. Owen O'Kelly grinned at her from the doorway, running a hand through his tousled hair.

"Is the psychic in?" Owen's green eyes flicked to the sign in the window, then back to Ava. There was a hint of a smile in them.

"Excuse me?" Ava was still trying to shake the image of Noah and Lexie from her mind. She wasn't sure she'd heard Owen correctly.

"The tarot readings. You still doing those?"

"Uh," Ava started, fumbling for words. "Yeah. Sorry—that's not what I was expecting you to ask."

"Why? I don't look like the type to be curious?" Owen's eyes were teasing, but there was something serious behind them, like he truly wondered what her answer would be.

Ava felt her face flush. She caught Riley's half smile before the girl went back to her book. She couldn't blame Riley for having a crush on Owen—he was handsome, and there was something about his demeanor that seemed flirtatious, even if harmless. She'd sensed it at the barbecue, and it was back now. But he'd figure out soon enough that she wouldn't be reciprocating. "It's less to do with you, and more to do with the fact that I'd kind of given up on anyone in town actually wanting a reading. By now, I figured I'd have to wait for people coming in from Lincoln and Omaha."

Owen shrugged, rocked back onto his heels. "Well, that's Shiloh for you. A lot of good church-going folk around here. But don't let 'em fool you. They'll be around, eventually. They've just got to get warmed up to the idea."

"Maybe." She caught the hint that "good church-goers" would be against any such satanic activity. "Anyway, what can I get you?"

"Well, one of those tarot readings," Owen began, tilting his head to the side as he finally moved his eyes from her to scan the menu board. "And I guess I'll have a dark roast."

"Sure," Ava said, already filling up a mug with steaming hot coffee. She set it on the counter in front of him. "When do you want to book the reading for?"

Owen looked surprised. "Well, I kind of thought we could do it now..."

"Um..." Ava glanced out the window again, searching the streets for any sign of life. She preferred to do readings in the evening, after hours. But it wasn't as though the business district—let alone her place—was teeming with customers. And besides, if someone else came in, Riley was there to take over. "Alright. Let's go sit over there."

Ava laid her apron on the counter and pulled out two chairs

at a nearby table. She placed her velvet pouch of tarot cards onto it and slid into a chair, gesturing for Owen to sit, too.

"So," Ava said, shuffling the cards. She could still feel Owen's eyes on her. "What kind of reading do you want?"

"I wasn't aware there was more than one kind." Owen studied Ava's hands as she shuffled. "What are my options?"

"We could do a Celtic Cross," Ava suggested. Almost as soon as the words were out of her mouth, she regretted them. The Celtic Cross was a complicated spread. Did she really want to sit there for half an hour delving into the loaded details of this man's personal life? Suddenly, the whole undertaking seemed uncomfortably intimate. But it was too late—Owen was already nodding.

"Sure. No idea what that is, but it sounds interesting. Hit me."

"Are you guys reading tarot?" Riley asked from her armchair, peering over the top of her book.

"You bet we are," Owen replied, flashing Riley a smile over his shoulder. "My first time."

"Can I watch?" Riley's gaze moved to the deck in Ava's hands.

"Next time," Ava said, jumping in before Owen could respond. It was her first reading in the new shop, and although Owen may not have minded if Riley sat in on it, she wanted to be as professional as possible.

Riley nodded, her gaze moving back to the page she was reading, but not without a wistful glance at the tarot deck.

Ava finished her shuffling and smoothed the deck into a neat pile, which she set in front of Owen. "Cut the deck twice, so you've got three separate piles."

"Alright..."

"Now stack the piles again in whatever order you want."

"Okay..."

"Good. Now, this spread is going to give us a look into a certain aspect of your life. There are ten cards total, and we'll lay the cards in different positions, which each represent different things."

Ava drew the top card, lay it face up in the very center of the table.

"The king of pentacles," Owen read aloud, studying the card with curiosity.

"Right," Ava said, taking over. It always amazed her how easily she could slip into the professional reader role when the situation called for it. "So, the first card in the Celtic Cross spread is the basis of the spread. It's the matter at the very heart of everything else we're going to see. The king of pentacles refers to someone who's an expert in their craft, who's mastered their personal area of business and remains grounded and solid in his material existence. My guess is this'll have something to do with your store—you own the hardware store, right? From the looks of the spread so far, you're in a pretty good spot."

Owen ruffled his hair. "Okay. Keep going."

Ava drew the next card. It was the six of swords. "Interesting."

"Why interesting?" Owen asked, bending forward to study the picture on the card. "Looks like somebody poked holes in his boat."

"Well, I guess in a sense they did," Ava said. If you went by the imagery, he had a point. "But this card signifies moving on from a painful situation. It's in the cross position of the spread, so it'll either support or oppose your basis card. To me, this looks like you're coming off the heels of something that didn't feel so great, but you've learned to turn it into something profitable, something solid that serves you."

Owen's eyes narrowed. He said nothing, only nodded at her to continue. And so, they settled into a flow, with Ava pulling each card, giving her honest assessment, translating the intuitions that came to her into words as well as she knew how, and then glancing over at Owen for his response. With every card she pulled, Owen studied it a moment, then nodded, as though he were gathering the cards into a mental pile to look through later. He remained tight-lipped about what the cards might mean for him, and Ava found herself hoping she might hit on a soft spot at some point. The soft spot came at the ninth card, when she turned it over and slid it into its place in the spread.

"The High Priestess," Owen read, and Ava could tell there was something different in the way he held the words in his mouth before speaking. "Who's she?"

Ava looked at him in surprise. It was the first card he'd asked a direct question about, and it surprised her he'd taken the image to represent a specific person. "Well, it's a major arcana card, so while it can represent a certain person, it's more likely to indicate a life lesson you need to learn. And, since it's the ninth card in our spread, that means it's in the hopes and fears position—meaning the lesson of the High Priestess is either one you fear or one you yearn for. It could also be both, as is often the case with things we want in life."

Owen was silent a moment, pondering the imagery on the card. It was a striking card, and one Ava had always felt a special connection with. Inner knowing was how Zaidy had described it. And the wisdom to know how to trust yourself.

"So what does it mean?" Owen said, raising his eyes to Ava's.

"Oh. Right." She laughed, slightly flustered. "It signifies intuition. Actually, she represents the feminine side of the divine, which in Hebrew we call the *shekhinah*. The High Priestess is all about sacred knowledge, the subconscious mind. It's about realizing that you hold the knowledge inside you, and that you only have to look inward to feel your correct path."

Owen looked doubtful for a moment, but then the lines in his forehead smoothed out. "Well, I guess that is something I struggle with—trusting what I know... inside..." His voice trailed off as though he were embarrassed at the string of words that had just come out of his mouth.

"I think a lot of us do," Ava said. "I know I do—all the time."

Owen stared down at the spread before them, his hands clasped together, elbows resting on his knees. When he spoke, his words came out slow, thoughtful, like he was weighing how much to share. "There have been things that I... knew... but didn't want to believe. I don't know how I knew, but I did, and then when they finally made themselves clear, it was too late."

"So maybe that inner sense is something you're kind of afraid of?"

"Yes," Owen said, still thinking. "But I think I'm also a little afraid that I lost it. Or rather, that I'll be so paranoid at missing another whisper—because that's the only way I know how to describe it—that I'll start convincing myself I hear it when I don't. If that... makes sense."

"I think so," Ava said. In truth, it was a feeling she'd also felt, and Owen had done a pretty good job of explaining it. "Well, let's see what the tenth card is. That'll show us the outcome—or rather, a potential outcome. The thing about tarot is that it's always changing, along with the decisions we make of our own free will. Nothing is set in stone."

Ava turned over the final card and set it into place at the top of the spread. It was the five of cups. Keeping her face passive and stoic at all times during a reading was something Ava had worked to perfect throughout her years reading the cards. As the imagery on each card was not always pleasant, the person whose cards were being read would often look to the reader for comfort—and a grimace or look of resignation would not make things better. So, as Ava turned over the five of cups and studied the man on the bank with the spilled cups around his feet, she kept her face immovable.

"Well, that doesn't look like a good one," Owen remarked. Ava couldn't tell how seriously he was taking the reading, but she was at least glad to hear a chuckle in his voice.

"It depends on what you call good," Ava said, keeping her voice steady. "We could argue that all the cards in the tarot are good, since they shed light on the issues of our lives and facets of ourselves that we need to be aware of."

"Alright. You can skip the consolations," Owen said, his tone playful. "What does it mean in English?"

"It means you're hung up on whatever it is you lost, or whatever didn't go as planned. But as a result—as you can see here by these two standing cups that the figure in the card is overlooking—you're missing the good stuff that's right under your nose. And since this card is in the outcome position of the spread, it means you're likely to continue doing that unless you change something and divert the path."

"Huh." Owen crossed his arms over his broad chest and leaned back in his chair. His gaze moved to the window, where the odd pedestrian now strolled past the shop windows. "Actually, that kind of hits home."

"Yeah? Well, good. I'm glad."

They sat in silence a moment longer, listening to the faint chatter of voices from outside, the rustle of Riley's book as she turned the page. As Ava studied the cards, she felt the heat of Owen's gaze on her. When she looked up, their eyes met. The hold of his mouth, in that same small smile he'd worn throughout the entire reading, like he was trying to decide whether to laugh or say something deeply profound, was soft and kind. It was the kind of reading that piqued her interest. What was this thing he had lost? What was it that was holding him back, making him so nervous to trust himself? And what was it he was overlooking? Growing up, Ava had repeated to her friends until she was blue in the face that tarot was not about telling the future or being psychic—but suddenly she wished it were. Owen's reading had roused her curiosity, but of course, she wouldn't ask him. She was a professional.

"It's kind of private," Owen blurted out, as though reading her mind. Ava was sure the shock on her face was more than apparent.

"Oh," she stammered. "That's fine. These readings can dredge up some stuff that's kind of uncomfortable. No need to say anything else about it. I'm just the conduit."

"Alright." Owen scooted his chair back from the table, got to his feet. "How much do I owe you?"

Ava could feel her cheeks warming as she busied herself with returning the cards to their pouch. This was the part she hated. "For a Celtic Cross, it's twenty."

Owen grinned at her. Then, making his way back over to the counter, he stuffed three ten-dollar bills into the tip jar. "If what I saw on the internet is right, that's a pretty cheap Celtic Cross. There's a tip for excellent service."

Ava laughed. He was right—but she needed to test out the waters first, see how much Shiloh was willing to pay for their readings. "Thanks. I appreciate it."

They stood in awkward silence for a moment before Owen's eyes drifted to the window. Craning his neck, he glanced out at the sidewalk. "Huh. Looks like—"

His thought was interrupted by the creak of the heavy front door, and in lumbered Greathouse, thumbs hooked inside his belt. He wandered to the counter, eyeing the menu, before noticing both Ava and Owen staring at him.

"You two look like a pair of deer in headlights," Greathouse remarked with a chuckle. He placed a hand over his ample belly. "Either that, or you saw a ghost."

Ava's eyes narrowed. It was the first she'd seen of Greathouse since the night of the search warrant, and she wasn't all too thrilled to see him in her shop. Her voice was icy when she spoke. "Can I help you?"

"You sure can," the chief chuckled, rocking back on his boot heels. He seemed not to notice the frosty tone in Ava's voice. "The first thing you can help with is a dose of caffeine. What do you recommend?"

"That depends. You like brewed coffee or lattes?" As she spoke, Ava noticed Owen was still hanging around near the doorway, apparently intrigued by Greathouse's cheerful demeanor.

"Normally I'm a regular old drip coffee person," Greathouse replied. "But do me something fancy today. And speaking of— have you got any sweets?"

Ava glanced at the empty pastry case. With the stress of the past couple days, her plan of baking homemade cookies to sell at the shop had fallen by the wayside. "Unfortunately, no. For coffee, are you good with a vanilla cappuccino?"

Greathouse clucked his tongue. "That'll work. You really ought to think about adding some baked goods to your menu, though, Goldberg. Bet business would pick up."

Ava allowed herself a strangled sigh as she headed to the counter to prepare his order. "I'm working on it."

The chief flashed her a wink, paid for his coffee, and tucked two crisp dollar bills inside the tip jar before starting to whistle. Ava eyed him as she steamed a pitcher of milk. There was no denying Greathouse's demeanor had changed. *What is he up to?*

The cappuccino made, Ava slid it across the counter to Chief Greathouse's waiting hands. He seemed to be waiting for something other than just his coffee—as did Owen, who still stood, perched next to the door. "You're suspiciously nice this morning. What's the other thing you need?"

Chief Greathouse stroked his chin. When he spoke, it was more of a drawl. "Here's the thing. I'm gonna need you to talk to Rose for me. Calm her down. As you know, things aren't looking great for her husband, and I'm worried about her."

"Oh, well, that's rich," Ava said, all thought of feigned civility gone. She crossed her arms over her chest, avoided Owen's gaze as she felt it move to hers. "You're the one who's accusing her husband of murdering a woman. How do you expect her to react? Why don't you calm her down yourself? I know Joel Robinson, and he would never so much as hurt a—"

"Now, now. Calm down there, little lady. You know I'm only trying to sort this all out."

From the doorway, Owen cleared his throat. He moved to stand next to the counter, where Ava and Greathouse stood facing each other down. "I think, chief, that what Ava would *like* to hear—and honestly, I would too—is what else you know that you're not saying. Because it seems like there's something."

Greathouse's eyes moved from Ava to Owen, then back again. No one spoke. Finally, the chief sighed.

"Alright," he said. "Here's the story. Audrey Wilson's found dead in the fountain Friday morning. Now, those cobblestones out there are in bad need of repair, and we've got sober folks tripping over 'em all the time. Given that Audrey had consumed a few drinks at the committee dinner the night before, it first appeared to be an accident. You know, maybe she tripped and fell, drowned in the fountain.

"But after the medical examiner had a look at her, he concluded she died of blunt force trauma to the back of the head—not drowning like we'd thought. He puts the time of death around 4:30 am. Furthermore, there was no water in her lungs, meaning she must have already been dead before her face hit that water. Now, even if we were to speculate that she tripped on those cobblestones and hit her head, it wouldn't explain the placement or the shape of the lacerations. Nor would it explain how, having been dead already, she could have dragged herself over to the fountain where Donna found her. You following?"

"I'm following," Ava said, leaning back against the counter, arms crossed. "I don't see at all how any of this points to Joel Robinson, but do go on."

Owen shot her a warning look, as if to say, *don't push it.*

"Yeah, yeah," Greathouse said, waving a hand. "I'm getting to that. Obviously, the first thing we had to check out was who the last people to see Audrey alive were. Turns out that was Chris Mitchell and Ed and Elaine Walsh, having all walked out to their cars together with Audrey after the committee dinner. We checked 'em all out, took all their statements. None of them saw Audrey after she turned toward her car. All got alibis for after that. Chris went straight home and crashed, which his wife can attest to. Ed and Elaine had their grandson stay over, took him to school the next morning.

"Now, I'm in the middle of taking these statements and figuring out what's what, when we get an email at the station from one of those burner emails saying they've got it on good authority that Joel Robinson's been having an affair with Audrey Wilson and, when she threatened to tell Rose about it, he had to take action. The tipster seems to think Joel lured her downtown to hash things out—kiss and make up, if you will— and then he killed her. Tried to make it look like an accident, only he didn't do a very good job."

Ava scoffed. "So, you're telling me you were able to get a search warrant based on this ridiculous tip you received? That tipster could have been anyone."

"She's got a point, chief," Owen remarked. He stroked his chin, glancing out the window.

"Well, yeah—if the accusation didn't check out, that is." Greathouse shrugged. "Joel himself has admitted that Audrey 'came onto him', information that he didn't bother to share with his wife, and then there's the matter of the note..."

"Which anyone could have written," Ava said, still indignant.

Greathouse shook his head. "We got our hands on some handwriting samples, and the script looks pretty darn similar. It's unfortunate, and we're still waiting on the handwriting analysts for confirmation, but our suspicions are not unfounded."

Ava sighed, exasperated. "Chief Greathouse. With all due respect, I was very clear with you about what I heard that night at the committee dinner. Audrey Wilson threatened to drive Ricky Birch's business into the ground because of—well, some kind of misunderstanding, I guess—and he responded by threatening to have her killed. What part of this are you not getting? Did you even check Ricky out?"

Chief Greathouse chuckled. "If I didn't find you so entertaining, Ms. Goldberg, I might remind you it's not usually a good idea to take that tone with law enforcement. Anyway, we heard you loud and clear. The thing is, we questioned Mr. Birch for well over two hours, and he's also got an alibi—which is more than Joel Robinson can say, seeing as he's got no one else to vouch for his whereabouts at 4:30 that morning."

"What do you mean Ricky Birch has an alibi?" Ava was flustered. She was sure of what she'd heard. Ricky Birch threatening Audrey the very night before she was found dead? It was too coincidental to not add up. She looked to Owen for help, but his eyes were narrowed, his brow a worried, furrowed line.

"Just what I said, little lady. Ricky was home all night, eating chicken wings and falling asleep in front of the TV with that woman of his, Jodi Laughlin. Ms. Laughlin says she woke up around 4:30—the time Audrey apparently died—to use the bathroom, and Ricky was right there in the armchair, snoring up a storm. Ricky isn't a suspect."

This time, it was Owen who spoke. "So, because Ricky allegedly has an alibi, you've automatically concluded that Joel Robinson must be responsible?"

Just then, the door to the shop opened. Ava, Owen, and Greathouse all whirled around, tensing when Ricky Birch sidled in. His face was freshly shaven, a far cry from his usual scruffy self, and Ava wondered if he was trying to appear more friendly to garner sympathy. He gave the both of them a crooked smile full of yellow teeth.

"You three look like you've been caught red-handed," Ricky said, still grinning. "Did I walk in on somethin'?"

Ava shot a glare at Chief Greathouse. *Good going, Chief.*

"Actually, Ricky, I was just explaining to Ms. Goldberg that you do, in fact, have an alibi for the night Audrey Wilson was murdered."

Ricky's smile faded. His face got serious. "That so? Why, do Ms. Goldberg here have some reason to think otherwise?"

Ava's face grew hot. She'd been caught out, and Chief Greathouse had thrown her under the bus without a second thought. "Well, Mr. Birch, I..."

"I'm listening. And give me a mug of that dark roast there, while you're at it, would ya?"

The thought flashed through Ava's mind that Ricky Birch's teeth would be better off without a mug of dark roast, but she poured the coffee anyway and handed it to him. Her hands were shaking, both with embarrassment and fear. If this Jodi Laughlin was Ricky's "woman" as the sheriff stated, of course, she'd lie to save his ass from the law. From where she stood, Ricky Birch still looked guilty.

"I just—well, I heard the two of you arguing in the hallway the night before..."

"At the committee dinner, you mean? Yeah, we got into it." Ricky nodded, then threw his head back and laughed. It sounded more like a villain's cackle, and Ava had to restrain a shudder. Owen also looked uncomfortable. "She brought her Audi in for repairs and didn't like the diagnosis. By the way, Goldberg, you got anything sweet?"

"Nope," Ava said, more tersely than she meant to. She was desperately wishing for the conversation to be over. She didn't like the smug way Ricky was looking at her.

Ricky shrugged his shoulders. He took a loud slurp of his coffee, smacked his lips in satisfaction. "That's some good stuff right there, lady. What do I owe ya?"

"D-d-don't worry about it," Ava said, forcing her mouth into a weak smile. "On the house."

God. What was she doing? She was already worried about business, and she was going around giving out free coffee? She kicked herself the moment the words left her mouth. From across the room, she saw Riley's brow furrow.

"Thanks a million, Ms. Goldberg." Ricky tipped his head back and drained the cup of scalding coffee. Ava couldn't imagine what the state of his throat must have been. Ricky slapped his empty mug on the counter and sidled back out of the shop.

Owen, Ava, and Greathouse watched Ricky meander down the sidewalk and out of view. Greathouse turned to Ava with an amused expression. "On the house? You're that scared of him? You really are new to town, aren't you, Ms. Goldberg? That's just Ricky. He runs around town spouting off that big mouth of his, but he doesn't mean anything by it. A little rough on the outside, sure, but Ricky Birch is harmless."

"I've got to agree that's generally the case," Owen said, his eyes following the sidewalk down which Ricky had just disappeared.

Ava raised her eyebrows. "I'm not sure I believe that, but regardless—that tip sounds like a framing, and the note you found in Audrey's pocket sounds like planted evidence."

"Or," the chief cut in, "a good citizen trying to do the right thing while fearing the repercussions of a murderer. Anyway, Audrey's father—barely even hanging on by a thread these days, god help him—is so distraught he's announced he's offering a reward of $50,000 to anyone who comes up with information leading to Audrey's killer. I'd expect we'll start getting some more leads, so who knows? Things could go either way for Joel, but right now, it's not looking good. And by the way, I'll make one thing clear: This jurisdiction doesn't mess around with psychics on our cases. Just so you know."

"Noted," Ava replied icily. She wasn't a psychic, but she doubted Greathouse even knew the difference.

Greathouse moved toward the front door, coffee still in hand. "Now, regardless of whether you agree with the potential charges against Joel Robinson, I'd say his wife could use some company. And, of course, if you come up with any new information, I'd be happy to hear it."

"I should get going, too," Owen said, glancing at his watch. Giving Ava and Riley a wave, he turned to follow Greathouse out of the store.

Ava stood for a moment behind the counter, watching the two retreating figures as they moved further down the street and rounded the corner. All hope of returning to normalcy was long gone.

"Owen's interested," Riley said, looking up from her book and flashing Ava a playful grin.

"As if *that's* what's on my mind after that ridiculous conversation," Ava retorted. Truth be told, she wasn't sure what *was* on her mind. It felt too jumbled with information and emotions to even begin to untangle the mess. The intrigue of the tarot reading and then Greathouse's suspicions—topped by Riley's commentary—only further muddled her mind.

She couldn't shake the sound of Ricky Birch's spit-riddled rasp as he'd threatened Audrey that night in the hallway, couldn't rid her mind of his eerie, echoing cackle today. If Greathouse wasn't going to take him seriously as a suspect, she had no choice but to do it herself. She'd wait until the next day when Ricky would be back at work in his shop, and then? Ava knew what she had to do.

8

Ava burst out into the bright morning sunshine, glad for the earthy scent of the fields drifting in from the edge of town. The balmy warmth of the early June day felt fresh on her skin, but she didn't have time for basking. Riley had agreed to open the cafe on her own that morning, but Ava had promised she'd be in by nine o'clock at the latest—which meant she needed to get straight to work.

Right next door to Joel's fitness center, Ricky Birch's auto shop was an eyesore of a place. As Ava eyed the chipped painted bricks of the main garage and the streaked windows of what passed for an office, she wondered if Joel had chosen the adjacent lot for his gym so it would look even more sleek and pristine by comparison. She surveyed the building for a moment, hand shading her eyes, and then crossed the street to the grocery store to buy herself an ice cream cone. The sun, at its highest point in the sky, was hot, and she'd need refreshment during her stake-out.

Ice cream cone in hand, Ava sat down on the bench next to the grocery store doors. From her perch, she had a prime view of Ricky's auto shop so she could wait for him to exit while staying far enough away to not appear to be loitering. She wasn't sure *exactly* what she was going to ask Ricky or how she would frame it in a way that didn't arouse the man's suspicions —especially after Greathouse throwing her under the bus the day before—but she'd think of something. Joel and Rose were depending on her.

Ava munched her ice cream cone, chancing glances down at her phone to appear less conspicuous should anyone passing by wonder what she was doing. Movement flashed through the windows of the office and a few loud clanks drifted from the closed garage—both good signs that Ricky was indeed there— but no actual humans had come into view yet. Ava's phone buzzed. She glanced down, frowning as an email notification from Sara Goldberg popped up. Given the high likelihood of it being a chain email, Ava almost didn't open it. But she did— and immediately regretted her decision.

Hi. Just saw this in the news—
Pretty cool!

Below the brief message was the article Sara had forwarded. Ava scrolled down and stopped, the sight of her ex-husband's dashing grin causing her to stiffen. Just below the photograph, in which Noah stood against a bare wall looking as handsome as ever in a button-down and tie, was the head-line: *Noah Shapiro Named Recipient of Distinguished Service Award by American Pediatric Surgical Association.*

Wow. Good one, Mom. Some days, Ava swore she would never understand her mother. What on earth had possessed Sara Goldberg to think her daughter would want to be informed of *that*? It made no difference to her these days, affected her life not at all. If anything, it was just another mark on the score-board, another piece of evidence showing how much of a success Noah was—and how much *she* wasn't. Then again, maybe that had been her mother's motive in sending the article.

Out of spite, Ava took an angry bite of her ice cream cone. She was already lamenting the numbness in her front teeth when someone sat down beside her on the bench. A sharp burst of pain struck through her forehead as she turned to see Owen O'Kelly.

Ugh. What is he doing here? Doesn't he ever go away?

"Well, you're not conspicuous at all," Owen observed, amused.

"Pardon?" Ava croaked out, tongue still stuck to the roof of her mouth. Her brain freeze was subsiding. She shoved her phone in her pocket, still trying to clear her mind of Noah.

Owen leaned against the back of the bench, gestured toward Ricky's shop. "I said it's not at all obvious what you're doing here, sitting alone, eating an ice cream cone, just staring across the street."

Ava turned to glare at him. It was then she realized Owen was holding his own ice cream cone. He gave her a merry smile as he tore off the wrapper.

"You think you're cute, huh?" Ava said, training her eyes once again on Ricky's auto shop. A clang sounded from inside the garage.

"What makes you say that?" Owen didn't turn to look at her. He kept his eyes on Ricky's shop, but Ava sensed he was dying to see her expression. She remained stony faced as he contin-ued. "I was headed inside for a Red Bull, but then I saw you out here with that ice cream, and I realized I needed some, too.

Besides, it looks like you could use an extra eye and I've got a little time before I open the shop."

Ava cocked her head to the side, turning to look at Owen fully. Was he planning to help nail Ricky for his involvement in Audrey Wilson's murder?

"I know you didn't ask," Owen said, as though reading her thoughts. "But you shouldn't have to be the only one doing what Greathouse and his team should be doing. I still think that so-called tip is a bunch of bull."

Ava turned her gaze back to Ricky's garage, not wanting to miss a single movement. If help had come in the form of Owen O'Kelly, then so be it, but she'd be damned if she was going to let him distract her.

"I mean," Owen continued, taking a bite of his cone. "It makes no sense that Joel would've done it. Joel gets along with everybody in town! I've known the guy my whole life—our grandpas used to play chess together in the park on Sundays after church. He may be a little full of himself, but that hardly makes him a murderer."

Ava smothered a smile. Owen was right. Joel was the kind of guy to flex his pecs and nod in satisfaction every time he passed a mirror—but it wasn't malicious. It was part of his charm.

"And Ricky...?"

Owen pursed his lips in thought. "I could go either way. I always thought the guy was harmless, just rough around the edges, but considering what you overheard the night before it all happened... Well, alibis aside, I'd say Ricky's the better suspect."

Just then, a side door of the office opened, and a figure poked its head out. Owen and Ava both straightened, their attention now fixed across the street.

"That can't be Ricky," Ava murmured, frowning. The person was of a willowy build, and looked taller than Ava remembered Ricky being, at least as far as she could tell from across the street. She thought she got a glimpse of a short ponytail.

Owen snorted. "Keen eyes! He'd be proud of you for not mistaking him for his partner." He was suddenly serious. "The question is, what's she doing looking up and down the street like that?"

Jodi Laughlin did indeed seem to be on the lookout for something—or someone. She stood for a moment with one hand on her hip, the other holding a cell phone to her ear. Ava was too far away to hear what she was saying to the other person on the line, but Jodi continued to look up and down the street as she waved her free hand in gesticulation. Then, apparently satisfied that the coast was clear, she slid her phone into her pocket, pushed the door shut behind her, and veered around the side of the garage.

Ava hopped off the bench. With hardly a glance behind to see if Owen was following, she chucked her ice cream wrapper in a bin and began a brisk walk in the direction Jodi had gone. Ava could still see the woman up ahead, sticking to the sidewalk, heading north. If she kept a good distance behind, she could keep an eye on her and avoid being spotted. Ava wasn't even sure what she hoped to find, but she knew it was better than sitting around waiting for Greathouse to change his course of action.

"Hold up, hold up," Owen said, moving to walk backwards in front of Ava. "Are you seriously going to follow her?"

Come on. Was this guy in, or was he out? "Sure. I thought you'd figured that out already. Why wouldn't I?"

Owen gave up on his backward trot and switched directions, falling into step with Ava's swift stride. "Well, first, you don't even know she's up to anything. She and Ricky live down this road, if you take it all the way out of town."

"Right, but I don't buy it. She was literally checking to make sure the coast was clear."

"Or she was looking for her ride that didn't show. Or any other explanation. But okay, then secondly—don't you think if Ricky really *did* kill Audrey, you might be flirting with a little bit of danger?"

"Not any more than you've been trying to flirt with me since the moment I came to town." The words came out more biting than she'd meant for them to sound, but she hoped it'd shut him up. Owen's ears were already turning red.

"Wow, you're a prickly one," Owen said, managing a grin despite his embarrassment. "I'm just trying to be friendly."

"Great," Ava said, trying to keep her eyes trained on Jodi. "Glad we're on the same page. Let's keep on, shall we?"

To their left was the Methodist church, its elegant stone facade and towering steeple reaching to the sky like hands in prayer. Ahead of them, lining both sides of the street, were rows of houses. Ava knew that on the upcoming cross street alone were two more churches: Lutheran and Catholic. So many houses of prayer, and not a single synagogue. Oh, well. Shiloh wasn't exactly her demographic.

Suddenly, Owen grasped her upper arm, pulling her to a halt. "She's turning! She's not going home."

Sure enough, Jodi had passed the row of houses and was rounding the corner of Boyd Street, right near the elementary school. She disappeared from view as Ava and Owen hustled to pick up the pace.

"Does she have any grandkids?" Ava wondered aloud. "Why would she go to the elementary school?"

"Nope. Ricky's got a granddaughter, but she's older. Definitely not elementary school age."

Ava and Owen rounded the corner, too, and hung back a bit, trying to keep a close enough distance so Jodi remained in sight, but far enough back that they wouldn't appear to be following her. And good thing, too, because as Jodi passed the Catholic church, she came to an abrupt stop and glanced around.

"Is she going inside the church?" Ava whispered, looking up at Owen.

He jutted his chin in Jodi's direction, as though to remind Ava to keep her eyes on the target. "No—look. She's passed the building. But there's nothing over there..." Owen's green eyes narrowed, his brows knit together. "...except—oh, that's it." His eyes lit up, and he turned to look at Ava with excitement.

"What? What's it?"

"Come on," Owen said, grabbing Ava's arm again and tugging her along down the sidewalk, sticking close to the bushes that were luckily overgrown from the yards nearby. "We've got to get closer, but I think..."

Just before reaching the Catholic church, they stopped. Jodi couldn't have been more than ten yards away, and Ava prayed Jodi wouldn't turn around. She and Owen were in plain sight.

"I knew it," Owen breathed, looking almost gleeful. For someone who had been trying to dissuade Ava from following the woman only a few moments before, the idea seemed to have grown on him.

Ava followed his gaze, puzzled at first as to what exactly Owen was talking about. Jodi seemed to have entered some sort of small glass enclosure. Ava squinted. What was she *doing*? After a moment, Jodi stooped down, stood up, and then backed out of the enclosure. She backed up almost to the street, then stood in the middle of the sidewalk, her gaze scanning the glass box she'd just emerged from.

"Is that a payphone?" Ava whispered incredulously, glancing at Owen. "Those things still exist?"

"They do in Shiloh," he said, grinning back at her. "Well, one does. They left it because it's so close to the elementary school. Apparently, there are still a few kids who don't have cell phones yet and might need to call their forgetful parents to come pick them up."

"So... it's functioning? As in, you can actually make calls on it?"

"You bet. And even better, you can make untraceable calls on it." Owen's grin was wicked.

Both Ava and Owen turned back toward Jodi, who was now walking around the back of the payphone box, her gaze fixed on the top. After a quick glance inside, her gaze searched the roof of the box once more. Then, almost before they realized it was happening, her gaze turned back behind her and fell right on Ava and Owen.

"GO BACK!" Ava hissed, already bolting back the way they'd come. "Act like we're just out for a walk."

"It's too late for that," Owen hissed back. "She saw us plain as day. No way your face didn't look guilty as hell. You look like a kid who just got caught with her hand in the cookie jar!"

"*My* face?" Ava fumed, still power walking. "You look like you just saw a ghost!"

"We may *be* ghosts soon if Jodi tells Ricky, Audrey's potential murderer, that she caught us following her. Come on—my store's only a block away after we turn this corner." Owen steered Ava straight on down the street. His grasp on her arm was solid, in charge.

As Owen unlocked his shop and they stepped inside, both panting, Ava chanced a glance out the window. "There's no sign of her."

"But she still saw us." Owen rubbed his face. "And she was clearly looking for something."

"That's what I thought, too," Ava agreed, following Owen behind the counter where he sank into a swiveling office chair. Around them, the smell of rubber and freshly sawn lumber was strangely comforting. "But what? If she'd been making a call from the payphone, that would've been one thing. But what would she have been looking for?"

"I don't know—something she or Ricky lost during a previous visit to the payphone?"

"But up high like that? She was definitely searching for something up above." Ava frowned, trying to make sense of it.

"Maybe it's nothing," Owen said, slinging an arm over the back of the chair. His biceps rippled beneath his t-shirt. "Maybe we're trying too hard to find something when there isn't anything to find."

Ava shook her head. "No. You have to admit it—it's weird. When's the last time you used a payphone? And anyway, it's not like she doesn't have a cell phone. We saw her using it, for god's sake!"

"That's true," Owen admitted. He moved to the cash register and began to sort the bills.

Ava sat in silence for a moment, watching the street outside. There was no sign so far of Jodi Laughlin.

Suddenly, Ava sat upright. Something had clicked. "Cameras. Are there security cameras in the payphone booth? Or outside it?"

Owen paused his counting, recognition dawning in his eyes. He opened them wide. "You're right. That makes sense! Someone had to have lured Audrey out of her house yesterday morning, and whoever that was would've wanted to cover their tracks. It would be stupid to make that call from a personal cell phone."

"Exactly." Ava's blue eyes were snapping. They were on to something.

Just then, the door of Owen's shop swung wide open, banged against the wall with a clatter. Jodi Laughlin stood in the doorway, her frizzy blond hair silhouetted against the noonday sun behind her.

Owen looked up, registering her presence but keeping his cool. "Hey, Jodi. Unfortunately, I'm not open yet—"

"Owen O'Kelly, I saw you following me," she declared in a raspy voice that suggested one too many cigarettes. She pointed to Ava. "And this one here—this newcomer who best learn to keep her perky little nose out of other people's business."

Ava was sure the look on her own face must have been one of horror, but Owen remained unperturbed. His face was smooth, his smile cheerful as always. "Actually, we were on our way to check out the menu of that food truck up north of town, and we saw you standing in the middle of the sidewalk. You looked lost. Everything okay?"

Jodi's gray eyes narrowed. "Everything is perfectly fine. I lost an earring—an expensive one—when I made a call to my cousin the other day."

"Oh, shoot." Owen looked genuinely concerned for Jodi's missing earring. Ava wondered if Jodi even owned earrings. "Did you find it? Also, Jodi, this is Ava Goldberg." Owen gestured to Ava, still grinning his friendly smile. "She owns the new coffee shop downtown. Maybe you knew her grandfather? Melvin Goldberg? He used to come by here often."

Her grandfather had been a frequent patron at Owen's hardware store? Ava hadn't thought about the possibility before, but it made sense. Her grandfather was always working with his hands when he wasn't studying. He'd once built her a treehouse when she was a small girl.

"Sure, I know the name," Jodi conceded, letting her furrowed brow momentarily smooth over. "But your grandfather wasn't a nosy man, ma'am. You oughta take a page out of his book. Stay in that shop where you belong, readin' those cards."

"We just wanted to see that menu," Ava offered, glad that Owen had thought up an alibi so quickly. It helped to know like the back of your hand what was on that side of town, she supposed. "Couldn't find it online."

Jodi gave a grunt and a nod, as though satisfied, and made to be on her way.

"So that payphone's still working then?" Owen asked, his voice nonchalant. "I know it used to, but I figured now it was just around for history's sake. You know, preserving the character of the town and all that."

Jodi shrugged. "Worked just fine for me. Lost my cell phone one night last week—found it later, under Ricky's armchair cushion—so popped down here to check in with my cousin. They'll charge ya an arm and a leg, though."

"Well, that's good to know. Alright, it was nice seeing you, Jodi. Tell Ricky I say hello." Owen's smile was sincere as Jodi gave him a wave and left the store.

As soon as Jodi was gone, Ava blew out her breath. "Well, that was some quick thinking. I'm a little scared to ask what else you're able to lie about so fast."

"Helps to know the town, I guess," Owen said, ignoring her comment. "For what it's worth, I recommend coming up with a story before you start tailing random people in town. I may not be there to save you next time."

Ava sniffed. She hated to admit he was right. As she had no intention of pulling any sort of dynamic detective duo stunt with him, she'd have to figure out how to frame things on her own. If Owen hadn't been there, what would she have told Jodi? Her cover would've been blown. Maybe it was just the big city side of her speaking, but the last thing she needed was to be slapped with a restraining order from Ricky Birch and Jodi Laughlin. She was sure Chief Greathouse would be all too happy to oblige.

Owen had busied himself with replacing a roll of receipt paper in the register when she looked over at him. He felt her gaze on him and looked up, a small smile at his mouth. *Nope.* The voice in Ava's head was firm. Owen O'Kelly was beginning to appear a little too casual, a little too friendly. She appreciated him not viewing Joel Robinson as a suspect in Audrey's murder, but beyond that, she wouldn't trust him. She'd moved to Shiloh to rebuild herself—not let someone steal in and tear her down again. If Owen wanted to keep hanging around while she tried to tease apart the circumstances of Audrey's murder, there wasn't much she could do about it. But she wouldn't let him waste a moment more of her attention, not when her friend's husband was likely very close to being arrested for murder.

"I'd better get going," Ava announced, her words cutting into the comfortable silence. "Thanks for the help today. I'll be sure to come up with a cover story next time. See you around!"

Ava strode out of the shop and into the sunshine of the golden June day. She had to get back to Arcana. There was coffee to be brewed and hopefully customers to be served—and if she got really lucky, tarot cards to be read.

9

———————

The day dragged on at a snail's pace. Since she'd returned to the shop that morning, a whopping total of three customers had meandered in off the street. Ava tried to reassure herself that it was still the early stages; this was how businesses *all* began. Still, if she was going to keep Arcana open, she'd have to spend more time on her shop and less time chasing down leads. She knew it was only the first week, but she was already feeling nervous about not having come out the gates roaring. Her mother would have been shaking her head. Well, Sara Goldberg didn't have to know—about Arcana's slow start *or* about Joel Robinson being the primary suspect in a murder investigation. Ava would just have to trust that Greathouse would wake up and smell the coffee. Pun absolutely intended.

By four o'clock, Riley had left for a doctor's appointment, and Ava had already cleaned the espresso machine, sorted the bills in the cash register, wiped down the tables, and brewed fresh pots of all the roasts on offer. Other than a takeout order here and a phone call inquiry there, traffic to the shop was still sparse. Ava was debating whether to scour the sinks or scrub out the already immaculate refrigerator when the doorbell tinkled. She breathed a sigh of relief. It was a group of three older ladies, each with a stylish leather purse slung over her shoulder. They were laughing amongst themselves as they entered the shop, sliding their sunglasses back onto their perfectly sprayed hairdos in unison as they gazed at the menu.

"Good afternoon," Ava offered cheerily, flicking her rag into the sink and stepping up to the register. It was a cheeriness she actually *felt*, so happy was she to see another human face inside the shop.

"Oh, good afternoon, dear," the lady nearest the front said, pursing her magenta lips into a contented smile. It was the same sort of look a grandmother might make at her cooing baby grandchild. "We're just in for a cup of coffee next to our Bible study—whatever you've got for a medium roast today. Right, girls?"

The other two women chimed their agreement, nodding emphatically.

"Ah," Ava said, her cheer somewhat deflated. *Bible study?* If Donna Schroeder were any indication of how the church communities in Shiloh would receive her business, Ava's wariness was warranted. Still, these women had come of their own accord. *And they seem friendly enough...* "Well, we can manage that. A little afternoon pick-me-up sounds perfect right about now."

"Absolutely," exclaimed one of the other women, swiping a strand of silver hair behind her ear. She winked at Ava. "We've been meaning to come see what this place is all about. We've never had a coffee shop in Shiloh before—it's quite exciting!"

"Glad to hear it," Ava said, reaching for the mugs and filling them up with hot, steaming coffee. Yes, this was a good sign.

The third woman, decked out in a leopard print duster and sporting velvety red lipstick, pushed her way in front of the other two, handing Ava a crisp ten-dollar bill. Before the other two could protest, she jutted her nose in the air and announced in satisfaction, "It's my treat, ladies!"

The first woman, the one with magenta lipstick, began to pipe in, but leopard lady cut her off with a jerk of her close-cropped dyed-red head. "No, no, no—I won't hear of it, Flo. You covered the tickets to the ladies' luncheon."

"Oh, just let her, Marge," the silver-haired woman said to the friend who'd been about to protest, giving her elbow a squeeze.

Ava smiled as she handed the women their coffees. "Is this something you three do regularly? Do your Bible study together, I mean?"

"Oh, yes," the woman called Marge said, cupping her hands around her mug. "Every Monday afternoon. We're Catholic—except for Flo here, she's Lutheran—so for a long time we met at St. Patrick's, but then the break-ins happened, and even with the cameras they put up we just didn't feel safe. So now we hop from place to place around town, and *boy*, are we glad there's a coffee joint." Then, as though remembering her manners, the woman clapped a hand on her chest to introduce herself. "By the way, I'm Marge. Marge Harding." She gestured to the other women, who had chosen a table near the window. "On the left there is Flo, and that's Juanita—with the silver hair."

"It's lovely to meet you. I'm Ava Goldberg." Ava stuck out her hand, and the woman shook it heartily. Ava noted the woman's last name. Could she be any relation to the Officer Harding that had been following Greathouse around?

"Say," Marge said, recognition dawning in her face. She

turned and called over her shoulder. "Juanita, this girl's name is Goldberg. Didn't you know a Goldberg here in town?"

"Goldberg? I knew a Melvin Goldberg." Juanita took a long sip of her coffee, looked at Marge through dark, round eyes.

"Well, *she's* a Goldberg," Marge said, sticking a thumb in Ava's direction.

What? These Bible studying women had known Zaidy Mel?

"That was my grandfather—Mel Goldberg," Ava offered. "How did you know him? Other than the given that everyone knows everyone around here..."

"You're catching on quick, honey," Marge said to Ava. She winked, gestured to Ava to follow her over to the table where the other women sat.

Juanita clapped her hands. "Oh, how fabulous! Mel was my tarot reader! I went to him for years. That man must've been one of the most insightful humans I've ever known, especially once he got those cards in his hands. Got me through some real low points."

Juanita was nodding at Ava, as though Ava must surely know what she was talking about. Which was true. Zaidy Mel had always had a way of *feeling* what was going on, and then helping you sort it out.

Something inside Ava jolted to life. This was the first she'd heard reference to her grandfather's tarot practice from someone in town. "You mean he read tarot for you?"

"Oh, heavens, yes," Juanita said, laughing. "More times than I can count. He helped me when my cat had to be put down, when I left my job. I believe he also had some advice for my son's wife when she miscarried. I tell you what, we loved your grandpa in our family!"

Ava felt her eyes misting over. How many times had Zaidy

Mel found wisdom in the cards for Ava when a boy she liked wasn't interested, or when the college she favored sent back a rejection? She'd always wondered how things might have been different if Zaidy Mel had still been around when things turned sour in her marriage. What would he have found in the cards? Would he have been able to offer a different perspective?

"That makes me so happy to hear," Ava said, blinking with a smile. "I miss him a lot." It felt good to admit.

"Well, so do we! He was loved here in our community—you can be sure of that. But it would seem we've now been blessed with his granddaughter, and from the sign I saw there in the window, might Melvin Goldberg's granddaughter also offer tarot services?"

Ava blushed. "I do. I wasn't sure anyone ever noticed that sign. I've had only one person ask about it, and I think he did it as a favor."

All three women at the table scoffed.

Flo leaned in conspiratorially, a twinkle in her pale blue eyes. "Actually... That's why we decided to do our study here today. To find out about the tarot."

"Well, yes. *And* to get some hot coffee," Marge added, raising her penciled-on eyebrows at Ava.

"Oh, I'm so excited," Juanita said, balling her hands up into little fists and shaking her ample shoulders. "We have a *tarot reader* in town, girls! And she's a *Goldberg*!"

At this, Ava laughed out loud. "I think my mother would have a heart attack if she knew that's what our name was known for around here."

"Why, is she one of those skeptics?" Marge asked with a tilt of her head. "I have to say, I never have been able to quite understand how it all works. Father Henley doesn't speak very highly of this sort of thing."

"Actually," Ava admitted, unable to resist asking now that Marge had brought it up. "I was wondering about that. I don't normally see a lot of church-going folks getting excited about tarot and divination. I wasn't sure if Bible study with a side of tarot cards was even *allowed*..." She didn't want to dissuade these ladies, but it felt important to understand their beliefs on this.

"Oh, Father Henley would speak ill of Mother Teresa if she so much as hummed the hokey pokey," Flo scolded, batting a hand at Marge. She turned to Ava. "We think it's fun. Now we don't go broadcasting it around *church*, mind you, but if you ask me, there's nothing wrong with using a few pretty pictures to help you think through issues."

Ava nodded. "I hear you. I think my mom's aversion to the cards falls more in line with your, uh, Father Henley's ideas. Let's just say a lot of people in the Jewish religion don't look very favorably on tarot either—you know, occult practices and all that."

Juanita nodded. "Yes, I heard Melvin say something along those lines. Reminds me of my abuela—devout Catholic, but always kept the family's *brujería* alive."

"I will say, though," said Flo, cutting in with a pointed look at Ava, "You seem to have stirred up some resistance over there at the Methodist church."

Ava sighed. She'd been trying not to think about Donna Schroeder. "You saw Mrs. Schroder's letter, too?"

The women exchanged glances.

"We did," said Marge, taking a prim sip of coffee. "And

according to Janet, our Methodist friend, your cafe even made it into Reverend Schroeder's sermon this morning."

"What?" Ava felt her face flush. "There's *more*?"

"Well…" Marge shifted in her seat. "He preached on Saul and the witch of Endor, which led to the reminder to resist being drawn in by occult practices, which led to some thinly veiled allusions to a certain establishment in town."

Juanita rolled her eyes. "Wasn't that story about summoning a prophet or something?"

"I think so," Ava said, wishing she'd paid better attention in Hebrew school. Her recollection of the story the women were referring to was vague at best. She managed a weak smile. "I've got no idea how to contact a spirit. I'm pretty sure that's an activity my grandfather would've frowned on."

"Exactly." Juanita gave the table a light slap and leaned back in her chair. "Don't worry. Donna's always on some vendetta or other. Shiloh's a conservative little town, but no one minded that your grandfather used to give readings to his friends. These people will come to their senses soon enough."

"I hope so," Ava said, gazing out the window at the nearly empty Main Street. At least not *everyone* was against her.

"Speaking of senseless," Marge mused, blowing on her coffee as she spoke. "It's so tragic about Audrey, isn't it?"

There was a chorus of murmured assent. Ava tensed. She'd somehow pushed the memory of police lights outside Joel and Rose's house to the back of her mind, and now there it was again.

"Just *terrible*," Flo agreed. Then, with a quick side glance at Marge, she pursed her lips. "All I'm saying is, Lucas being back in town is *awfully* good timing…"

Marge clucked her tongue. "Now, now, Flo. Let he who is without sin—"

"—cast the first stone," finished Juanita with a roll of her dark, snapping eyes. "We know. We'll refrain from speculation, but there's no denying Flo *does* have a point."

Ava's ears perked up at the mention of Lucas Wilson. Audrey's brother *had* seemed quite suspicious when he'd stormed into the cafe during her meeting with Greathouse. *Could he really have killed his own sister?*

Not wanting to come off as a gossip, Ava flashed the group of ladies a smile and turned to head back behind the counter.

"It was nice to meet you, Ava," Juanita called, causing Ava to turn back around. "You let me know when you have time for a reading. I'm absolutely *itching* to book one."

As the women thumped their study Bibles onto the table in unison, Ava stopped, pulling her phone out of her apron pocket and swiping through the calendar. "What about tomorrow night? I could do eight o'clock."

"Perfect," Juanita said, nodding her head as though to seal the deal. "I look forward to it, Madame Goldberg."

As she left the women to pore over their Bibles, tracing delicate fingers down wafer-thin pages, Ava felt a surprising pang of happiness. Every once in a while, an eruption of laughter would bubble up from the table, with Juanita wiping her eyes as she guffawed at something Marge or Flo had said. It was certainly a different kind of Bible study than the weekly Torah studies had been, when she'd sat on a metal chair next to her parents in the temple basement, munching on a bagel and listening to the group debate the meaning of a certain passage. These ladies weren't debaters, but they seemed to find joy in their holy text. That is what her Zaidy Mel would've said was most important. It was surprising—and happily so—that this quirky group of Christian ladies had given her the first glimmer of belonging she'd felt since she'd first opened her cafe's doors. This—*this* was the feeling of community, the sense of togetherness she'd had in mind when she chose Shiloh to be the home of Cafe Arcana. She hadn't been sure her matzo-eating, Santa-disbelieving, tarot-reading self would *ever* fit in here, but it looked like she was three clients closer to seeing her vision pan out. Now all she needed was a murderer behind bars, and maybe things would finally start taking shape.

SHILOH'S WINE BAR, Looking Glass, was bustling when Ava walked in after closing Arcana for the night. She'd only been in a couple of times before, and one of those times had been for takeout, but the place was always alive with the clatter of silverware on china and the pleasant hum of friendly conversation. Although business was still dragging, she hoped someday Arcana would be the same.

Glancing around the room, Ava spotted a small vacant high top along the far wall. Perfect. She'd feel like a heel taking up an entire table to herself, but taking a seat at the bar made her feel too much like a lonely wino, come in for the company of the bartender and the comfort of the booze. Some might have shaken their heads in pity at a woman eating by herself, but dining alone had somewhere along the way become one of Ava's favorite pastimes. She'd been hoping for a little peace after the chaos of the past few days.

A server waltzed by and flashed her a grin, sliding a crisp, white menu in front of her.

"Let me take care of this table over here, and I'll be back in a few minutes with water," the girl said, tipping her head toward a table of middle-aged couples. She was gone in a ripple of long, blonde ponytail.

Ava surveyed the menu. She already knew she'd order the hummus board, so the important thing was wine. What wine paired well with hummus, anyway? Coffee was her specialty—she was hardly a wine connoisseur. She'd have to ask the server for recommendations. Then again, they'd most likely all taste the same to her, anyway.

"Hey."

Ava nearly jumped out of her skin as Riley slid onto the stool next to her. The girl dropped her backpack down to the floor below in a heap.

"What are you doing here? This is a wine bar." Ava tried to keep her tone light, but the words still sounded accusatory.

Riley shrugged. "It's not technically a bar. Lots of kids from school come in here. Good food."

"Huh."

Well, my mulling things over will just have to wait. Ava turned the menu toward Riley. "What do you feel like? I was thinking the hummus board."

"Yeah, hummus is good. And extra olives."

They gave the server their order, along with a Coke for Riley and a pinot noir for Ava, at the woman's recommendation. Moments later, Riley set her glass down on the papery coaster the server had left.

"Weird couple of days, huh," Riley remarked. She fiddled with the edges of the coaster.

"Stop right there," Ava commanded. She'd come to Looking Glass to unwind—*not* to rehash the horror of Audrey's murder and Joel's alleged involvement. God knew she'd done that a million times already, even if only within her own mind. "There will be *no* talk of Audrey Wilson over the next hour. No murder, no bodies, no fountains, no mention of Joel Robinson. Got it?"

"Geez," Riley said, raising her hands in innocence. "I didn't even *say* anything. Don't have a cow."

"Well, consider yourself warned."

They sat then, sipping their drinks in awkward silence, neither sure what to say now that the obvious topic of conversation was off limits.

After a few moments, Riley spoke up. "So, do you have those cards on you?"

"Yep," Ava said, a bit surprised that she'd asked. "They're always in my bag. You want to see them?"

Riley's brown eyes glowed. She nodded. Rummaging around in her bag, Ava drew out her cards, slipped them out of their sachet. Although she carried her cards in her bag everywhere she went, she'd never imagined herself laying them out on the table of a wine bar. It was so... out in the open. Well, what was the harm? People in Shiloh would have to get used to it anyway, what with Arcana being—fingers crossed—a fixture in town. As long as that Donna Schroeder woman didn't saunter on in—which was unlikely assuming that a pastor's wife would not be frequenting a wine bar—she'd be golden. She fanned out the cards before them.

"Can I touch them?" Riley looked hesitant, like Ava had handed her some sacred relic forbidden to the hands of humans.

"Of course!" This time, Ava grinned. There were, of course, tarot readers who didn't allow anyone else to touch their cards in order to preserve their own energy within the deck, but Ava wasn't one of them. Zaidy Mel had always let her fan his cards out on the kitchen table, much like Riley was doing now, and Ava wasn't going to break the tradition.

"So, how do they work?"

"You mean, what's the story behind them? Or, like, how do you read them?"

"I don't know. Both, I guess. I saw you reading them the other day for Owen, and they looked pretty cool. I didn't realize it was a thing actual normal people could learn to do."

"Well, I'm glad to hear I'm an actual normal person," Ava quipped. Ava scooted her stool closer to Riley and took the deck in her hands again. "May I?"

Riley nodded. Ava began separating the deck, deftly flicking cards into two specific piles. Riley watched, enraptured, as Ava's fingers blurred with the cards, until she laid the last card on its respective pile. She looked up at Ava expectantly.

"Okay," Ava began, excitement fluttering in her belly. She'd tried before to explain how the cards worked to various friends, but no one had ever been very convinced. And certainly no one had *asked* her to explain. This was a first. "So, a standard Rider-Waite tarot deck has seventy-eight cards—"

"What's Rider-Waite?"

"It's a kind of tarot deck. There are several types of tarot decks, and Rider-Waite is the one most commonly used nowadays. I think it was first published in 1910 or something, by A. E. Waite—"

"Okay, I got it," Riley said, cutting Ava off with a wave of her hand. "Continue. Seventy-eight cards."

Ava gave Riley a pointed look. "Fine. So, those seventy-eight cards are split into two groups: the major arcana and the minor arcana." She patted the respective piles as she mentioned their names. "The major arcana signify life lessons and universal archetypes. You know, the phases we all go through or big lessons we have to learn. The minor arcana show more of the nitty gritty, day-to-day stuff."

Riley nodded, waited for Ava to go on.

Ava took one of the piles in her hands. "Let's start with the minor arcana. Some people call these pip cards. They're split up into four suits—just like regular playing cards—but the suits have different symbols. See, you've got wands, cups, pentacles, and swords."

She separated the minor arcana pile out into the four smaller suit piles and set them in front of Riley. "Each suit has cards for numbers two through ten, along with an ace. Each suit also has their own set of court cards—page, knight, queen, and king. Make sense?"

"I guess so," Riley said, taking in the cards in front of her. "But how can you tell what they mean?"

Ava's eyes sparkled. "That's the fun part. Okay, so staying with the minor arcana, remember how we have four suits? Each of those suits represents a different facet of life. Cups represent emotions, wands represent passion and creativity, swords stand for intellect, and pentacles symbolize more material stuff, like work and finances."

"Alright..."

"So," Ava went on, fanning out the wand cards in front of them. "For example, here's the suit of wands. Excluding the court cards for a minute, we can see how they go from ace all the way up to ten. I won't go through all the meanings now, but the ace of wands signifies a golden opportunity, the potential for a creative endeavor, the spark of a passion. And that spark continues on, as it's cultivated, so that the higher the card number, the more developed the stage of the spark's journey. So, like, once you get to the ten of wands, you're almost at the finish line. See how the guy in the image is loaded down with the sticks on his back? Things are getting heavy, and you've got to keep pressing on."

Riley gingerly picked up the ten of wands and studied it for a moment. "I think I get it. What do the court cards mean?"

"Right. So, the court cards often represent people—ourselves, family members, people around us, someone we don't know yet but are going to meet soon, someone we're in search of. They can also represent various types of personality traits, as well as line up with certain ages. For example, the pages can often symbolize children, knights stand for teenagers, and then the king and queen are male and female adults. But I don't always take the genders into consideration. Women can often show a lot of king energy, and vice versa."

"Okay, so which court card are you?"

"Oh, that's a good idea," Ava said, her blue eyes snapping. Plucking the four court cards from each of the four piles, she placed them in a neat row. "Different court cards can represent us in different ways and in different contexts, so there's technically no one court card we *are*, but you tell me what you think. Which one seems to embody my personality the most?"

"But how can I tell?" Riley asked, spreading her hands. "I don't know what they mean."

"A lot of tarot is intuition," Ava said. "Look at the pictures and trust your gut."

"Hmm." Riley spread all sixteen court cards out and sifted through them, taking in the still vibrant images of the old deck. While she studied the cards, Ava searched the room for any glimpse of their server. She didn't want to hover over Riley as she thought through the cards, and she was getting hungry. It had been a while since they ordered.

"This one," Riley said, pushing one card toward Ava and stacking the rest into a tidy pile.

Ava looked down. Riley had chosen the queen of swords. There she sat, rigid and dignified on her throne of stone, ready to slice through lies with the razor-sharp sword in her right hand. Huh. Ava would've pegged herself as more of a queen of wands, especially since opening Arcana, but Riley was still learning. It would be interesting to see why Riley had singled this card out.

"Alright," Ava said, settling back on the stool. "The queen of swords, huh? What's your reasoning?"

"Well," Riley began, averting Ava's gaze. She twisted her fingers in her lap. "She looks independent."

Independent. That wasn't bad. That was, in fact, desirable. Ava could see it.

"...and cold."

Ava stopped short. That had gone from good to insulting real quick. But, now that she thought about it, hadn't Riley used that word to describe her once before? "Okay. Explain."

Riley shrugged, pushed a strand of blue hair out of her eyes. "I don't know. Just trying to be honest."

"I see," Ava said. Apparently, she was cold—like stone, like sword-wielding warrior queens, like stratospheric air. What was she supposed to say to that?

"Isn't that what you want, though?" Riley cocked her head.

"For people to think I'm cold?"

"Not exactly, but for people to leave you alone. To do everything on your own."

Ava scoffed. She laid the queen of swords back onto the pile of court cards and mixed them in with the rest of the deck. Tarot lesson over. "I don't want people to leave me alone. I'm sitting here about to have dinner with you, aren't I?"

Riley shook her head. "That's not what I mean..."

"Well, then what?"

"I don't know," Riley repeated, clearly uncomfortable with the can of worms she'd opened. "People around town are saying you're not very friendly. They can't figure you out, you keep them at arm's length."

"I do not," Ava protested. "I'm very friendly! When customers come in, I always say hello. I'm very attentive."

Riley gave a small smile. "Even that couple with the matching t-shirts?"

Ava scoffed. "That was *one* time. Those shirts were asking for it."

"Fair enough," Riley said, tilting her head to the side in thought. "But what about *outside* the cafe? Do you, like, say hi to people at the grocery store?"

"I don't know. I don't pay much attention—I usually just like to get in and get out."

Riley folded her hands on the tabletop. "Exactly. See, that's not how a small town rolls."

"Well, I'm sorry," Ava said curtly, feeling annoyed. It wasn't as though sullen-faced *Riley* was the epitome of friendliness. "I hate small talk, and I'm a private person. I don't need everyone knowing my business. That's how *I* roll."

Riley stared at her for a few long seconds. She nodded as though she understood, then spoke haltingly. "So anyway, will you still teach me?"

"About... what? Tarot?"

"Yeah, to read it." Riley looked at the floor.

Ava looked at the girl, sitting there fidgeting on the bar stool, her eyes flicking back and forth from the ground, and remembered how she'd sat cross-legged on the ground while her grandfather spread out the cards in front of them. "Sure. We can find a time outside of work to really start looking at them together, if you want. Just don't ever use them to accuse me of being cold again." She offered Riley a small smile to let her know she was half joking.

Riley returned the smile, nodding. "Noted."

Ava placed the cards back in their pouch and dropped them into her bag. Their server reappeared, sliding the hummus board they'd decided to share onto the high top, along with two delicate ceramic plates. Ava and Riley dug into their meal, something softened and even familiar emerged between them now. But even as they ate, the memory of red and blue lights flashing in the Robinsons' driveway lingered at the edge of Ava's thoughts, and try as she may, she just couldn't shake it.

10

—————

By the time she parted ways with Riley after their meal at Looking Glass, Ava knew what she had to do. She needed to see the scene of the crime for herself. If Greathouse could be so easily convinced that Joel was the one responsible for Audrey's death, overlooking crucial facts when it came to others in Audrey's periphery, perhaps there was also *physical* evidence he'd overlooked. Either way, she needed to get a sense of what had actually happened to be able to accurately picture it in her mind.

The town plaza wasn't empty like she'd hoped it would be, even though the sun was already sinking. Shoot. She'd have to be discreet, so as not to attract questions—or worse, prompt anyone to alert Chief Greathouse that she'd come back to examine the crime scene uninvited. Would people around town recognize her by now? Regardless, she figured, if no one was meant to come into proximity with the place Audrey's body had been found, then Greathouse would've kept it roped off. But the police had cleared out all the yellow tape, and the fountain was as before. You'd have never known there had been a body floating in it just a couple days prior.

Sliding on her sunglasses, which were only barely necessary in the early evening sunlight, Ava sat down at the fountain, on the side facing away from Main Street. She hadn't been able to get close on the day of the murder, but from what she *had* seen, this side was the side on which they'd discovered Audrey's body. Flicking her eyes back and forth to ensure no one was watching, she drew her tarot handbook out of her bag and opened it to a random page.

Ava traced her finger down the lines of the page, but behind her sunglasses, she examined the fountain. She tried to imagine where exactly Audrey's body had been, the angle it might have fallen at—or rather, been dragged to. The police would've taken photos of the crime scene, of course, but she wondered if any nosy bystander had snapped a picture. Then again, what would it tell her? The autopsy results showed Audrey had been bludgeoned, which meant that she hadn't died *in* the fountain. Someone had moved her there. And unfortunately, Joel Robinson, with his broad shoulders and muscled chest, was more than strong enough to have done the job with little effort.

Just then, a flash of light caught Ava's eye.

Yes! Something on the floor of the fountain had caught the sunlight at just the right angle, sending a glint of gold up through the clear, moving water. Ava set her book down beside her, leaning over to peer into the fountain. The bottom mosaic glittered up at her, dotted with coins tossed there by gleeful children and interstate tourists. Pennies, dimes, the occasional quarter... The number of coins at the bottom of the pool seemed sparse, and it occurred to Ava that the city must have swept the fountain recently, collecting the change and donating it to whatever charity the city deemed fit. In fact, it had seemed much more full of coins when she'd strolled past the week before—like the bottom of a treasure chest.

Ava dipped a hand in the water, enjoying the coolness of it in the surprising heat of the almost setting sun. As her hand touched the surface, the water rippled once more, and her gaze fell on what had caught the light before. There, among the pennies and nickels, was something larger. A gold dollar maybe? One of those Sacagawea ones they once circulated circa her elementary school years? Ava scooped it up. Once she held it in her palm, she glanced around to make sure no one was watching. Then again—who cared if they were? For all they knew, she was simply out basking in the glorious pre-sunset evening, enjoying the trickle and splash of the plaza fountain.

Ava studied the object in her hand. The coin was not a coin at all. It looked, instead, to be a gold button—the kind with holes jutting out from the back, rather than running through the middle. Peering at the button's front, she saw a single triangle engraved in the center.

Closing her fingers over her palm, Ava held the button and tried to think. What was the triangle for? Some kind of design? And anyway, what was it doing in the fountain? It seemed like a weird thing for someone to throw in with their change, even if by accident...

This time Ava took a thorough look around, taking in the elderly woman with her dog across the plaza and the sporty-looking mom pushing a stroller. Satisfied that she was unobserved, Ava slipped the button into the pocket of her bag along with her book, and headed to the street, where she'd parked her bicycle. She called Rose.

"Hey—are you home?"

"Just walked in the door. What's up?"

"I found something. I've got a hunch."

She heard Rose draw in her breath. "What?"

Telling Rose she'd found a button in the plaza fountain seemed suddenly like a gigantic letdown. She needed to show her, explain her theory. Besides, there was still the matter of Jodi Laughlin's shady visit to the payphone to discuss.

"You need to see it. I think it could be what we were looking for. A clue the police overlooked."

Rose was silent for a beat. "Okay. Come over." The line clicked off.

Ava hoped the discovery of the button would be the match to spark Rose and Joel's hopes alive again. But, as she fingered the button she now carried in her pocket, a tingly feeling of apprehension nagged at her. Maybe she should've run the discovery by Owen first. Or consulted the cards? That would at least be better than dragging overly friendly Owen further into her investigation. The more she thought about it, the more she realized that getting Rose's hopes up before she was sure of anything might be the wrong way to go. Well, it was too late now. Rose would want to know what she'd found. Ava could only hope the button would lead them toward the actual killer.

ROSE'S FACE looked grim as she swung her front door open and ushered Ava inside. Ellie was in her exersaucer in the middle of the living room, the entire contraption rattling as she thumped her chubby feet and wobbled from side to side. She gave Ava a drooling, toothless grin, blissfully unaware of the nightmare her parents were living.

"How are you holding up?" Ava asked Rose, eyeing her friend. She was afraid to ask whether Greathouse had come up with anything else that he would claim pointed to Joel's culpability. They didn't need more ammunition against them.

"I've been better," Rose replied, sinking down onto the sofa. Ava took the armchair opposite her. "Anyway—what's all this about? What's this thing you need to show me?"

"Well—" Ava started, digging into her pocket for the button she'd found in the fountain. She opened her palm to Rose, who gingerly picked the button out of Ava's palm. "I found *this* in the fountain. And I think it got there recently. There are hardly any coins in there now, and there *were* when I passed by there a few days ago—the day before the committee event. Which means they must have swept it between now and then. My thought is—"

"What? That the killer dropped it in the fountain when he planted Audrey's body there?" Rose's face had gone white.

"Something like that, yeah." The look on Rose's face was worrying Ava. This was not the reaction she'd expected.

Rose gazed out the window. "This button is from Joel's fraternity jacket, Ava."

"What?" Ava gasped, almost cursing before she caught herself. Ellie was in the room. She lowered her voice. "Are you positive? There's no way…"

Rose nodded grimly, then shrugged. "I mean—I think so. Delta Tau Delta. His Delta jacket's got buttons like that, with the Δ on there. Gold."

Ava's shoulders sank. *Of course.* Her mind had completely

skipped the possibility that it was something to do with campus Greek life. Not surprising, though—she'd dropped out of her sorority by the end of freshman year, much to her mother's dismay.

"Okay," she said. Her mind was whirring, trying to figure out how to remedy the situation she'd just made infinitely worse. *Why* had she thought this would be a good idea? "I haven't told anyone about it yet..."

"You can't just find what you think is evidence and then not say anything to the police, Ava." Rose crossed her arms over her chest. "If it came to light that you'd taken evidence from a crime scene and held onto it..."

"But it's not a crime scene anymore!" Ava protested. She glanced at Ellie, who was now babbling as she smacked at a squeaky toy. "The crime tape's gone, the plaza is back to normal. There's been foot traffic all day. And anyway, we can't be sure it's even *from* that day."

"What if..." Rose began, tipping her head back to examine the ornate plaster ceiling. Her dark eyes grew round as she brought her gaze back to Ava's. "What if we look at Joel's jacket? We'll know pretty fast if it's missing a button."

"Right," Ava confirmed. It made sense, as terrifying as it was to imagine the jacket *would* be missing a button. "And then if Joel's jacket has all its buttons—which I'm sure it will—we can hand the button over to Chief Greathouse for him to handle. He can decide whether it's a good enough lead to figure out where else the button might have come from."

"But what if Joel's jacket is missing a button?" Rose's face fell. "What do we do then?"

"I don't know," Ava admitted. She hadn't wanted to mention the possibility aloud. "We'll cross that bridge *if* we come to it."

"Alright." Rose slapped her hands on her knees and got to her feet. "Come on."

With Ellie absorbed in trying to bite her reflection in a smudgy, plastic mirror, Ava followed Rose to the bedroom. Rose threw open the closet doors. She rustled around in the back for a moment, sliding hangers up and down the rod, wrinkling the plastic wrappings protecting suits and fancy dresses. She emerged from the closet, her hair mussed and empty-handed.

"It's not there," Rose said, her eyes darting around the bedroom as though in search of somewhere else the jacket could be.

"Front closet?" Ava suggested.

A thorough search of the front closet yielded a polyester neon jacket that Ava couldn't believe Joel owned, but no Delta jacket. At least the neon jacket brought about a little nervous laughter.

"Alright," Ava said, taking charge. "As my grandfather would've said, this calls for coffee. You always do your best thinking with a mug of hot coffee in hand."

Rose nodded, sinking down into a chair at the kitchen table, and Ava set to work brewing the coffee. She hadn't been to Rose and Joel's house too many times before, but the kitchen was small and cozy, with everything organized intuitively, almost as though Rose had stuck little labels around. Rose had always been like that—even as a kid, her Lisa Frank binder had been meticulously organized and her Barbies' outfits were always color coordinated. As the coffee percolated, Ava leaned her hips against the counter and she and Rose discussed their theories aloud.

"Alright, so if Joel's jacket isn't here—any ideas where it could be?"

Rose shook her head. "He doesn't wear it very often, ever since I told him it looked lame to be going around in his fraternity duds as a grown-ass man. Honestly, I'm not even sure when the last time I saw him wear it was..."

Ava tapped her chin. "Okay, now *that* makes things even weirder. Why would Joel, *if* he was going to lure Audrey Wilson to the fountain or wherever the murder happened, decide *that* was the night to put on the Delta jacket? Especially if it wasn't one he would've normally put on?"

"It's anyone's guess," Rose said, spreading her hands out onto the table in a helpless gesture. "Anyway, he went for a run. Wouldn't it have made more sense to take care of the dirty business while on the run, if that's what—and mind you, I'm speaking hypothetically—he was planning to do?"

"Exactly. And you wouldn't wear a bulky letterman jacket on your morning run, anyway. Still, I think we've got to find it. The fact that it's not here makes it even more suspicious if we were to go to the police with the button."

Ava poured out two mugs of coffee and set one down in front of Rose, who was already flipping through her iPhone's recent calls. She pressed speaker, then set the phone down in the middle of the table. Both women wrapped their shaking hands around the warm mugs in front of them.

"Hello?" Joel's voice was fuzzy on the other end of the line. There was a clanking sound, followed by a few distant grunts.

"Hey," Rose said, louder than necessary. "It's me. Ava's here, too. You okay?"

Joel's voice sounded strained and tired. "Yeah, as good as I can be, I guess. A few of the guys have made some jokes, and a couple of aerobics teachers have been giving me looks, but other than that..."

"Well, you can tell them where to get off. It's not funny." Rose's voice was firm.

"Rose, we've been through this." Joel's voice was also firm, and Ava could almost picture the set of his chiseled jaw as he spoke through the other line. "I've got nothing to hide, and the last thing I want is for people to think I take these accusations seriously. I'm trying to keep things lighthearted."

"Listen—Joel," Ava said. "Do you know where your fraternity letterman jacket is? We were looking for it in the closet and we couldn't find it."

"My Delta jacket?" Joel sounded puzzled. "I took it to the dry cleaners. It was super dusty. Why?"

Ava looked up at Rose, her eyes alight. "When did you take it? Do you have the receipt or anything?"

"As a matter of fact, I do," Joel said. "And actually, I think the cleaners must have lost the jacket. It was missing when I picked up the rest of the laundry a couple weeks ago, and they said they would look for it. I've been meaning to go down there and see what on earth's up. Do you mind telling me *why*, though? What's this got to do with anything?"

"Well," Rose said, jumping in for Ava. It seemed she wanted to be the one to let her husband in on the potential fresh evidence Ava had found. Ava couldn't blame her—Rose's voice was calm and sweet and would do a better job of delivering the news if things did indeed go south. "Ava was just at the plaza fountain today after work"—she looked up at Ava for confirmation, who gave a yes-no sort of nod— "and she spotted a button in the fountain. It looks exactly like the ones off your jacket."

Joel drew in a sharp breath. "You're kidding. It's got the delta engraved?"

"Yeah. I knew right away when I saw it," Rose said. "Unless

there's another jacket around with gold buttons and deltas on them..."

"I mean, there could be," Ava was quick to point out. "It's not impossible. Lots of other people belong to the fraternity, I'd imagine."

"No one else in Shiloh, though, to my knowledge," Joel pointed out. They could almost hear the whir of his thoughts. "But how do you know that button hasn't been in the fountain for ages? It could have gotten mixed in with the coins that people toss in there. The police might not have seen it. Heck, *I* could have dropped it in there at some point! Although I'm sure I would've noticed if a button was missing."

"Oh, the police missed it alright," Ava said. "But that's the thing—I always ride past the fountain on my way into work, and I distinctly remember that the day of the committee dinner —that is, the day *before* the murder occurred—I could see the bottom for once, when just two days before, it was full of coins. They must have collected the coins the day before the murder."

"I see. Did you alert the police yet?"

"No," Rose admitted. "We wanted to check out your jacket first—" She stopped mid-sentence, as though realizing what she had just been owning up to.

"It's okay, Rose," Joel said, sounding weary. "You wanted to make sure my jacket wasn't missing a button before making any next moves. I get it—it was the logical thing to do."

Rose sat in silence. Ava picked up the slack. "Okay, well— I'd recommend you check out the situation at the dry cleaners. If we take this piece of evidence to the police *and* you can prove your coat was at the cleaners that entire time, I would think it'll strengthen your alibi."

"It's tough to say," Joel said. "There's no way to tell if the killer was the one who dropped that button, anyway. It's just as possible that the killer left no evidence at all at the fountain."

"But *still.*"

"Alright," Joel agreed. "I know Todd at the cleaners stays late on Mondays. I'll run over there before he leaves and see what's going on."

AVA HAD BEEN HOME for an hour when the whisper hit her. She'd just put a tray of roasted vegetables in the oven when it happened the way it always did, like a feather at the back of her mind, making the skin on her neck prickle. She knew exactly what it was and wondered why she hadn't thought of it before. Then again, that was what the whisper was there for—to remind her that some things that couldn't be explained could offer an explanation. Setting a timer for the oven, she sat down cross-legged on the rug in front of the coffee table in her cozy little living room. The summer nights were way too warm to light the stove her grandfather had left in the corner, but she looked forward to colder weather when she'd be able to snuggle up with a blanket by the light of the crackling fire.

Lighting a single white candle, Ava took a moment to ground herself. The memories of her grandfather, of what seemed like a lifetime gone by, and of the love he'd showered on her when her parents were busy running with their careers, swirled around her in a warm embrace. Ava didn't know if she believed in ghosts, but she was positive that a part of her grandfather lived here still, watching over her from the tall, pointed eaves of the farmhouse. Outside, a faint breeze rustled the leaves on the tree near the kitchen window, crickets chirping.

She placed one palm over the cards, feeling the tingle of energy rise through her as it always did when she got the whisper. She shuffled the cards, fanned them out in front of her, and selected three. *Which spread? What are these three cards meant to be?* She was half asking the cards themselves, half asking Zaidy Mel.

Overt. Covert. Next move.

Alright. Well, there it was. She had her answer. Ava laid out the three cards she'd selected in a row and turned over the first. She sucked in her breath. Of course—it was so spot-on she almost laughed to herself, managing not to, though, given the gravity of the situation. The Death card stared back at her once again, its horse and skeletal rider looking every bit as menacing as it had just a few days earlier at her shop, the day before Audrey's murder. If only she'd known that day what the card was alluding to—but then again, thank god she hadn't. She might've turned tail and gone right back to Chicago. Well—no. No, she wouldn't have. Her mother would be waiting for that to happen, greeting her with a smug, triumphant expression. Ava would have rather faced off with the killer themselves than give her mother that satisfaction.

Ava turned over the second card. The five of swords. Interesting. There were several things the imagery on the card could pertain to, several ways one could interpret it, but one thing was for sure: The five of swords showed deception. Someone wasn't being truthful. *Well, duh.* It didn't take a genius to figure that one out. Still, she was sure now the cards in front of her were, in fact, referencing Audrey Wilson's murder; everything added up to what she already knew—or the direction she was headed in her little private investigation. The question was... who? *Who* was not being truthful? And how could she find out? Before she turned over the next card, Ava sat back for a moment, settling the nerves that were simmering inside her. She needed a clear head for this card. She needed to keep an open mind, to be open to whatever the cards were trying to tell her. There was a time and place for her own theories, but it was the tarot's turn to talk in this conversation. Drawing a deep breath, Ava turned over the final card.

The two of cups, reversed. The picture glimmered up at her, the surface of the card matte and faded from years of use. Zaidy Mel had read with these very cards, and Ava often imagined his energy still flowing through them, now flowing through her and giving her strength. She didn't know what to make of the card at first glance. The figures with their golden goblets in hand—*l'chaim!*—were cheesy, and the sacred union she knew the card represented felt different. To make things even more difficult, she'd never been good with reversals—there was something about the upside-down imagery that tumbled her feelings along with it. She couldn't get a good grasp on the sense that normally flowed through her when reading the cards. And trying to link it to the rest of the cards in the spread? Forget it.

But then a thought occurred to her. How would Zaidy Mel have read this card? She closed her eyes, pictured his calm, lined face, his thick white hair. He would've stroked his equally white beard, flipped his skullcap over in his hands a few times before placing it back on his curly head. And then he would've said, "Well, here's what I see..." This was what he'd always done, from the very first reading he'd ever given her, all the way through the lessons they'd had together. *What do you see?* Ava felt the hair stand straight up on her arms now. It was like

Zaidy Mel had spoken aloud, so clear was his voice in her mind.

Ava gazed at the card, taking the imagery in. She knew in theory that reversals often signaled an imbalance of energy; literally turning the card on its head was a metaphorical reversal of the card's meaning. If the upright two of cups represented partnership, harmony, and mutual, romantic love, was the opposite of that... distrust? Ava laughed softly to herself. It wasn't farfetched in the slightest; she'd been down that road and back over the past couple of years. But surely the tarot wasn't suggesting that her next move should be to *distrust* others? And more to the point, what did Ava's personal relationships have to do with Audrey's murder and clearing Joel's name? Perhaps the two of cups reversed was not suggesting *distrust* of others but was pointing to Ava's need to trust *herself*... After all, trusting Greathouse's (lack of) intuition was proving disastrous, and so far, the town of Shiloh seemed more interested in reading about the scandal in the Shiloh Gazette than they did in tracking down the real killer. Who *could* she trust but herself? But something still bothered her. She was stuck. The whisper was gone, floating away like a puff of smoke, and Ava sat alone on the floor of her living room. The rattle of branches on the roof seemed fitting for the darkness of the night.

Stacking the five of swords and Death cards on top of the deck, Ava pushed the cards aside. She placed the two of cups card up on the mantel, giving it a solid stare. It could prove useful to keep it in her line of vision in case something clicked later, or in case the whisper returned with some new sense of imagery she'd missed before.

Ava's phone buzzed on the coffee table. *Rose*. She snatched it up.

"Any word?"

"The dry cleaners don't have it."

"What?! What do you mean they don't have it? What happened to it?"

"They don't know. Their best guess is that it got in with another customer's belongings and was taken home by mistake. The only thing they can do for right now is offer a refund. They said they'll let us know if anyone brings it in."

"God, talk about poor service," Ava grumbled. "So, where does this leave us? Anyone in town could have Joel's jacket!"

"I know." Rose's voice sounded glum through the phone, desperate. "Still, Joel is adamant that we're giving the button to Chief Greathouse." She lowered her voice in imitation of Joel. "'I've got nothing to hide. Give him the stupid button—we have to catch who did this.'"

"Hmm." Ava didn't know what to think. Obviously, Joel was right. The right thing to do was to hand any potential evidence over to the police, but it didn't seem like it would do much for Joel's case. Unless— "Rose, do you think the cleaners would give us a list of all the customers who came to pick up their dry cleaning since Joel took his coat in?"

"We can ask," Rose said, seeming to think it over as she spoke. "Why? Are you planning to narrow down the list of people who could've ended up with the coat? I know it's a small place, but it could be dozens, Ava!"

Ava's excitement fell. Rose was right, of course. Even if they *could* convince the cleaners to give them a list of their recently picked-up orders, following up on every single lead would be exhausting and not at all efficient. No, they needed a faster solution. But Ava's mind was at a loss. She glanced up at the card on the mantel. *Think.* No whisper. She hoped one would come, eventually.

"You're right," Ava conceded. "It would take far too long, even if we could get our hands on a list. But I want to be the one to take the button in to the station tomorrow. I've got a few things I want to discuss with Chief Greathouse."

11

———

Martin Lombardi, the receptionist at the Shiloh Police Station, was in the middle of a donut break when Ava strode into the station the next morning. She'd already been to Arcana early to open up, brew the coffee, and get Riley set up with cleaning instructions to keep her busy when business was slow, promising to be back in thirty minutes.

Martin had already stopped by Arcana for his morning cappuccino. Seeing Ava, he stuffed the rest of the donut in his mouth, catching puffs of powdered sugar in his beard.

"Morning again, Ava," he said, swallowing down a hunk of donut. "What can I do you for?"

"Hey, Martin. I'm here to see Chief Greathouse."

Martin raised his eyebrows but gestured down the hall. "You're welcome to see him, but I'll warn you—he's grouchy. I don't think he slept at all last night."

"Wonderful. Thanks for the heads up." Ava shot the man a weak smile and strode down the hallway in the direction he'd pointed.

The door to Greathouse's office was ajar. Ava rapped twice,

to which a gruff voice responded that whoever it was could come in.

"Chief Greathouse?" Ava poked her head in, then opened the door wider to slide the rest of her body inside the office. "May I shut the door?"

The chief nodded gruffly, gesturing with his head for her to take a seat on the opposite side of his polished mahogany desk. He sat with hands folded neatly on the tabletop, his mustache twitching. "Yes?"

Ava set the button down on the desk in front of him. The chief took it in his rough fingers, turned it in the light for a moment, then looked up at Ava, waiting.

"I found that in the fountain. Don't worry—the crime tape was all gone."

"Alright? What's it to me?"

"Well, I like to ride past on my way in to work in the mornings. The water is calming. Anyway, I went past the day of the committee dinner, and I distinctly remember noticing the fountain had been cleaned—when it had been full of coins just the day before. That means they must have removed the coins sometime around the day of Audrey's murder and someone dropped this button in there *after* they cleaned."

"Let me guess," the chief said, his expression amused. "You think this button belongs to the killer, that it came off while he or she was committing the murder."

"Well, either committing the murder or precisely *after*, given that whoever killed Audrey planted her body there when she was already dead," Ava corrected tentatively. She sensed the chief wasn't buying it.

"Could be." Greathouse shrugged his wide shoulders and

leaned back in his swivel chair. "Could just as easily not be. Hang on a second."

Greathouse held his iPhone at arm's length, frowning at it as he jabbed thick fingers at the screen. When he held the phone up to his ear, his mustache wagged.

"Yeah, Greathouse here. Morning. Say, when did y'all last sweep the Main Street fountain?" Greathouse frowned, stroking his giant chin. Ava sat in silence, waiting. "Okay, got it. Yeah, you too. Have a good one."

The chief drew the phone away from his ear and scowled at it, stabbing his sausage finger at the screen in finality. He settled back in his chair. "City Hall says they swept the fountain the day before Ms. Wilson's body was found."

"So the day before the murder," Ava said, crossing her arms to meet the chief's stance.

"It would appear so, yes." Greathouse raised his eyes to the ceiling, stroked his mustache. He was silent a moment, thinking. "That's a button off a letterman jacket. That means we're looking for something academic-related that has something to do with the Greek letter delta. You know who was in a fraternity during their college days, Ms. Goldberg?"

Ava sensed this was not going in the direction she'd hoped. Before the chief could continue, she pounced on his bait. "I know Joel Robinson was, sir—Delta Tau Delta—but his jacket's been at the dry cleaners for at least the past two weeks and—"

"And he's got proof of that? That he both dropped it off *and* didn't pick it up?"

"Well," Ava began, stopping as abruptly as she'd begun. "The jacket's not there. Joel has the drop-off receipt, but apparently someone else picked it up by mistake."

"Or *he* picked it up."

"But I swear, Rose and I searched their house inside and out, and there was *no* jacket."

"Of course, there wasn't," Chief Greathouse said, scoffing. He looked almost disappointed. "Really, Ms. Goldberg, I thought you'd have thought things through better than this. The first thing Joel Robinson would've done with that jacket would've been to get rid of it. You don't keep evidence lying around!"

"But why would it even *be* evidence? As far as I understand, Audrey didn't die from blood loss, and you can brush something like hair off with a lint roller, so there'd have been no *reason* to get rid of the jacket. Not unless Joel—hypothetically, of course—knew he'd dropped the button."

The chief scratched his chin. "Which maybe he did know, and why he got rid of it. I hate to say it—this just makes Joel look *more* suspicious in my book. You know anyone else in this town who was a Delta?"

"I'm not exactly up on who was in what—"

"There aren't many Shiloh folks messing around with fraternities, ma'am. Now, if you want me to take this button into evidence, I sure can—but it's not going to help Joel's case."

The chief was right, of course. She and Rose had told Joel as much when he'd insisted they deliver the button to the station that morning. Ava let out a flustered sigh. "*Joel* was the one who insisted I bring this in to you. I'm well aware of how it looks, but Joel has nothing to hide, and as he said, every shred of evidence could help find Audrey's killer."

Chief Greathouse gave Ava a long look. He reached over and grabbed a baggie from his desk, dropped the button in, and zipped it. "Alright. Into evidence it goes." He shook his head. "I tell you what, between this, that tip, and the note found in

Audrey's pocket, Joel Robinson doesn't need *any* more evidence against him."

That's right! The note. How could she have forgotten? She'd wanted to see that note for herself, decide if the handwriting really *was* Joel's, but there was no way Greathouse was going to allow *that*.

Greathouse grunted a dismissal and got up to shoo Ava toward the door. "Police work is for police, and the last I checked you were making coffee and reading fortunes. Keep your nose out of police business, little lady."

He placed a firm hand on Ava's back, swung the door open, and all but shoved her out into the hallway. The door slammed shut.

Ava made her way back to the station lobby unbothered by Greathouse's rudeness. He'd reminded her of something important—and he wasn't the only one in the building with access to evidence.

"Oof," Martin said. "What did you do? I heard the door slam."

"Well, I guess the chief doesn't like concerned citizens trying to help a case along unless it fits his agenda," Ava said, sidling up to the counter and leaning her elbows on it. From the look on his face, she sensed Martin was no stranger to Greathouse's pompous nature. In fact, she thought she had found her ally. "I can't believe he actually thinks Joel Robinson could've killed that woman."

Martin nodded sympathetically. It was clear he understood all too well the moods Chief Greathouse could get into. "It's shocking, I agree. The note is pretty damning, though."

Perfect. Ava had to work to hide her smile.

"I know," Ava said, pursing her lips together to look glum. "I still don't want to believe it."

Martin nodded. "It's a bummer. They're still comparing handwriting samples, but as someone who used to copy notes from Joel in chemistry—I'm telling you, it's his writing."

Ava felt herself growing hot. She swallowed hard, praying that her cheeks would not redden from panic any more than they already had from anger. She had to keep her cool, keep Martin on her side, keep him from knowing just how adamant Greathouse was that she keep her nose out of Joel's case.

"Oh, I never got to see it," Ava said, trying to keep her voice nonchalant. "I wonder if I'd be able to confirm the writing."

Martin was already coming out from behind the desk and waving Ava down a separate hallway. "We're waiting for the analyst to sign off on it, of course, but having someone else who knows Joel's writing give a preliminary confirmation can't hurt."

"Right," Ava said, her thoughts humming. Just what did this note say that was so damning? *Dear Audrey, here's a whack on the head for you. Sincerely, Joel Robinson?*

Martin unlocked the evidence room and held the door open for Ava to enter. He led her past the rows of shelves packed with drawers and bags, finally coming to one at the end of the row. Flipping through the drawer, he pulled out a sealed, flattened baggie and smoothed it out onto a nearby desk. Inside was a crumpled, half sheet of purple dotted notebook paper, with a few lines scribbled onto it.

Audrey–

We need to talk. Please.

I don't want to lose what we have.

Joel

Ava looked up at Martin. Her insides felt like solid lead.

There was no doubt about it—it matched the writing that had been on every Christmas card she'd received from the Robinsons over the past eight years. Sharp, angular, and scratched up and down across the lines—like a heart rate monitor.

"Well?" Martin was eager to get her opinion. "What do you think? Did he write it?"

Ava wasn't sure how to answer. She wasn't sure her opinion even mattered if they were going to be calling in experts, but she didn't feel great about throwing Joel under the bus by saying the sample seemed legitimate. Instead, she settled for a vague: "I really can't say."

Martin looked disappointed. His shoulders slumped. "Well, I guess we'll find out soon. It fits, though, given what we know about their affair and all..."

"What the chief *thinks* he knows," Ava corrected. "That was an anonymous tip. It could easily be some crazy person who just wants to win instead of Joel in next year's Mr. Husker Body or whatever."

Martin laughed. "It could be a crazy, I guess. But paired with the note? I dunno, Ava. My guess is Joel wasn't planning to kill her, but he lost control—got a little too angry. It certainly wouldn't be the first time something like that happened to someone."

Ava frowned, trying to integrate all the new information that was now coming to light. First the tip, then the note, and then—Ava swallowed hard at the memory of the button she'd just handed over to Chief Greathouse. Three hard signs pointing to Joel Robinson as Audrey Wilson's killer. Could that be the truth? Could Joel Robinson, the man she'd watched marry her childhood friend, who she'd come to love like her own brother, really have murdered this woman? Nothing was making sense. She needed a sounding board, a voice of reason. There was Rose, of course, but it was Rose's family whose future was on the line. No, Ava needed someone else, someone objective, outside the tangled web this murder was now becoming.

"I've got to get going." Ava pushed the baggie back into Martin's hands and headed to the door. She shot him a grateful glance on her way out of the room. "Let me know what the experts say."

She'd just had a flash of an idea, as much as she hated herself for it. Owen O'Kelly had turned out to be a pretty good help the last time around, when her tailing of Jodi Laughlin had gone wrong, and god, could she use some good help.

IT WAS all Ava could do not to hurl herself inside Owen's hardware store. Still shaken from her visit to the police station, she forced herself to pause outside the door, gulping a deep breath. Things really did *not* look good for Joel, and she needed to turn them around fast. There had to be *something* she was missing. As she entered the shop, the glass door swung shut behind her, the bell atop it nearly giving her a heart attack with its jarring clang. Owen was in the tool aisle, pointing out a package of variously sized wrenches for a customer. Both men looked up.

"Well, you're jumpy this morning," Owen remarked, hiding a smile. "I'll be with you in just a sec."

She pretended to busy herself with her phone, more than once glancing up over the screen to see whether Owen's customer had made up his mind about the wrenches and would be getting out of their hair. She really didn't have time to waste—time was of the essence if she was going to convince Greathouse that Joel was innocent, that Ricky was the real killer.

Owen rang the man up at the register, sent him on his way. "Take care, Phil."

"Ava Goldberg," Owen said, offering her a pointed, bemused look. He pulled himself up to sit on the counter and patted the spot next to him. "To what do I owe the pleasure?"

"There's been a development," Ava said, ignoring his teasing manner. She hopped onto the counter next to him.

Owen raised his eyebrows. "Everything okay? You made it pretty clear yesterday that this little investigation was none of my business."

"I know, I know." She waved her hand. "I need help, though. I need a sounding board, and I don't want to drag Riley into it."

Owen studied her for a moment. "Alright. I'm listening."

Ava drew a deep inhale, looking anywhere but at Owen while trying to think where to begin. "After work yesterday—after we saw Jodi searching the payphone booth—I took a little walk to the plaza to sit by the fountain. You know, to read a book and get some fresh air."

"Right," Owen nodded, smirking. "As one does."

"As one does. And, while I was sitting next to the fountain, I looked over and saw something glimmering under the water—a gold button with a triangle etched into it." Owen's brow knit, but he said nothing. Waited. Ava went on. "Which could have been nothing, right? Except for—let me see if I can explain this right—I remembered that when I'd passed by the day before the murder the fountain had been freshly cleaned. As in, no coins at all. Which means—"

"That the button had to have fallen in *after* that day. Meaning that it could—potentially—have come from Audrey's killer."

"Exactly. And yes, I know Joel Robinson was in that Delta fraternity."

Owen's face had gone serious. "Did you tell the chief?"

"Yes. In fact, Joel insisted I should."

"What's the chief say?"

Ava sighed. "Chief Greathouse sees the button as even more evidence in the case against Joel. And I talked Martin into letting me see the note."

"Note? Like, the one they said they found in Audrey's pocket?"

"Right, the love note. Or *something*. Which was allegedly written by Joel. And... *God*, Owen, it matches. The handwriting matches."

"Hmm." It was all Owen said, but from his concentrated expression, Ava could tell he was taking his time to put together a response. A gush of appreciation flooded through her. They sat for a minute, both swinging their legs and listening to the whir of the ceiling fan. When Owen finally spoke, his words were short and to the point. "It's too obvious. It's too perfect."

Ava turned to look at him. Their eyes met, and she knew they were thinking the same thing. "Like he's been framed, right?"

"Yep."

"But by *whom*? Why would someone have it out for Joel? I know he was kind of a jock in high school, meaning some people might not like him, but *god*. This is on another level."

Owen chuckled. "He wasn't so bad. Anyway, it might not be

anything personal against *Joel*. Maybe Joel was just the easiest target. Maybe he walked right into the plan."

"You mean, like, someone wanted to kill Audrey and Joel just happened to be the easiest person to frame?"

"Something like that." Owen shrugged. "But wait—does Joel's jacket have all its buttons? *Tell* me you checked that."

"Of course, I checked," Ava scoffed, crossing her arms over her chest. Then, remembering the answer to his question, her face fell. "But we couldn't find it. Joel says he took it to the dry cleaners two weeks ago and never got it back with the rest of his clothes."

Owen's eyes widened. "So somebody else in town has got Joel Robinson's Delta jacket."

"Or, as Chief Greathouse so kindly put it, Joel most likely got rid of it after he wore it while murdering Audrey Wilson."

"Yikes. Didn't think of that. So, what now? Got anything new on Ricky?"

"No," Ava admitted. "Not since we saw Jodi hanging around the payphone. I *do* have a shop to run, you know."

"Well, gee—so do I. And look who keeps coming in to disrupt my business."

Ava snapped her gaze to Owen's, readying a retort, but found he was grinning, dimples just barely glimmering in his cheeks. He held up his hands. "Don't get riled up now. I'm just teasing."

Ava sniffed. "Well, I'm glad you can be so lighthearted in the face of dire circumstances."

"That's what I'm here for. Anyway—back to business. Who do we think could've framed Joel? Or, perhaps more correctly worded, who might have wanted Audrey Wilson dead?"

"See, *this* is where I need your help," Ava said. "I'm new here. I keep to myself. You're the one with the town gossip."

"*You* keep to *yourself*?" Owen snorted. Ava ignored the remark. "Alright, well, I hate to speak ill of the dead, but Audrey Wilson wasn't the number one most liked person around Shiloh. She's always had a bit of an ego."

"So I gathered," Ava remarked, remembering the disgust on Rose and Riley's faces the day Audrey had visited Arcana. "She was nothing but friendly to me, but Rose and Riley didn't seem to like her."

Owen chuckled. "I don't know about Riley, but I'm sure Rose didn't. Audrey was always flipping that red hair of hers around, puckering her lips at Joel. They were a thing in high school, but ultimately Joel chose Rose."

"That... doesn't sound great considering the accusations against Joel right now." Ava grimaced.

Owen shrugged, ran a hand through his wavy hair, which sprang right back down over his forehead. "I mean—just because Audrey never got over him, doesn't mean the feeling was reciprocated." Then he turned to look at Ava, keeping his green eyes trained on her until she looked up, reluctantly meeting his gaze. "What do *you* think? You know Joel Robinson just as well as I do, if not better. Do *you* think the accusations are true?"

Ava paused. Somehow, speaking the words aloud seemed dangerous. "About the affair? I don't know. I'm not in a great spot to be making that kind of judgment. But I'm *certain* Joel isn't a murderer."

"Why aren't you in a good spot to make that judgment?" There was no missing the glimmer of curiosity behind Owen's eyes.

Ava shook her head. "Not important."

Owen nodded. They sat in silence for a moment.

"So," he said, breaking the silence. "I heard the police were over at Lucas Wilson's last night. Chris Mitchell—one of Audrey's coworkers at the law firm, remember?—was in here this morning to pick up an order and was catching me up to speed. He said that Ted Finkenbaum, one of Audrey's law partners and the Wilsons' family attorney, wanted to talk with Greathouse because Audrey was set to inherit their parents' estate and Lucas wasn't happy about it. Apparently, there's been some past drama with Lucas who feels he's got more right to the inheritance than Audrey, with her being the stepsister and all. And it's not like they've ever gotten along..."

"No," Ava breathed, recognition dawning. "Well, his behavior the day of the murder makes a lot more sense now..."

"What do you mean? You talked to him on the day they found Audrey?" Owen's voice was sharp.

"More like Riley and I had to listen to him go off," Ava remarked. "Greathouse was taking our statements at Arcana after Audrey's body was found, and suddenly here comes this guy in off the street. I had no idea who it was until Greathouse called him 'Lucas', and then I put two and two together. He said he wasn't sorry about Audrey being dead, but he seemed pretty pissed he was going to be questioned."

"Well, Greathouse must've known the situation with the will, so good on him. Do you know what became of the questioning? I mean, the will doesn't *prove* anything, but..."

"I have no idea. Greathouse isn't exactly offering up information. But this *does* give us another person with a motive. Did Chris say anything else?" Finally. Maybe they were finally getting somewhere, finally had a lead.

Owen shook his head. "No, but we can head over there right after we close up shop. Grab a bite to eat after?"

Ava tensed. She was here for Owen's sleuthing skills—not for a dinner date. This was exactly what she'd hoped to avoid. She hopped down off the countertop, slung her bag over her shoulder. "Actually, I need to get back to Arcana. I left Riley alone, and she'll freak out if I'm gone too long."

"Mm." Owen stared at her, a small smile on his lips. "Alright. Well, let me know if you—"

Owen was cut off by a piercing scream. Ava's blood turned to ice. They hurried to the door and to the sidewalk, where someone from the salon across the street had also stepped out to see what on earth was going on. The scream came again, shattering the spring air.

"Help—police! *Greathouse!*"

Ava shielded her eyes. Across the street in the police station parking lot, a woman was running frantically between parked cars, trying to get around to the front side of the building and screaming as she went. Was that...?

"Jodi?!" It was Owen who recognized her first. He broke into a sprint, barely sparing a glance behind as he dashed across the street toward her. Ava was on his heels.

When they reached Jodi, her eyes were frantic, her frizzy blond hair even more huge than normal. Her shoulders shook with silent, tearless sobs, shrieking, "Call Greathouse! Call 911!"

"Hey," Owen soothed her, wrapping a brawny arm around Jodi's shaking shoulders. "Hey, hey. We're here. Ava's calling." He raised his eyebrows sharply at Ava, but she already had the station on the phone.

"He got—somebody tried to—Ricky—" Jodi was in such a panic she could barely get the words out.

Ava was frantic to know what had happened, but with the way Jodi was heaving in gasps of air, it was clear she was in no state to be answering questions. Instead, Ava patted the woman's arm, casting a worried glance around the parking lot.

Chief Greathouse and Officer Harding were out in no time, sprinting across the parking lot. The chief cleared his throat, making his mustache wobble, announcing his presence.

Owen gave Jodi's shoulders a supportive squeeze, released her, and moved to stand next to Ava. Jodi, still frantic, sucked in a deep breath as though willing herself to calm down enough to speak. After a moment, she let out a shuddery breath and turned toward Greathouse.

"They got Ricky," she wailed.

12

"Jodi, you've got to tell me what happened," Chief Greathouse said, his voice firm and rumbling. His mustache didn't even twitch so serious was his face. "*Who* got Ricky? And where *is* he?"

And what does 'got Ricky' mean? Ava barely resisted crying out. Jodi's shrieks had filled her with a white-hot fear that was getting hard to contain. She chanced a glance at Owen, who stood next to her, his hands shoved deep into the pockets of his jeans. His green eyes were clouded with worry.

Jodi, still struggling to get her sobs under control, took a deep, rasping breath. "I don't know *who*, Matt! All I know is I left the shop to go get some smokes and when I came back, Ricky he w–was on the ground—and the b-blood…" Her face went white.

Chief Greathouse said something sternly under his breath to Officer Harding, who turned on his heel and was gone. His expression, though still commanding, was softer when he turned back to Jodi. "Dan will have the paramedics here in just a minute, Jodi. But right now, I need you to breathe so you can tell me exactly what happened."

Jodi nodded, her face still stricken. She looked dazed. "I don't know, Matt. The door was slightly open when I got back to the shop, and I thought it was funny 'cause Ricky don't usually like it open—it rattles. And then when I got inside, he was laying on the floor, arms and legs bent kinda weird. I couldn't see his face, but I saw the pool of blood leakin' out from under him, and that's when I come over here to get help."

Ava felt Owen tense. Neither of them had spoken since Greathouse took charge of the situation, but Ava wasn't sure how much longer she could hold back. What was going *on*?

"And you saw nothing else?" Chief Greathouse pressed, concern in his eyes. "No sign of anyone else inside the building?"

Jodi shook her head. "No—but I didn't look very well, Chief. I got out of there. All I could think to do was to get help."

Chief Greathouse nodded. "You did the right thing."

"I *told* you Ricky didn't kill nobody," Jodi said then, crossing her arms over her chest and shivering despite the summer heat.

"Alright, Jodi," Chief Greathouse said. "The EMTs are on their way, and Dan will radio once they've assessed the situation. Let's get you into the station and a cup of coffee in your hands. That'll make things a tad better while we wait to hear from them."

Reluctantly, Jodi let the chief lead her inside the station. Chief Greathouse shot Ava a warning look, as though aware of the thoughts racing through her brain. And sure enough, it was all Ava could do not to take off in a sprint toward Ricky Birch's auto body shop that very second. Someone had attacked Ricky? The obvious question was *why*? And just as concerning, *who*? Ricky had been the prime suspect in Ava's mind—had Jodi reported that Ava had been tailing her, leading him to stage the attack on himself to throw Ava off his trail? It seemed far-fetched... But then again, so did everything about the entire situation.

Owen eyed her warily. "You're thinking of going over to Ricky's shop, aren't you?"

She met his gaze with defiance. "I need to know what's going on."

"I hear that," Owen said, a small smile briefly overtaking the concern on his handsome features. "But don't you think we ought to wait to hear what Officer Harding says? A second murder isn't something you want to get yourself tangled up in."

"You think he's dead? And it was murder?"

Owen shrugged his broad shoulders. "I don't know, but whatever it is, it doesn't sound good. What—you don't think this was staged, do you?" He looked incredulous.

"I'm not ruling anything out," Ava said, shrugging right back at him. "I have no clue what the details are yet, which is why I'd like to find out."

"Okay," Owen said slowly. He raked a hand through his tousled hair. "But if Ricky was attacked—by someone other than himself—I think it's best if you back off. Who knows? Maybe whoever killed Audrey saw Jodi at the payphone and thought she and Ricky were onto him. I know you want to clear Joel's name, but..."

As much as she hated to admit it, Owen was right. Investigating Audrey's murder on her own had been iffy enough, but if there really was a murderer on the loose who was willing to kill a second person to avoid being found out, things were looking dangerous. It would mean this whole thing was bigger than Audrey Wilson. No one was safe.

Suddenly, Ava had a thought. "That's it! It's only the middle of the day. Joel will have been at New Heights all morning, which means he'll *definitely* have an alibi this time."

Owen's brow furrowed. "I'm not sure I'm following…"

Ava took a deep breath, still working things through in her mind. Her blue eyes gleamed. "Like you said, maybe Ricky's attacker and Audrey's killer are the same person. And if they are, the fact that Joel has an alibi *now* would also preclude him from having murdered Audrey. I've got to call Rose!"

Owen laid a hand on Ava's arm, which she shrugged off. His expression was still wary. "I'd wait a bit until we know more about what's happened. I mean, we don't even know if Ricky's… still alive. For all we know, he could've slipped and fallen, making this whole thing an accident and Joel's being at New Heights irrelevant."

Ava sighed. He was right, of course—but would it have killed him to let her stay hopeful for one minute? Not that she wanted Ricky to be dead or for him to be the victim of attempted murder…

"Fine. I'm headed to Ricky's garage then." Without so much as a glance backward to see if Owen was following her, Ava turned on her heel and stalked down the sidewalk toward Main Street. She needed to find out what had happened—and fast.

The paramedics were already on the scene when Ava stopped short across the street from Ricky's garage. Behind her, she could hear Owen's heavy footsteps. Two police cars were parked in the lot next to the shop, the garage door open. A group of people were already gathered outside the shop, standing around by the curb, waiting to see what was going on. As Ava crossed the street, Owen caught up with her and they joined the small crowd.

"What happened?" Owen asked one of the men, whom Ava recognized as Tim Meyer from the gallery next to Arcana.

"Ed Walsh came into the gallery just a few minutes ago, saying someone attacked Ricky." He shook his stylishly combed gray head. "I guess Ed was headed back to the tasting room after his lunch break, and he ran into Dan Harding, who said Jodi Laughlin was down at the station in an awful state."

"We ran into her, too," Owen said, gesturing to Ava beside him. "We came down here to see what happened. Is he alright?"

"Don't know yet."

The group of rubberneckers moved closer to the shop, inching toward the gaping garage door, only to be pushed away by a very all business Officer Harding. He clapped his hands, waved everyone away from the door and toward the parking lot.

"Everyone, get out of the way! We've got a man coming through. Enough rubbernecking!"

All Ava could see from her spot near the parking lot was a flurry of EMTs inside the open garage, kneeling around something on the floor. A moment or two later, they emerged, a figure strapped into the stretcher, a thin blanket pulled up over it and its head covered in bandages. Officer Harding and another police officer stood somberly by.

Ava gasped. "Oh, my god!" She looked up at Owen. His face was dark.

"They got him good, alright," he said.

There was a hum of voices up ahead, a buzz that made its way through the crowd, ending with Tim. He turned to Owen and announced, "Elaine Walsh is near the door and says she heard Harding say someone took a wrench to Ricky's head and started going to town. They found the wrench nearby."

"Good god," Owen breathed. His face had gone from dark concern to outright alarm.

Ava stood on her tiptoes to try to peer into the still open door. Had they found anything else? Did Ricky have security cameras in his shop? She craned her neck and bumped the top of her head on Owen's chin. Embarrassed, she came down to her heels with a thud and drew away.

"Sorry," she mumbled.

"No need," Owen said. He wore a strangely wistful expression.

"I said everyone get going!" Officer Harding was not having any of the crowd's nosiness. "We're not finished here, and we need you all gone if we're to do our jobs right. For the love of god, Shiloh, get back to work!"

After the sobering ordeal they'd just witnessed, neither Ava nor Owen needed to be told twice to get out of there, although Ava wondered just how much work anyone would do that day. When they parted ways at the plaza, each headed back to their own store, Ava stopped for a moment, watching Owen's broad back as he disappeared down the street. She'd seen Ricky carried out on that stretcher, his head covered in bloody bandages, with her own eyes. There was no way he had done that to himself. Audrey's killer was still out there. Ava was struck by a sudden pang of fear. If whoever had killed Audrey had also attempted to kill Ricky, they must have been keeping an eye on who was on their trail—which meant that she and Owen may have already gotten themselves in too deep.

Swallowing back the fear that was burning in her chest, Ava strode off toward Arcana. It wasn't too late. This newest development would bring its own evidence and—hopefully—clear Joel's name without anyone else having to get more involved. Joel would've been at his fitness center all morning, meaning it couldn't have been him who attacked Ricky or, if her hypothesis was correct, killed Audrey. *There's no way they can pin this on him now.*

13

The air was cool and surprisingly fresh when Ava stepped out of Arcana that evening. As she hopped on her bicycle and made her way down Main Street, the warm breeze that whipped through her hair was a welcome change from the dim dullness of the afternoon. Business had dragged once again, with Riley passing the afternoon leaning sullenly against the counters and Ava busying herself by wiping tables that hadn't been used since the last time she wiped them. She even turned a blind eye to Riley's phone, which the girl kept in her apron pocket and sneakily withdrew when she thought Ava wasn't looking.

Ava pedaled harder, pushing her way up the hill with effort. She was on her way to New Heights to talk through Ricky's attack with Joel, but with how out of breath she was by the time she reached the top of the hill, she wondered if she ought to be signing up for a membership while at the gym. *Ha.* She stopped her pedaling, let herself coast down the other side of the hill, picking up speed as she went and relishing the wind as it streamed through her hair. It was these small things, like the crunch of loose pebbles beneath her tires in the stillness of the summer evening, that made her understand why her grandfather had loved small town life so much.

Suddenly, Ava's heart stopped. *No no no no no. It can't be.*

But it was. Up ahead, she could see the blue and red flashing of police lights, glowing ominously in the still light sky. She pedaled faster, moving closer and closer to the scene she was still hoping was somehow only a nightmare. She had half a mind to turn tail and escape, pinch herself, slap herself awake —anything that would make the scene she knew was coming dissolve into imagination.

But as she flew down the few blocks that remained between her and New Heights, the police lights became ever more glaring, their brightness even more sinister. Sure enough, as the fitness center came into view, so did the police cars parked out front. Ava's heart was beating wildly in her chest. She jumped off her bike, propped it next to a tree, and without even bothering to chain and lock it, began striding toward the building. There had to be some explanation other than what she feared —right? But then again, as her mind flicked through all the other possibilities that would've meant police cars at New Heights, they all seemed pretty grim. She set her jaw, braced herself.

Just then, the front door of the gym opened, and Ava sucked in her breath. There was Joel, his gaze downcast and hands behind his back, stepping carefully down the sidewalk with Greathouse lumbering behind him. Without even thinking, Ava broke into a run.

"Joel! Joel, what's going on—"

"Whoa, there. I'll have to ask you to take a step back." Officer Harding had stepped out of one of the police cars, and now stood directly in Ava's way. His hands were on his hips, and his face looked dark with regret.

"What? This is ridiculous! I just need to—" Ava was indignant, floundering for words as she tried to sidestep the officer. He blocked her way, crossed his arms over his chest.

"Ms. Goldberg," Officer Harding said in a low, warning voice. "I understand you're upset, but I can't let you approach the suspect."

Ava stood helplessly in the middle of the parking lot, craning her neck around Officer Harding as Joel and Greathouse made their way down the sidewalk. She could see now that Joel's wrists were cuffed. Her heart plummeted. If only she had gotten here sooner...

"Ava!"

This time it was Rose's voice that cut into the chilly evening air. Ava snapped her gaze in the direction of the voice and saw Rose slipping through the front door of the gym, rushing across the grass toward her. Her pixie-like face was ashen, her dark eyes wide with shock.

"What's going on? Where are they taking Joel? Why...?" Ava was struggling to even find the words. She grasped Rose's forearm with a shaky hand, clutching at her.

Rose drew in a shuddery breath, steeling herself for the words she was about to say. "He's under arrest. That note in his pocket, the missing jacket, him not having a solid alibi for the time of Audrey's murder—Greathouse still says the evidence points to Joel. And now with that flashlight..."

"What flashlight?"

Rose glanced at the building behind them, her face taut. "After Ricky's assault this afternoon, Greathouse showed up here with a search warrant. They tore the place apart, and of course, I thought they wouldn't find anything—but I was wrong. They found a flashlight in one of the closets. It's got blood residue on it and is all dented up on one side, like somebody really took some vicious swings with it. They'll test it for Audrey's DNA, but with all these things together..."

"But what grounds did they have for another search warrant?" It was all Ava could do to keep her voice from shaking.

"According to Greathouse, Ricky Birch has been trying to track down Audrey's killer so he can snag the reward money. The police think Ricky was targeted because of that, so they decided to make a move—and Joel is their prime suspect."

"But Joel was *here* when Ricky was attacked today!" Ava hissed, throwing an angry glance in Greathouse's direction. "If the police are thinking Audrey's killer and Ricky's attacker is the same person, Joel has an *alibi*."

Rose shook her head. The fear was clear on her face. "He wasn't here. He went to Omaha to pick up some supplies."

"Well, we'll call the shop then! Get them to vouch for him, confirm he was there when he said he was."

"The shop was closed. He didn't speak to anyone, just drove back here."

"No way," Ava said, shaking her head in defiance. "I don't believe it. This whole thing is too perfect—especially that flashlight. If Joel had killed Audrey, why would he have kept the murder weapon in a place that could implicate him? Why not —I don't know—throw it in the lake? It makes no sense. Joel's not an *idiot*."

The creak of a car door opening pulled their attention away from their speculations. Officer Harding had opened the door to the police car that sat parked at the end of the sidewalk, and

Joel had stooped to enter the car. Greathouse placed a firm hand on the top of Joel's head. Ava knew the move was just protocol, but she couldn't help but feel offended on Joel's behalf. Did they think he wasn't going to go willingly? When the car door slammed shut, Rose jumped. Ava grabbed her wrist and squeezed.

As Officer Harding pulled out of the parking lot, gravel crunching under his tires and lights still flashing, Joel didn't turn to look at Ava and Rose through the window. His gaze remained straight ahead, trained on the seat back in front of him. Unmoving. Ava felt a well of sympathy rush up inside her chest. That they'd arrest good guy Joel Robinson was already unthinkable—but to arrest him in front of his wife while she stood helplessly by, watching him being driven away to an undetermined fate, was even worse. Ava was suddenly glad Ellie wasn't there. Although she was only a baby, there was no doubt she would have picked up on the tension reverberating through the air, the grief etched in her mother's face. The police car turned at the intersection, disappearing around the corner, and the evening was still.

Greathouse tromped over to where Ava and Rose stood, still facing the direction the car had gone. His face was solemn, lined with regret, but the hold of his mouth was firm.

"I'm very sorry," he said to Rose, placing a hand on her shoulder. "I didn't want it to be Joel. He was always a standup kid. Even now, I keep asking myself how... Well, never mind." He shook his head.

"I know," Rose said, not looking at Greathouse.

"Chief," Ava cut in, unable to stand it any longer. "With all due respect, I think you should investigate this more deeply. If Joel had killed Audrey, he wouldn't have—"

Greathouse raised a hand, silencing her. "With all due respect to *you*, Ms. Goldberg, I don't believe you went to officer training. As I've told you before, we will pursue all avenues."

Ava was about to protest when a hesitant voice sounded behind her. "Is everything okay?"

Ava, Rose, and Greathouse all whipped around. There was Riley, hands sunk deep in her jeans pockets, looking like she'd just seen a ghost.

"We've arrested Joel Robinson on suspicion of murdering Audrey Wilson and attacking Ricky Birch," Greathouse announced, drawing himself up straight. He turned to Rose. "I'll be in touch tomorrow about where we go from here. And again, I'm really sorry."

With that, Greathouse got into the other police car and left. On his way out of the parking lot, he nodded solemnly at the three women still standing stunned in the parking lot. No one acknowledged the gesture. Instead, they remained silent, all avoiding one another's eyes.

Finally, Ava broke the silence. "Rose, do you want me to stay with you tonight? I'm happy to if that would make you feel any better at all..."

Rose managed a weak, grateful smile. "No, I'll be okay. Ellie's been at Mom's all day, and I figure I'll just stay there tonight, too. She's already tried to call me forty times since Greathouse showed up—she'll want me there with her."

"If you're sure," Ava said, following Rose as she began moving back toward the building. "And we'll get this sorted out. I know it sounds ridiculous but try not to worry."

Rose gave a bitter laugh. "Too late."

"Hey," Riley said suddenly, stopping short of the building as

Rose opened the door. "Ava, didn't you and Juanita say you were going to do that reading tonight?"

Ava groaned, let her head fall back. She'd completely forgotten about that. "Damn it all. You're right. And I don't have her number either, to call and cancel."

"You should go." Rose spoke from the doorway. "Ellie and I will be fine at my parents. I need some time to... process. First the alleged affair with Audrey, now a *murder* charge..."

Ava looked warily at her friend; she hoped she was telling the truth and not only trying to make Ava feel better about leaving her. But if Rose wanted time alone, just her and her family, to come to terms with the nightmare that had fallen into her lap, Ava wasn't going to encroach. She sighed, nodded her head reluctantly. "Okay. But I'll keep my phone on. You let me know if you need anything at *all*."

"I will." Rose gave her a halfhearted hug, then turned and disappeared inside the fitness center, leaving Ava and Riley alone in the parking lot.

"Thanks for reminding me about Juanita," Ava said to Riley, more out of a feeling of obligation than actual gratitude. She was categorically *not* in the mood to give a tarot reading and almost wished the girl hadn't remembered.

Riley shrugged, scuffed the toe of her shoe in the dirt. "Actually, I was wondering if maybe I could come along. You know, during Owen's reading you said I could watch the next time..."

Ava frowned. The girl had a good memory. "You're right—I *did* say that. But tarot readings can really dredge up a lot of stuff for people. They might not be comfortable with someone else sitting in on the reading."

"But I *know* Juanita," Riley pressed. "She used to babysit me back in the day. Can't we at least ask her?"

Ava sighed, no longer having the strength to argue after the night they'd both had. "Fine. We'll *ask*. But if she so much as hesitates, I'm sending you home. Got it?"

Riley's eyes sparkled. "Got it."

"I REALLY DON'T THINK Joel Robinson killed Audrey Wilson," Riley announced into the chilly night air, her voice slightly out of breath as she worked to keep up with Ava's brisk stride.

"Obviously not," Ava snapped. She was already beginning to regret letting Riley come along with her to Arcana. She knew the girl wanted to see tarot in action, but Ava could've done with a little silence. Her mind was overstimulated the way it was.

"Well, it's not *obvious*," Riley countered, flashing Ava a quick glance as though to check if she'd pissed her off further. "I just mean, if it were *obvious*, Greathouse wouldn't have arrested him..."

"Yeah, well, Greathouse is being an idiot." Ava shrugged her shoulders.

"He should at least be looking at Lucas Wilson," Riley agreed. "We both saw what he acted like that day Greathouse took our statements. Guy was *weird*. I don't think he cared at all that his sister was dead."

Ava only nodded, not even sure Riley noticed the gesture. She was right, though—Lucas was where Ava's mind had gone, too, as soon as it sank in that someone had actually attacked Ricky Birch. It was horrible to think someone would've wanted to kill their own sibling, but it had happened before. From what Ava had heard around town, Lucas had ample motive.

The lampposts lining Main Street glowed hazily in the half dark ahead as Ava and Riley passed by the now notorious fountain. Ava saw Riley cast a wary glance at it, but neither said anything. What else was there to say? The whole town had done nothing but rehash the murder since it happened.

"Ava! Riley!"

A cheery voice cut into the twilight, and Ava snapped her head up to see a silvery-haired figure coming toward them down the sidewalk. Sure enough—Juanita was waving a hand in excitement, like a child at a parade. Somehow, even though she'd met Juanita only once before, she felt a sense of relief just seeing the woman's beaming, red-lipped smile.

"Hi," Ava said, managing a weak smile. There was no way she could match Juanita's level of enthusiasm—especially not tonight—but she felt somehow that she owed it to the woman to at least attempt a grin.

Riley offered a shy smile in Juanita's direction and, head down, unlocked Arcana's front door and headed inside. Ava had hoped that Riley would take the initiative and ask Juanita's permission to sit in and observe her reading, but apparently not, from the looks of it. Ava sighed.

"Riley is interested in learning to read tarot," Ava began hesitantly, pulling the door shut behind Juanita as the three of them traipsed inside the cafe. "Would it be alright by you if she sits in on the reading to observe? Feel free to say no—I already told her it was a possibility you would."

Juanita waved a hand, huffed herself down onto the sofa. "Oh, heavens, no! I don't mind one bit."

Giving Riley a brief side glance, Ava saw the corners of the girl's mouth turn up just slightly. Ava set her tarot deck down onto the coffee table in front of Juanita and was just sinking back into the armchair next to her when Riley spoke out of nowhere.

"They arrested Joel." Riley's face was blank. She looked almost as though she expected Juanita to make sense of it for her.

Juanita started. She looked from Riley to Ava, then back to Riley. "Are you sure? Joel Robinson? Arrested him for..." Her voice trailed off as though she didn't want to finish the sentence.

Ava's throat was tight. She hadn't been planning to bring it up. Speaking the words aloud gave them power, and the last thing she needed while giving this woman a tarot reading was the nightmare of the past hour hanging over her head. She turned to glare at Riley, but the girl simply tossed her electric blue head defiantly. *Yeah—I said it*, the gesture seemed to say.

"We're sure," Riley said, her voice unwavering. "Ava and I were both there. We saw it all go down."

"*Ay, dios mío,*" Juanita breathed, sinking against the back of the sofa. "Well, things have certainly taken a turn. They must have evidence, though, I suppose."

Now it was Ava's turn to speak. "Actually, I find the evidence in question to be a bit suspect."

"Oh?" Juanita's dark eyes snapped in interest. She leaned in eagerly, rubbing her hands together so that her rings made clacking sounds. "Tell me."

"Well," Ava said slowly, gathering her thoughts. "Let me start at the beginning. When I attended the committee dinner the night before Audrey's murder, I overheard Audrey arguing with Ricky Birch—like, bad arguing. Threats. I mentioned this to Greathouse, of course, but he seemed convinced that Joel was the killer, so I decided to look into it on my own."

Juanita frowned. "Oh, sweetheart. 'I decided to look into it on my own' is never a good start to a story. But go on." She waved her hand for Ava to continue.

Riley was leaning forward, elbows on her thighs, her full attention on Ava. Aside from bits of gossip from wagging tongues around town, Ava realized this was probably the most information Riley had gotten since Audrey turned up dead in the fountain. She looked both horrified and mesmerized.

"What I saw seemed pretty good at first—good as in pretty damning of Ricky," Ava continued. "Owen O'Kelly and I happened to spot Jodi coming out of Ricky's garage looking pretty suspicious, so we followed her. And where did she end up? That old payphone next to the Catholic church."

Juanita's eyes were wide. Ava had to hand it to her: She was a pretty good audience. Ava could tell by the transfixed expression on Riley's face that she, too, was enjoying the story as it unfurled. "You mean across from the elementary school? What was she doing over there?"

"We *think* she was looking for a security camera. To make sure Ricky's tracks were covered. Because *someone* had to have called Audrey to lure her back downtown that night. And the payphone would have been untraceable."

Juanita gasped. Recognition dawned on her face, and she slapped a hand down on the coffee table. "That makes total *sense!* Marge said—well, Officer Harding's her son, you know, and she said that Ricky Birch was in possession of *Audrey's phone.* Says Ricky came in the station saying he found it in the bushes near the assisted living center—the one where Audrey's father lives—and picked it up, hoping to find something that'd get him that reward money the family is offering. The police checked through her recent calls, of course, and the last call, which would likely be the call that lured her back to town at four in the morning, was saved in her contacts as the *assisted living center*. But when they called the number back, it just rang and rang…"

"Clearly not the number for the assisted living center," Riley remarked.

"Clearly," Juanita agreed. "I'm sure they've traced it by now, but unless we're completely mistaken, I'd say it's safe to say that number belongs to the payphone. I also assume that Ricky did some of his own sleuthing, figured out the number belonged to the payphone, and sent Jodi to check for any camera footage. She wasn't covering Ricky's tracks—she was trying to close in on the killer, too."

"One thing's for sure: Someone wanted to make sure Audrey answered the phone when they called her," Ava said.

"That's kind of sick!" Riley said, looking horrified. "Using someone's unwell dad to lure them to their death?"

Ava snorted. "I guess you could say that killing someone in the first place is also 'sick'."

"Touché," Juanita said, nodding. She crossed her arms in thought, then gestured at Ava with a wave to continue. "So now what? You were thinking it must have been Ricky who killed Audrey, right? And that Jodi was in on it. But *now* things are looking different, what with Ricky having been nearly killed *himself*…"

"Exactly. So now, with Ricky being attacked, Greathouse is even *more* convinced that it was Joel who killed Audrey. He went and got a search warrant—for New Heights, this time—

and apparently found what he thinks is the murder weapon stashed away in a closet on the premises—"

"A flashlight with dried blood on it," Riley cut in, her eyes wide.

Ava shot her a look and finished her sentence. "—after which he led Joel out in handcuffs and pushed him into the police car."

"Okay," Juanita announced decisively, clapping her hands. She patted the coffee table in front of them. "That's it. Forget my reading. We're doing a reading for the *case*. There's got to be something we're not seeing."

Ava looked doubtful. "Really? I promised you I'd read for *you*. I hate to take up your time..."

"Nonsense," Juanita said, waving the idea away with a hand. She rubbed her hands together. "Let's lay these cards down and see what we can come up with!"

"Alright," Ava agreed, a rush of excitement flooding her chest. She was never quite sure *what* she believed about the cards, whether there was any sort of supernatural element to them, but there was one thing she was sure of: human intuition. And the tarot cards were a wonderful tool to get the intuitive juices flowing.

Ava slid the cards out of their velvet pouch and began shuffling. Zaidy Mel had taught her to shuffle as many times as felt right, and for her that was always four times—no more, no less. She cut the deck into three, then laid the piles on top of one another until they once again formed a single stack. She placed a delicate hand on top of the pile, closing her eyes for a moment to center herself. Beside her, Riley and Juanita were both still, their breathing muted, each focused on the deck of cards on the table in front of them.

"Okay," Ava said, opening her eyes. Her hand still covered the deck of cards. "I'm going to draw three cards. The first will represent the situation as we know it. The second will be what we're not seeing—that is, something we still need to figure out. And the third is *how* we figure it out, what steps we take to get there." She looked around at the other two and raised her eyebrows. Riley and Juanita both nodded.

Ava drew the first card, lay it face up on the table. "Here's our situation."

"The ten of swords," Riley read, peering at the card. "Looks about right."

The image on the card depicted a man lying face down on the ground, ten swords stuck clean into his back. The card was definitely a grim one.

"Okay, I feel like this one speaks for itself," Ava said, giving a hesitant laugh. "It can definitely represent death, whether physical or emotional, and often also alludes to betrayal."

"I would say betrayal fits right in with what we know about that number being programmed into Audrey's phone," Juanita remarked. "Somebody really used one of her vulnerabilities against her. But let's see about the second—the stuff we're not seeing."

"Right." Ava drew another card. She frowned. "The five of pentacles..."

"What's it mean?" Riley asked, glancing toward Ava uncertainly. "This one doesn't look as violent."

"No, it's nothing to do with violence," Ava said, still parsing her thoughts. She always tried to keep an open mind in her readings, but this card seemed unexpected. "Pentacles are associated with earth, the material world, and financial issues. The *five* of pentacles suggests financial troubles—like poverty, feeling worried about money, a mindset of lacking..."

"And this is what we're *not* seeing?" Riley asked. She looked skeptical. "Did Audrey have some kind of financial issue nobody knew about? Seems weird—her family's *loaded*."

"Well," Juanita said, stroking her chin in thought. "Speaking of Audrey's family, didn't they say her brother stands to inherit the estate now that Audrey's gone? Now, *he* is someone who could've used the money. Family cut him off ever since that time he got arrested for drug paraphernalia, and as far as I know, he's been on his own ever since."

Ava felt her heart speed up. Juanita was right. It *had* to be Lucas the card was referring to. Not that needing money made him a murderer, of course—but she and Riley had both seen with their own eyes how *smug* he'd seemed at the news of Audrey's death. And now with the card backing up their prior intuitions...

"Alright, third time's the charm," Riley said. "Give us the last one."

Ava turned over the final card, half praying as she laid it flat in front of them that she would understand it.

"The Moon," she announced, feeling her hopes fall. It was a bit of a given, really. She wasn't sure it told them anything new. "This card usually means that there's more going on than meets the eye."

Riley looked annoyed. "That's it? We knew that before we started the reading."

"I know," Ava admitted. "It's not the most revealing. Basically, it's telling us that, just like how the moon has a dark side that's not visible to us, so do circumstances. So do people. Which means, I guess, that not everyone around us is who they appear to be." As soon as she said the words aloud, Ava thought of Joel. That's how Greathouse would've taken the card.

"I hope that's not in reference to a *certain* person," Riley said, meeting her eyes from across the table.

"I hope not, too." Ava turned back to the card. Perhaps there was a meaning that hadn't come to her yet.

"Well, if you two are talking about Joel Robinson, we could just as easily say the same thing about *anyone* in this town," Juanita pointed out. "That's Reality 101. People aren't always who they seem to be. I mean, this could just as easily be pointing to Lucas Wilson."

"Didn't you say this was the *how* card?" Riley asked. "That it represents *how* we figure out what we need to find in the second card?"

Ava nodded. She pushed a wisp of dark hair behind her ear. "Yes. I guess it means that we have to look at things from a different angle. But as of right now, I have no idea what it's getting at..."

Juanita sighed. "Well, maybe we all ought to sleep on it. Let's do my reading another time and let this one soak in. These things have a way of taking on new meanings with a little distance. Some sleep'll do us all good."

They sat in silence for a moment, their eyes fixed on the spread of cards on the coffee table, their minds whirring. The only sound in the shop was the rattle of wind at the huge bay windows and the crunch of dusty cobblestones on tires as the odd car rumbled by. The heaviness of the night fell over the room, draping itself around them. Riley yawned.

"Alright. I guess we ought to call it a night," Ava announced, sliding the cards back into a pile and giving them a shuffle. She returned them to their pouch. "Riley, I sure hope you let your parents know you'd be here."

Riley waved a hand. "Trust me. They don't care."

"Well, regardless, you've got to be back here early tomorrow. Surprisingly—or maybe *unsurprisingly*, actually—having a murderer running loose around town hasn't affected people's need for caffeine."

Juanita chuckled, rising from the sofa. "Well, I'll keep my eyes peeled and my brain cells working. I'm sure this will all get solved soon enough."

"I hope so," Ava said. She placed her tarot cards inside her purse, slung it over her shoulder, and followed Riley and Juanita as they traipsed toward the front door. Once outside in the cool night air, Juanita bid them good night, promising to sleep with her thinking cap on and let them know if Marge dropped any more hot gossip.

Riley stood for a moment next to Ava on the sidewalk, rocking back and forth on her heels, watching as Juanita pulled out of her parking spot and disappeared down Main Street.

"I'm going to stick around a bit longer. There's some stuff I've got to do for tomorrow," Ava said, turning to go back inside the shop. Really, she was planning to sift through the day's receipts to see how bad the numbers really were, but Riley didn't need to know that.

"Sounds good," Riley said. She pointed a thumb behind her. "I'm going to swing by the convenience store for a Diet Coke before heading home."

"Okay," Ava said. "See you tomorrow."

She watched the girl disappear down the sidewalk before heading inside.

14

Cafe Arcana was cozy at night, dimly lit by the naked bulbs that hung glowing from the ceiling. The place smelled of coffee, which gave Ava the feeling of being inside someone's warm, comforting kitchen. It almost made up for the tediousness of having to go through the books, pore over the numbers that, if Ava were honest with herself, weren't looking so hot. Almost—but not quite.

Ava sank down on the sofa, a mug of steaming coffee in her hand. She set her purse on the seat of the sofa and spread out her binder, stuffed full of receipts but organized to a tee, on the coffee table in front of her. She glanced at the clock on the wall. Eight fifteen. She hadn't had dinner yet, and crunching numbers was about the last thing she wanted to do. Still, if she were going to stay on top of expenses, she needed to know how bad the situation was. The money she'd received in her divorce settlement was dwindling, a thought she kept trying to push to the back of her mind.

"Alright," Ava said aloud to herself, grabbing the notebook she kept in the front of the binder. "Here goes nothing."

At the end of each day, either Ava or Riley would print out a receipt from the cash register, showing the total amount in sales for that entire day. Ava wasn't sure whether Riley ever looked at the receipts before tucking them inside their respective envelopes and handing them off to Ava—and if she did, perhaps she didn't have a frame of reference to compare them to—but the last few days, Ava had had to suppress a grimace when she caught sight of the paltry totals. It wasn't *nothing*—visitors came to the shop and a handful of regulars—but it certainly wasn't *good*. The rent needed to be covered, the equipment maintained, the coffee beans ordered, and Riley's wages paid. And that wasn't counting the utilities that were bound to take a chunk out of the account, nor the loan Ava had taken out to even open the place. Arcana had only been open a week, but if no one was interested when the buzz was fresh around town, what made her think they'd gain interest with time?

Ava groaned. She had just laid her head back on the top of the sofa when a loud crash from the back of the store jolted her back to reality. An icy coldness crept down her spine. Sitting stock still, Ava listened. Aside from the beating of her heart, which was thumping harder than she'd ever felt it thump before, the shop was silent. If someone had entered the store, she would've heard footsteps... or at least their breathing. She nearly shuddered to think about it. Still, the place was quiet, empty. Maybe a broom had fallen over in the supply room, or a case of beans had slid off the counter. She thought suddenly of the grisly murder that was supposed to have occurred in the building, the ghost stories she'd heard.

Trying to ignore the icy feeling that had taken hold of her limbs, Ava rose from the couch and made her way down the short hallway to the back of the shop. On one side of the hall was the restroom, and on the other was the supply room, where Ava stored a supply of fragrant, bagged beans. The hallway was still. She strained her ears for any rustle of movement. Her heart was still beating in her chest as she turned the knob to the supply room, peeking around the door as it opened inward. The shelves on the wall closest to her appeared untouched, lined with neatly stacked bags of beans—exactly how she'd placed them earlier in the week. The cleaning supplies on the far end of the counter, too, stood in a tidy line, the sink still clean. *That's weird...*

And then she saw it. As Ava opened the door fully and turned to take in the rest of the room, she drew a sharp breath. The entire windowpane lining the back wall, which looked out onto the alley behind her shop, had shattered. Shards of glittering, splintered glass littered the floor, tiny crystals glistening from every surface. *What the hell...?* She stepped back, almost involuntarily, froze. There on the carpet, in the center of the remains of the broken window, was a brick. An icy chill raked down Ava's spine. Someone had thrown the brick, shattered her window—that much was obvious. The bigger question was... why? And was whoever it was still *there*, lurking?

Knowing she shouldn't go near the broken glass but unable to help herself, Ava stepped gingerly over the crackling shards and turned the brick over with a shaking hand. Where had it come from? There was exposed brick in the building itself; was this the same—

Oh, god. On what had been the underside of the brick, but which was now facing up, was taped an ink-covered index card. All thoughts of the brick, the broken window, the vandalism were gone in an instant. Despite the sinking feeling that tugged at her, Ava bent down to inspect the card more closely. A wave of horror washed through her as she peeled it off the face of the brick and stood holding it, taking in the card's image. Drawn in shaky, feathery lines was the outline of a woman. The black ink was smudged in places, as though whoever had drawn it had been so absorbed in the grotesque imagery they hadn't waited for the lines to set, and from the dark, sultry waves of the figure's hair, Ava could tell that it was meant to be her. The woman's eyes were closed, a nasty scar drawn jagged down her cheek, and her toenails were jagged and black. Worst, though, was the noose drawn tight around the figure's neck, the black bruises creeping like smoke up into her jawline, swirling about her pale face. She dangled from the end of the rope like bait on a hook. And across the card, a title: *The Hanged Woman.*

Ava sucked in her breath. A cold claw of fear had clasped around her throat, was trailing its dirty nails down her spine. The tidiness of the room now felt cold and skeletal. She was alone. The store was entirely empty, and the darkening sky out the shattered window seemed capable of swallowing her whole. Everything was silent, save for the faint chirp of crickets in the alley. Ava stood, feeling the blood rushing to her head, and backed away from the scene. She glanced around the tiny storeroom, listening for any sign of movement from the rest of the shop. Someone had clearly meant to scare her. Was that *all* they had planned? Or was there more? Her hand made its way to her pocket, her fingers closing around the smooth edges of the lapis lazuli she never left home without. The cool smoothness of the stone was comforting, but her heart still thumped against her ribcage.

Suddenly, Ava knew she couldn't be alone. She needed someone to be there, fill some of the silence that now beat loud in her ears. Rose? She couldn't. The last thing Rose needed on top of her husband's arrest was to worry about what appeared to be a threat of potential violence. Riley was too young, didn't need to be subjected to something so disturbing. Almost without thinking, Ava slipped her phone out of her pocket and began digging through her purse. When she finally unearthed the business card she'd nearly forgotten was there, she dialed the only person she could think of whom she could ask to help her fill the silence.

He answered on the second ring, his voice deep and cheerful on the other end of the line.

"This is Owen."

"Owen, it's Ava," she said, her tone hushed. As she spoke, she stuffed the card in her jeans pocket and backed out of the storeroom, stalking briskly back down the hallway. She kept her eyes up, her gaze alert, darting through the shop, behind the counter, the sofas. If someone was there, had somehow gotten inside, she wouldn't let them catch her by surprise.

"Oh, hey! What's up? Did you think of another lead?"

"No. Someone's just thrown a brick through the window at Arcana."

"Wait, wait. Hold up." Owen's voice had lost its jovial tone. "What do you mean someone threw a brick through the window?"

"Exactly what it sounds like. And they taped this card to it. Owen, I think it might be some kind of—"

"Don't go anywhere," Owen broke in, his voice rising a few tones, like someone trying not to sound panicked. "Call the police, lock the doors, and stay inside. I'm coming to meet you."

"Okay." Ava was too shaken to argue. For a brief moment, she thought about telling him there was no need, that she'd buck up and wait by herself for the police to come, but the darkened sky outside sent a chill through her. If someone was indeed threatening her, who was to say they wouldn't follow through? Main Street was all but empty this time of night, and the shadows beneath the building overhangs were long. It would be all too easy for someone to slink up behind her, close their gloved hands around her windpipe. The locked doors were hardly a comfort. She'd wait for Owen.

"Good. I'm hanging up now. Call the police, Ava, and wait inside for me. Whoever threw the brick is still out there."

The line clicked off, leaving Ava standing in the dim, eerie silence of the empty shop. She dialed the police, then locked both the front and back doors, trying hard not to look at the gaping hole in the window of the back room. Back in the main room, Ava sat down and crossed her arms in front of her chest, shivering. Through the window, she could see the stately elms that lined each block of Main Street casting eerie shadows in the darkness. She drew deep breaths, trying her best to push back the image of the hanging woman on the index card. Who would've drawn it? And *why*? Whoever it was, and whatever the reason, Ava was almost sure it had something to do with Audrey Wilson's murder. She should have known better than to stick her nose into business it didn't belong in, especially with a very real killer on the loose in town, but what else was she supposed to do? She wouldn't let Joel Robinson hang for someone else's sins.

Headlights shone at the end of the street as a vehicle turned onto Main Street, bouncing over the cobblestones toward her. Not even bothering to kill the engine, Owen whipped his truck into a nearby parking space, jumped out of the cab, and strode toward her. Ava unlocked the front door and ventured out onto the sidewalk to meet him.

Owen held her at arm's length for a moment, peering anxiously into her face. His green eyes were wide, full of worry.

"Are you okay?" Owen let his hands fall from Ava's forearms. He was still studying her face.

Ava nodded. "I'm okay. Just shaken up."

"What *happened*?"

This time, Ava shook her head. She glanced behind her at the cafe, dark and silhouetted against the starry sky above. "I don't know. I was here crunching some numbers, and all of a sudden I heard this crash. I figured something had just fallen off the shelf in the supply room, but then I went to check it and —and there was a brick... with the card..."

Owen frowned. He, too, glanced at the shop, then back at Ava. "Card? Like, what? A greeting card?"

"No. A tarot card. But not a real one—someone drew it and left it there. I think it's supposed to be me."

Ava drew the card out of her back pocket and handed it facedown to Owen. She looked at the ground, not wanting to look at that horrible image again. Owen flipped the card over and studied it. His expression had gone dark. When he spoke, his voice was scarily calm. "You'll have to pardon my ignorance, Ava—I don't know anything about tarot. But... is this supposed to be a *real* tarot card?"

"A bastardization of one, I guess. The equivalent card is really the Hanged *Man*, but the imagery normally doesn't include a noose or jagged toenails." The blue and red lights of a police car flashed down the street.

"We need to give this to the police. We've got no way of proving it's connected to Audrey's murder and Ricky's attack, but I'll bet you anything it is. You've proven too smart, and the killer's getting nervous. First, it was Ricky. Now they're giving you a sign: If you don't cut it out, you're next."

"That's what I thought, too," Ava agreed. "I just hope the chief sees it that way. He might say it's just someone in town who doesn't like tarot trying to scare me off."

"Well, regardless of how he sees it," Owen said, "There's no getting past the fact that someone vandalized your shop. I'd even say this counts as making terroristic threats. At the very least, it's harassment on top of vandalism of property."

Drawing his phone out of his pocket, Owen snapped a quick photo of the grisly drawing. The flash of the camera lit up the night for a split second, landing like bony fingers on Owen's handsome face. Ava shuddered. A police car came down the street, lights still flashing, and pulled up next to Owen's truck. It was only as the officer strode nearer that Ava could make out it was Chief Greathouse.

"Ms. Goldberg. Owen," the chief said with a nod. "We got a call about a vandalism. Is that correct?"

"That's correct," Ava said. "I was here by myself, and someone threw a brick in the back window, shattered the whole thing. And this was taped to it."

She gestured to Owen, who was still holding the grotesquely drawn tarot card, to hand it over. Chief Greathouse took the card and gave it a long look, his mustache quivering.

"What in the blazes is that?" he barked. "Looks like one of them rock band album covers."

Beside her, Ava heard Owen stifle a laugh, which she ignored. "Well, it's playing off a tarot card called the Hanged Man—which I can assure you does not use the same imagery, and certainly doesn't feature me."

"I see. Well, it's ominous, alright," Chief Greathouse admitted. He stroked his mustache. "In fact, I might even say it's a message. I warned you about getting involved in things that don't concern you, little lady."

Ava was about to protest—if he called her that *one more time*—but then she looked at his face. His expression was only one of concern, like he'd just heard some very depressing news and wanted to spare her from having to hear them, too. Ava could tell Owen had been about to say something as well, but now he shifted uncomfortably on his feet. They were both waiting for the chief to speak again.

"Now, I appreciate that you want to clear your friend's name, Ava," the chief continued. It was the first time he'd used her first name. "But, as you know, police work is dangerous business. *Murder* is dangerous business. And I think it's time the two of you—yes, you too, Owen—hang up your Holmes hats and let us take care of things. Got it?"

"Understood," Owen said, shaking Chief Greathouse's hand. "I'll make sure Ava gets home safely and help her see about getting an alarm system installed tomorrow."

"Good man," the chief said. He nodded in finality. "I'll go in and look around, and then put *this*" —he waved the makeshift tarot card— "into evidence. There's a storm rolling in from the east, so you two best be getting on home. I'll put a tarp up in the back to keep the rain from getting in. You call me if there's any more trouble, alright?"

Ava nodded, handing her spare set of keys over to Greathouse. Despite his gruff demeanor, Ava was at least thankful for his help; the man was looking out for her. But something about what Greathouse had just said nagged at her. As she watched him move toward the front door of the cafe, a cog clicked into place.

"Wait," she blurted. Greathouse stopped, the key in the door. "One second. That thing you just said about clearing my friend's name? If this is a warning connected to Audrey's murder—that is, if whoever killed Audrey also threw the brick in my window to scare me off—that person can't be Joel. He's in custody."

She stood, eyebrows raised, looking at Chief Greathouse and Owen as they all three parsed this new realization.

Greathouse gave a grunt, seemingly unwilling to concede that Ava might be right, and turned the key. The door swung open. "I'll look into it, but let's not rush to conclusions, ma'am. You're not in a state to be solving any cases this evening."

Ava began to protest, but Owen laid a gentle hand on the small of her back. She stopped, words still in her throat, a tiny tingle of electricity jolting through her. She stepped away from his hand, gave a sharp nod. Again, her hand found her pocket, playing with the stone there.

As the chief turned on his heel, disappearing into the store, Ava and Owen stood on the curb, letting the tensions of the incident dissipate into the cool night breeze. The song of distant crickets filled the silence.

"I'm glad you called," Owen said, his voice low. He offered her a half smile, concern still etched on his face.

"I'm glad you came," Ava returned, smiling wryly. The twinge of electricity lingered in her skin.

They stood looking at each other for a moment, the easy coolness of the earthy air wrapping around them like crisp, clean sheets on a summer night. Then, giving Ava's free hand a quick squeeze, Owen nodded at Ava's bike, still chained to the rack next to the building. "You want to put that in the back, and I can give you a ride home?"

Her first instinct was to decline, but the thought of the dark ride home, the image of that terrible hanged woman filling her mind the entire way, stopped her.

"Sure," she said. Tonight, she'd permit herself to accept help. Tomorrow, she'd be back at it again, harmed by no one and needing no one. She'd learned the two went hand in hand.

"No," Ava groaned, rubbing her eyes in the darkness. Her hand darted out from beneath the covers and groped wildly on the nightstand for the snooze button. It seemed like just a half hour ago that she'd stepped down from the cab of Owen's pickup and gone upstairs to bed. *How can it be six already?*

Ava's hand slapped at the top of the alarm clock, but the alarm wailed on. *Stupid thing.* Hoisting herself up onto her elbows, she snatched the clock off its place on the nightstand and jabbed frantically at the off button. The droning continued.

"What the *heck*," she groaned, setting the clock back on the nightstand with a clatter. She sat upright, ran a hand through her tousled bedhead, and squinted into the darkness. Out the window, the moon streamed into the yard below. Clearly, it was *not* six in the morning. If it wasn't her alarm, then what *was* that awful wailing sound?

A terrible thought struck Ava's gut. Her limbs went cold. Hadn't Chief Greathouse mentioned something about a storm? She ran to the window, the cool touch of the hardwood floor a welcome jolt against her bare feet. Outside, the wind whipped violently through the trees, tearing at the branches like angry claws across a hated face. Lightning flashed across the distant sky. The force of the wind was astounding, causing the windows to rattle and the dormer that housed her bedroom to shake. That wailing wasn't her alarm—it was a siren. *A tornado siren.*

Ava sprang back from the window at the same moment a clap of thunder crashed outside. The boom reverberated in her ribcage. Ava wracked her brains for some memory of tornadoes during the summer weeks she'd spent with Zaidy Mel. Surely he'd mentioned it at some point, hadn't he?

"The basement!" Ava hissed aloud. Wasn't that what you were supposed to do in a tornado? Huddle in the basement until the sirens stopped and the storm passed? But did her grandparents' old house even *have* a basement? If so, she'd never seen it. Somehow, during all the time she'd spent with her grandfather in Shiloh, she'd missed out on the tornadoes. Still, the persistent wailing outside urged her to action. If the house didn't have a basement, she was better off staying low to the ground—right?

Ava snatched up her phone and flew down the stairs. How long did you have after the sirens started until a tornado came plowing through your living room, anyway? She wasn't sure how many minutes of the siren she'd slept through, but she could very well be on her way to Munchkin Land in a matter of seconds if she didn't book it. Just then, her phone screen lit up in the dark.

She paused at the bottom of the stairs, stared at the screen, still trying to orient herself in the middle of her half-awake rush.

You okay?

Owen's text stared back at her in the dark like a blinking gaze. Relief rushed through her gut, followed by a sharp pang. When they'd first been married, Noah would text her to check in—to make sure she was safe from the accident he'd seen happened on I-29 or the house fire they'd shown on the news. At what point had he stopped? It had been so gradual, she hadn't even noticed. All she knew was that now, fending for herself was second nature. There was no one now to let know she was safe. She made her way to the kitchen as she texted back.

I think so. Am I supposed to go to the basement or something?

She hoped he wouldn't think her an idiot, but hey—better to be safe and look stupid, right? Everyone loved to talk about the corn when you moved to a small Midwestern town, about how everyone everywhere knows everyone else. But the walking, talking guidebooks all neglected to mention local tornado protocol.

No sooner had she fired off her text than another came in—this time from Rose, asking the same question. Ava copied and pasted her reply, then plunked down at the kitchen table to wait for whoever replied first. Outside, the wind tore through the treetops, their branches rattling against the windows. She had the feeling that if she closed her eyes, the next time she opened them she'd be flooded with vibrant, living color and the merry cheers of dancing munchkins. *Ding dong, the witch is dead.* She shuddered. She hadn't had to be swept away to Oz to stumble across a dead body.

Her phone pinged. Rose had answered first.

Nope. Just turned on the TV—it's going north of us!

Ava eyed the windows, her heart still racing. A clip of lightning lit up the sky, and the bare yard flashed into view, eerie and skeletal in the naked light. As it flickered again, the wailing sirens faded to silence, a dying jack-in-the-box in the dark.

Thank god. She typed back. *The sirens stopped now. But it still looks pretty nasty out there.*

Ava laid her phone on the counter, still peering out the kitchen windows where rain pelted the panes. Rose seemed unbothered by the storm, and Ava hoped her friend's laid-back attitude was correct. Still, the wild whistling wind that shook the house from all sides was alarming—especially when she remembered the hole in Arcana's back window. She hoped Greathouse's tarp job had been adequate. So much for sleep.

Another ping of her phone. Owen's reply. *No need. Looks like it's staying clear of us after all. You good with the storm, though? No hail by you?*

Well, that was a relief, at least—that more than one person had heard the worst of the storm was bypassing them. If nothing else, it was good to know that the sirens worked and that she could hear them from her house on the edge of town.

Thanks, she typed. *And no hail yet. Just wondering how I'll be able to sleep with all this thunder!*

His reply was nearly instantaneous. *You will. Trust me. It'll be like a rainy nighttime soundtrack!*

Ava doubted that very much, but she switched her phone off without a reply and headed back upstairs to bed. As she listened to the booming thunder that still clapped overhead, her thoughts drifted to her shattered shop window, the awful tarot card taped to the back of it. *The Hanged Woman.* Alone in the dark, Ava shuddered. She didn't need a tarot deck to tell her that whoever had thrown that brick was the same person who'd killed Audrey Wilson and who'd gone after Ricky's head with a wrench. The murderer was still out there, and they were watching her every move. She would have to tread lightly. A tornado was the least of her worries.

15

"You found *what*?" Riley demanded, snapping her head up from the coffee she was grinding.

Ava and Riley had arrived at Arcana early the next morning, business as usual. Not wanting to scare the girl, but also knowing she wasn't likely to miss the gaping hole in the supply room window, Ava had decided to be straight with Riley and give her the option of taking the morning off. With the potential of customers present, a repeat offense wasn't likely to happen, but by this point Ava wasn't ruling anything out. All bets were off.

"Watch where you're grinding that," Ava said, nodding at the ground coffee that was missing the filter in Riley's hands and headed straight for the counter. "Someone threw a brick in the window, and they taped this awful fake tarot card to the back of it."

"What did you *do*?" Riley wrinkled her nose in horrified glee. She dusted the coffee that had fallen on the counter into her open palm.

"What do you think I did? I called the police." There was no need for Riley to know that Ava's first instinct had been to call Owen O'Kelly. She'd have called the police on her own. Owen was beside the point.

"Can I see it?"

"See what?"

"The card! *Duh*. It sounds terrifying." Riley still wore the same gleeful expression of disgust. She placed the filter into the brewer basket and slid it into place.

"Greathouse took it into evidence," Ava said. "Probably to dust the tape for fingerprints. Anyway, you wouldn't want to see it. Trust me."

Riley sniffed. "You act like I'm five years old. What are we doing about the window?"

"I'm still figuring that out," Ava admitted. She wiped her hands on her apron, watching the trickle of steaming coffee as it brewed into the urn. Much to her relief, the tarp Greathouse put up the previous night had done its job, but the window would have to be replaced. The hardware store in town was the obvious place to call, but Ava feared that calling right after Owen opened the shop would just seem like an excuse to talk to him, and she didn't want him getting the wrong idea. Better to wait a few hours. Someone could crawl in the back window if they wanted, but they'd end up with a whole lot of cuts for a safe full of... nothing.

"You turned the open sign in the door, right?" Ava asked Riley, who had pulled herself up on the counter and sat swinging her legs.

"Yep." She slid off the counter, busied herself with the knobs of the espresso machine. "Anyway. Do you think they'll be back?"

Ava frowned. "Who? Our customers?"

"No," Riley said, shaking her head, eyes flicking toward the supply room. "Whoever it is that's got beef with us. Do you think they'll try something else?" Riley's voice was nonchalant, but it was hard to miss the worry in her eyes.

"I don't know," Ava admitted. "I hope not. But regardless—I won't have you stay here alone. Sound good?"

"Sure." Riley shrugged, turning to carry the now full urn of freshly brewed coffee to its place near the espresso bar. The girl was quiet, as though something about Ava's answer wasn't quite what she'd hoped to hear. But what else could Ava do? Hire private security? She could probably get by with giving Riley a few days off until things calmed down, but somehow, she didn't think that was what Riley was looking for either. Summer was prime money-making time for teenagers, as Ava remembered well from her own high school years. Just then, the doorbell jingled as the door swung open and Owen stepped inside, a red Huskers cap pulled down low on his brow.

"Morning," Owen announced, setting a heavy plastic sack down on the counter with a thud. "Man, it feels good in here. It's going to be a humid one today."

"What's that?" Ava looked skeptically at the bag. To her relief, Owen didn't seem to be interested in a discussion of the previous night. That was more than fine—she would ignore it as well. What was there to say, after all?

"This?" Owen lifted the sack an inch and then let it fall back to the counter. He pulled a tape measure out of his back pocket. "Your new security camera. I had a couple in stock at the store, so I figured I'd install one this morning. I'm also going to measure the windows back there and see about getting some new panes put in."

"Oh," Ava said, genuinely surprised. "Well, I really appreciate that. Let me know how much I owe you—for equipment *and* labor."

"Like I'm going to charge you for labor," Owen said, his green eyes now scanning the menu behind Ava. "Tell you what, though. I'll trade you: camera installation for a cup of coffee."

"Deal."

Owen was quiet a moment as Ava poured his coffee. He cast a nonchalant glance around the shop. "So, I'm supposed to stop by Finkenbaum Law Offices right after work. I've got a meeting with Chris about some supplier agreements for the store, and I thought maybe you'd want to come along."

"To discuss supplier agreements? Why would *I*—" She stopped, realization dawning on her. Owen was grinning.

"Obviously, after last night, we have to lie low," he said, shoving his hands in his jeans pockets. He lowered his voice. "But if you were to come along with me and remember that Audrey had borrowed something from you which you haven't gotten back yet, it could be the perfect opportunity to look around her office without anyone on the outside being any the wiser."

"I don't know..." Owen's text the night before flashed through her mind. *You okay?* She pushed the thought down, turning to glance at Riley so Owen wouldn't see the heat rising to her cheeks. "It seems risky."

"Up to you," Owen said, running a hand through his hair.

"Then again..." Ava mused, carefully avoiding any glance at Owen. She was finally getting a grip on herself. "Greathouse didn't seem convinced that the incident with the brick last night had anything to do with Audrey's murder—and maybe he's right. I need to find a new direction *stat*."

Ava sighed, then flashed Owen a small smile. "Alright, I guess I've got to see this through. I'm in."

"Great!" Owen slapped his palm on the counter. "Anyway, I'm going to go measure that window, and I'll be back for the coffee. And Riley—I've got something for you."

As he moved toward the hallway, Owen slid his phone face up across the counter toward Riley. He was already out of sight when she peered down at it and gasped in satisfied horror. Her eyes grew wide, and she turned to hold the phone up to Ava, but Ava had already guessed what it was.

"He took a picture of the card!" Riley hissed, looking back down at the phone. She pinched the screen to zoom in. "Whoever drew this is kind of a good artist, but damn, that's *creepy*."

Ava closed her eyes and sighed. Leave it to Owen.

"Anyway," Riley continued, fixing a mischievous gaze on Ava. "I guess the police weren't the *only* people you called last night, huh?"

Ears suddenly hot, Ava flicked a dish towel at the girl, who cackled with glee and darted out of reach. The two of them straightened at the sound of the supply room door closing and Owen's footsteps in the hall.

"Everything you hoped and dreamed?" Owen asked Riley, taking his phone back from the girl, who nodded. He snapped his tape measure shut and shoved it back into his pocket. Then, turning to Ava, he added, "I'll have to order the panes, but hopefully they'll have them delivered by tomorrow. I'll stop by right before closing to install the camera, and then we can head over to Finkenbaum's."

Ava nodded, and Owen strode out of the shop, coffee in hand. The door clanged shut, and Riley turned to Ava.

With a toss of her ponytail, Riley crossed her arms over her chest, her eyes moving to watch Owen disappear down the sidewalk. "He's way cooler than you," she announced, giving Ava a sly grin.

THE AIR WAS thick and humid when Ava and Owen stepped out of Arcana early that evening and made their way to Finkenbaum Law Offices. As they passed by New Heights on their right, Ava fought back the wave of nausea that surfaced every time that dreaded parking lot came into view. The image of Joel being led out in handcuffs would be forever etched into her mind. As they neared the office, Owen breathed deeply, inhaling the sticky air that clung to their skin.

"You can sure smell that storm hanging around," he announced, swinging open the heavy glass door of the law firm.

Finally starting to recognize the smell of a storm herself, Ava walked through the door Owen held open. Inside, the crisp coolness of the air-conditioned office brought a blast of instant relief, cooling her clammy skin. Melanie, the office administrator, whom Ava had only met in passing, was still sitting behind the main desk, her perfectly polished nails clacking on the keyboard. When she saw Ava and Owen, she shot them a prim smile, then glanced at the clock. They didn't miss the undertones—Owen was the last appointment of the day, and they were to stay on task, make it quick.

"He's in his office," Melanie said, tipping her head down the hall. She looked at them over the tops of her half-moon glasses. "Do you need me to accompany you?"

"No—thanks." Owen matched Melanie's crisp smile and ushered Ava down the hall, his hand placed gently in the middle of her back. Under his breath, he said, "My god, she's like a vulture."

Ava stifled a laugh, picturing Melanie's long red nails as talons. It was a wonder she ever got any work done, typing with those things.

When they entered the office at the end of the hall, Chris was sitting behind his desk, ankle crossed over one knee, leaning forward to peer at his computer screen. Owen rapped on the door to get his attention as they stepped inside, and Chris got to his feet.

"Owen, hello," he said, gesturing them to the two chairs across from his desk. "Please, have a seat. And you're Ava Goldberg, right? I believe we met at the barbecue."

"Yes, it's nice to see you again." Ava shook his outstretched hand and took her seat, glancing around. Save for a scant few piles of rumpled papers spread across his desk, Chris's office was spotless, and, with its posh furnishings, not at all what Ava would have pictured for an attorney's office. The back wall was painted a deep red, which, paired with the floor lamps and the vibrantly colored painting that hung behind the desk, tied the place together.

Chris's eyes followed Ava's gaze to the artwork on the wall, and he smiled. "I like it, too. Painted it myself a few years back."

"Yeah, you've got a pretty nice space here," Ava offered lamely, once again hating herself for her paltry small talk skills. Beside her, Owen stifled a laugh as he sat down, slinging one arm over the back of the chair.

"Anyway," Chris said, folding his hands on top of the desk

and smiling at Owen. "I understand you have some questions about the wording in those agreements you mentioned." Then, casting a hesitant glance toward Ava, added, "Is this something you'd like Ava to be included in?"

Owen coughed. "Ah, no—not exactly. We're headed to dinner after, and I figured she could tag along."

It was the excuse they'd come up with on the way over: Act casual, as though Ava was along by chance. Ava suspected the excuse might give way to a rumor about her and Owen, but it couldn't be helped. She needed a glimpse into Audrey's world, her frame of mind, if she was to think of anything else that could serve as a potential lead. So, she played along with the charade, starting to rise. "I'm happy to wait out in the lobby if it's more convenient."

"Definitely not necessary." Owen waved a hand. "Oh— besides, didn't you want to ask if anyone here had come across your book in Audrey's office?"

"Oh, that's right," Ava said, as though remembering something she'd forgotten all about. "I was hoping you'd have seen it —or if not, maybe I could take a quick peek at her desk if her things are still there, just to check? She borrowed a book from me, but she never had a chance to return it. I figured I'd check here first, since I don't want to bother her family right now."

Chris looked surprised. "Really? She borrowed a book from you?"

"Something tarot related," Owen jumped in, flashing an easygoing smile in Ava's direction. Her chest loosened. *That was close.*

"Huh," Chris said, shrugging, although apparently satisfied with Owen's explanation. "Well, I didn't see anything like that when Melanie was going through Audrey's things, but the police have taken what they wanted, so sure, take a look. We haven't gotten around to clearing it out completely, but we did remove everything confidential, so no worries about stumbling across anything sensitive. Her office is the last door down this hallway."

"Perfect." Ava excused herself and headed back down the hallway she'd come from. Ava tried not to show the gleeful shock she felt—their plan had worked! She wasn't even sure what she hoped to find in Audrey's office, but having a clearer picture of her day-to-day life wouldn't hurt anything. She would be fine with *any* little clue that might point her in a new direction.

Audrey's office door was ajar. The darkness of the room was disconcerting. So weird to think that just a week before someone as put together as Audrey Wilson had been sitting here poring over cases, taking phone calls, reapplying lipstick before meetings. The light had been snuffed out, and you could feel it. Ava had never been so glad to flip on a light switch.

"Okay," Ava muttered to herself, scanning the polished oak desk. Although it felt silly, she continued in a low voice, half hoping Audrey herself would somehow hear her. "Who *were* you, Audrey? Who might have wanted to kill you? It sure as hell wasn't Joel Robinson. What am I *missing*?"

For having been cleared by both Melanie and the police, Audrey's desk was still covered in scattered papers. These, apparently, had been deemed of little interest to Greathouse and his staff, and mainly included meeting minutes, reminders to add calendar events, and the occasional receipt. Ava sifted through them aimlessly, having no clue what she was looking for, what kinds of things would even help. Letters or notes from

Joel? Or *to* Joel, from Audrey? Even if the affair had happened and the notes existed, the chief would have already taken them into evidence. She was also sure she would've heard about them. Briefly, she wondered if there might be an invoice from Ricky's garage lying around, remembering in frustration that even if there was, the point was now moot.

"Come on," Ava whispered, more to herself than to Audrey now. She opened the top drawer of the desk and began sifting through the pens and pencils. "What am I even supposed to find here? A memo pad saying who killed you?"

Then, somewhere between the memo pads and high-lighters, her fingers touched on something glossy. A... picture? Frowning, Ava slid it toward her, took it between two fingers, and held it up to the light. In the picture, Audrey posed in the middle of a set of railroad tracks, one hip jutted out to the side, her long slim legs made even sleeker by the pointy stilettos she wore. Her auburn hair was thick and shiny as always, cascading around her shoulders, but her face was younger, and there was something about the shine in her eyes that said she hadn't yet dealt with the woes of the world.

"Audrey's senior picture?" Ava frowned, wondering why on earth an adult would keep a picture of themselves as a senior in high school in the drawer of their desk at work. Living the glory days? Not likely. From what little Ava had seen of her, Audrey had been just as vivacious as a thirty-something woman as she had in her youth and was just as beautiful—perhaps even more so. Turning the card over, Ava's breath caught. There, on the back of the card, was a scrawled note. Or rather, *two* scrawled notes.

The first was a seemingly commonplace greeting in faded ink:

Hey bro, have fun next year. Love ya lots!

<3 Audrey

There was nothing very special about it. It was like any other cheesy dedication a senior might write on the back of their photos before handing them out. The second note on it, however, was different. The handwriting didn't match the first note, and the ink was distinct.

Remember: I remember.

Well, that was weird. Was it a good or a bad remember? And who had written it? The two sets of handwriting were different, but that didn't necessarily mean Audrey hadn't written both. Ava's own handwriting had, thankfully, changed a lot since high school. What bothered Ava was why the photograph was in Audrey's possession in the first place. If she'd written the first note *to* someone else, wouldn't she have then given them the picture? Somehow it had been returned to her. It seemed strange, and to Ava, it sounded a bit like a warning.

Were the items in the room still considered evidence? Seemingly not, as Chris had mentioned that the only things remaining were ones the police had deemed inconsequential. Hoping she wasn't about to get herself into hot water, Ava slipped the photo into her back pocket and swept through the rest of the drawer's contents. She rifled through the shelves in the corner bookcase, but nothing else turned up. Aside from the photograph, the office was void of anything that might shed further light on who had killed its former occupant.

Ava heard the faint click of a door, followed by voices that got louder as they moved down the hall. Throwing one last glance around the room, Ava switched off the light and, satisfied, moved out into the hallway where Chris and Owen were just coming to meet her.

"Find what you were looking for?" Chris asked, stealing a glance at his watch. "I'm hoping to squeeze in a quick workout at New Heights before dinner, but I can stay a few more minutes if you need…"

"Uh," Ava began, trying to remember what it was she'd claimed to have been looking for. Oh, right. The tarot book. "No, but it's fine—I'm sure I'll get it back, eventually."

Chris nodded. "Sure. I'll keep an eye out here, just in case it turns up." He smiled, gesturing Ava and Owen to continue ahead of him into the lobby.

"Alright," Owen said, clapping his hands together. "I've taken enough of your time, Chris. We're on our way to dinner, but after that I'm hoping there'll be enough of a break in the thunderstorms to get a full night's sleep. That siren last night woke me up at three, and I've been awake ever since."

Chris escorted Owen and Ava to the door. "I hear you. It woke me up, too, but Katie slept right through it. I guess even pregnancy hasn't hampered her ability to sleep through anything."

Chris stepped forward to hold the door open for Owen and Ava. He smiled. "Anyway, you let me know if you run into other questions, Owen. Or if you hear back from your brother."

"Will do," Owen said. "See you around, Chris." He gave a quick two fingered wave—the kind Ava had seen the farmers make as they rumbled down the cobblestoned main street in their pickup trucks—and followed Ava out the door.

They walked in comfortable silence for a moment or two. Then, once they'd reached a safe distance from the office, Owen spoke eagerly.

"Okay, so did you find anything?"

"Maybe, maybe not. But first—you have a *brother*?"

Owen shrugged his broad shoulders. "Yeah. Lots of people do."

"Okay, but Shiloh is, like, a hundred people. How did I not know this?"

"Correction: 2,500 people. And I don't know—he doesn't live here. We're not on great terms, but he's got a share in the business."

Ava was about to ask what had happened, but thought better of it after the sharp sideways look Owen shot her. Instead, she said, "Well—anyway. I found what appears to be one of Audrey's senior pictures inside her desk drawer."

Owen frowned. "Like, high school senior pictures?"

"Yeah. At least, it looked like that to me." Ava drew the photograph out of her pocket and handed it to Owen. "See, there's writing on the back. It looks like a note she wrote, planning to give the picture to someone, and then someone else wrote that thing below it about remembering that they remember."

"What? What is that even supposed to mean?"

Ava shrugged, taking the photo back from Owen. "Who knows? I mean, it could be nothing, but it seems weird."

"Well, I guess whether it's weird depends on who wrote the note and what it is they remember."

"Was there anything weird that happened to Audrey her senior year of high school—or something she did that someone might hold a grudge about? Some guy she might have snubbed? Someone obviously gave the photo back."

Owen thought for a moment, the scent of tacos wafting toward them. "Or maybe she never gave it to the person at all. I can't think of anything scandalous she was involved in. I mean, she was kind of the *it* girl, so technically, there's no telling how many guys' hearts she could have unwittingly broken. But no one in particular comes to mind."

"God, those tacos smell amazing," Ava breathed.

"Well, I wasn't kidding about dinner." Owen stopped in front of the curb and jutted his chin toward La Fontana. "You down?"

It was against her better judgment, she knew, but who said no to tacos? In fact, cheesy sustenance might even give them the brain power they needed to make some headway in the case.

"Sure," Ava said, and led the way into the brightly lit restaurant. "And the margaritas are on me."

"So, what do we think?" Owen dipped a tortilla chip into the bowl of spicy salsa and stuck it in his mouth, crunching. They'd already ordered their meals and were sitting in a red vinyl booth, munching on chips and salsa while they waited for their food.

"I don't know. I know Joel Robinson didn't kill Audrey, but that's about *all* I know," Ava said, shrugging her shoulders. She hoped the people around her weren't listening. They all seemed to be absorbed in their own meals and conversations.

"Okay. Let's go over the facts again," Owen said. He reached for another chip. "Audrey was found dead in the fountain, cause of death being blunt force trauma to the head. Presumably, the killer moved her body there *after* hitting her over the head to make it look like an accident, like she'd tripped on the cobblestones."

"Right. And then Ricky Birch finds Audrey's phone near the

scene of the crime, figures out that the last call she received—the one that lured her to her death—was saved as the care center her dad's at, but was *really* the number of the payphone across town."

"Which begs the question: Why was that number on her phone listed as the care center? I think the only way an identification comes up on a phone call is if the phone's owner—or someone else—programs it in the contacts list. Did *Audrey* save that number under that name? Was she involved in something we don't know about? Or did someone *else* save the payphone number under that name? Like after she died. But why not just take and toss the phone?"

"Exactly. We can't rule either option out, but *if* it was someone else who'd saved the number, two things follow: That person had less than honest intentions *and* they had access to Audrey's phone."

Owen blew out his breath. "Dang. This is just getting too convoluted."

"But we're so close," Ava pressed. "Let's back up a little bit. That's only half the story."

"Okay," Owen began, crunching on another chip. "So, Greathouse got that anonymous tip about Joel and Audrey having some kind of affair, which was backed up by the note they found in her pocket. In his handwriting. Ricky and Audrey had argued the night before, making him seem suspicious, but then the attack on him sort of shut that road down. Meanwhile, Joel doesn't have an alibi for the time of Ricky's attack, making him look even *more* suspicious to Greathouse. Although, really, why would he attack someone who could also be on the suspect list? It only narrows that list back to him... Anyway, the police get a warrant to search New

Heights, and boom—there's the murder weapon. The flashlight."

Just then, their server appeared next to the table carrying two enormous plates of steaming food: cheese enchiladas for Ava and steak fajitas for Owen. Both Ava and Owen halted their conversation to smile at the waitress as she set the food in front of them. Once satisfied that Ava and Owen had everything they needed, she bustled away from the table. Ava cut into her enchilada with the side of her fork, delighting in the cheese as it oozed out onto her plate.

"So, setting aside the flashlight for now," she began, in between bites of tortilla and cheese. "The thing that's bothering me is that senior picture I found in Audrey's desk. What does that mean, anyway?"

"Dunno." Owen shrugged. "It could be nothing. Not related to her death at all."

"Right. But what else do we have to go on now? I mean, it *might* mean something."

Owen nodded. "True. But maybe all she wanted was to remember the *glory days*. A lot of people are like that in small towns. You know, dads gathered on the deck drinking beer and rehashing the high school football games they carried to victory."

"Yes, but *her*? What, she somehow peaked during high school and has to constantly be looking back? I don't buy it— seems ridiculous. And anyway, that seems especially weird given that she'd meant to give the photo to someone else at one point."

"Okay, so what do you think it *did* mean?" Owen set down his fork and met her eyes across the table. His gaze was soft, yet unflinching.

"I don't know..." Ava said, lowering her gaze. Heat rose in her cheeks. Were Owen's green eyes really specked with gold, or was it just the light? She shifted in her seat, bringing her focus back to the case at hand. "The top part that Audrey wrote on the photo—which I took to be the original note meant for somebody else—said, '*Hey bro. Love ya lots!*' Could it have been a photo she was planning to give to Lucas?"

Owen looked dubious. "I don't know. Would she really have given her senior photo to her brother? Seems like they'd have a lot lying around at home, and they never got along very well, anyway."

"That's true," Ava admitted. "And *bro* is—was?—a fairly common thing to call your guy friends. But that does still narrow it down some, right? She probably gave that picture to a guy."

"Eh. It still doesn't add up," Owen said, shaking his head. "I mean, that may be true, but it doesn't answer any of our questions. Let's say for the sake of postulating that she gave that photo to Joel their senior year. And he gave it back to her with that second note. Why?"

She shrugged. "I know Joel's handwriting, but with only three words I couldn't guess if it was from his hand."

"Aside from who wrote the second note, what's it doing in her desk now? And what does the '*remember*' part have to do with anything?"

Ava thought about it for a moment. "The second note did seem kind of ominous. Like, a reminder from someone who had dirt on her and wanted to keep her in line."

Owen raised his eyebrows. "You mean like blackmail?"

"Could be. Do *you* know of anything Audrey might have been involved in, something that might have happened to her or something she did? If it was something in high school, it would explain the link between the picture and the warning. Like, the person who wrote it was saying, 'I remember that thing that happened in high school'…"

Owen scoffed. "Audrey was in her thirties. I'd like to think we've all moved past the pettiness of high school."

"No," Ava persisted, sawing at her enchilada more violently than necessary. "I mean something *bad*, not just petty cheerleader stuff." Suddenly, a thought occurred to her. "Owen, do you still have any of your yearbooks?"

Owen narrowed his eyes at her from across the table. "Probably somewhere. Why?"

"Well, maybe if you look through all the pictures in one place, it'll jog some kind of memory. Like, 'Oh, *yeah*, she dated *that* guy', or 'Oh man, they hated each other's *guts*.' Something like that."

Owen snorted. "I think you're overestimating how much I remember about high school."

"Oh, come on. You got any better ideas?"

Owen shrugged. "I mean, I'm not sure what we'll find other than a bunch of gangly teenagers in braces, but sure. What the hell."

"Perfect." Ava pushed her empty plate forward and waved to the waitress, imitating a check-writing motion and mouthing, "Two checks, please." No way was she going to let Owen pay for her. This dinner was strictly business.

It felt to Ava that the waitress took forever to return their credit cards. When she finally returned, clearing the dishes and depositing two black books onto the table, Ava scrawled her signature and left a generous tip. She'd wished they'd had time for dessert—fried ice cream was always her favorite—but she couldn't wait to get her hands on those yearbooks. She was still hoping they'd find something useful, although she wasn't sure what, but at the very least, she'd get to see what Shiloh had looked like in the early 2000s. And, of course, if Owen had been a dreamboat at sixteen, she'd just have to keep her mouth shut.

16

―――――

Owen loaded Ava's bicycle into the bed of his truck, and they both hopped into the cab, setting off down Main Street. As Owen turned into a driveway on the southwest edge of town, Ava realized she'd noticed the tiny house several times during her evening bicycle rides, had admired the sage green shutters and well-tended flowers below the windows.

Owen unlocked the front door and held it open for her. Once inside, Ava found herself in the middle of a tiny living room, complete with an antique coffee table and a plush, upholstered armchair. Opposite the coffee table stood a minia-ture sofa, and behind that were entire floor-to-ceiling shelves of books upon books that covered the entire wall.

Ava turned back to Owen in surprise as he pulled the door shut behind him. "You've got yourself a real home library!"

Owen shrugged, a faint blush creeping up into his chiseled cheeks. "Yeah. I'm a reader. My grandmother left me her collec-tion, and I've added to it some."

"They're beautiful," Ava breathed, stepping across the

creaky hardwood floor to examine the titles. "I always think you can tell so much by what books a person has in their bookcase."

"Yikes." Owen rubbed the back of his neck. "Well, you better not look too closely then."

"Oh, I already have," Ava laughed, wrinkling her nose at him. "Sherlock Holmes. Plenty of Dickens. I'm also seeing a whole row of Dan Brown here. I'd say your taste is quite well rounded."

Owen folded his arms across his chest and leaned back against the wall, watching her. "What about you? You read anything other than those cards?"

"Oh, sometimes," Ava said, a bit embarrassed she hadn't read more than a handful of books over the past year. "To be honest, I haven't read much fiction for the past couple of years. I didn't think I could handle any additional drama or tension, other than what I was already dealing with in reality."

Owen raised his eyebrows. "What happened?"

Ava shook her head. She hadn't meant to say this much. There was no way she was going to admit to someone she hardly knew that her ex-husband had cheated on her with her best friend. So, she said simply: "Divorce."

"Ah." Owen nodded, his face unreadable. Ava couldn't tell if the nod was one of acknowledgment or understanding. How could you understand, though, if you hadn't lived through it yourself? If Owen had ever been married, she was sure Rose would have mentioned it.

"Anyway. How about those yearbooks?" Being in Owen's house already felt strangely intimate, and she wanted to get down to business.

"Right," Owen said, pushing away from the wall and striding over to the rightmost side of the wall of books. He looked almost glad of the subject change, like someone who'd been snapped out of a sobering daydream. His fingers danced across the spines of several books on the highest row, pulling a couple out to better see the title. "Ah. Yes. Here we go."

He drew the book down, then sank down onto the plush sofa. Ava followed, already curious about the slim little yearbook he'd pulled down. It had to be half the size of her own, having gone to school in the Chicago suburbs. Then again, Shiloh was probably lucky to even *have* enough students to fill a yearbook.

"I know, I know," Owen said, sliding a finger into the book and closing it momentarily to shoot Ava an amused glance. "It's small. I once saw my buddy's yearbook—he's from Omaha—and literally laughed out loud. It looked like a real yearbook, like you see in the movies, but this..." He chuckled and reopened the book.

"Well, it'll be easier to look through! That's for sure. It must have been nice going to school with so few kids in your grade. You probably knew everyone."

"Yep, and that was exactly the problem." Owen grimaced. "Never any privacy. Still isn't—as I'm sure you've noticed by now."

"I may have. So what year is this? 2008?"

"This one's 2007. I graduated in 2008, but Audrey was a grade older, so if we want her in it, we've got to look at 2007 or before."

"Okay, even better. That would've been her senior year, so we can make sure the picture matches up, too, although I can't think what else it would be if not for a senior picture."

Owen flipped back to the front of the yearbook and began to flip through the pages, his green eyes scanning the pictures and lines of text as he did. They sat like that for several moments, rifling through the glossy pages, pointing out dated hairstyles to each other and laughing aloud at a page that listed the most popular songs of the year. The front pages were full of pictures from homecoming week, featuring four student-crafted floats—one for each grade—and a bunch of football pictures that all looked the same to Ava. Just as Owen was about to turn the page, Ava jabbed a finger at a blown-up photo of the entire football team, helmets off and lined up with arms slung over each other's shoulders. On the end of the back row stood a grinning, messy-haired boy whose eyes twinkled even in black and white. She knew that grin.

"That's you!" Ava tapped Owen's face in the photograph in triumph. "It's *got* to be."

"Oh, oops, turning the page now!" Owen laughed, nearly ripping the page in his haste to get past his own picture. "We're not looking for me. We're looking for Audrey. Stay on task!"

"Well, we'll get to your picture sooner or later," Ava said sweetly, her blue eyes scanning what looked to now be home-coming royalty pictures. "Oh! Is that Joel? Oh my god, was he homecoming king?"

"Oh, perfect. Here we are. You bet Joel Robinson was home-coming king. And—oh, *duh*. Audrey was homecoming queen that year. I remember thinking it was fitting, since they were going out back then and all that."

Ava bent closer to get a better look at the picture. Sure enough, there was Audrey Wilson, fifteen years younger but exactly the same: lush, auburn hair curling around her milky shoulders, eyes snapping, and the same severe half smile she'd been wearing every time Ava had seen her. The only difference now was the cheesy rhinestone tiara that sat atop her head.

"Well, of course she would've been homecoming queen," Ava remarked. "I suppose it's different at a smaller school, but the idea's the same, right? Homecoming's for the popular people and jocks, and prom's for the academics?"

"Yeah, more or less." Owen pointed to another photograph on the page. "There's Rose."

"Where are you?"

Owen waved a dismissive hand at Ava. "Enough with that. I'm sure I'm somewhere, but I was pretty low key. I tried to stay out of the spotlight."

"Oh, here are the seniors," Ava said, flipping the page to a full color spread. "Let's look to see if the picture I found was taken around the same time. You know, if she looks the same."

They both scanned the pages—there were only three or four total as the class was so small—until Owen tapped his finger atop one of the pictures. "There."

Ava leaned forward to peer at the photograph. Eighteen-year-old Audrey Wilson smiled coyly as she strutted along the Shiloh cobblestones, posing like she was on the red carpet. Her red hair shimmered in the light, and behind her—Ava sucked in her breath. Behind her was the very fountain her dead body had wound up in just two days before.

"Well, that's a pretty dark coincidence," Owen muttered, and Ava did not have to ask what he was talking about. "But there she is."

"There she is, and wearing the same outfit as in the picture I found in her desk drawer."

"Okay, so then it *was* her senior picture you found. But we already thought so—this doesn't change much."

"Right..." Although disappointed at the realization that Owen was, of course, correct, the wheels inside Ava's mind were still turning. "But it definitely seems like that second note on the back of the picture was referring to something that happened her senior year. Otherwise, why use that picture for it? Does any of this jog any memories?"

"Not really," Owen said doubtfully, flipping back to look through the last few pages. "I wasn't in her grade, though. She was on the student council and played volleyball. I was a football guy. Our paths didn't cross much."

Ava flipped back to the earlier grades, still scanning the faces. As her eyes flicked through the rows, she stopped. In the very last row of the juniors' section, the picture of a round-eyed, smiling blonde girl had been circled in a heart.

"Who's this?" Ava asked, casting a teasing side glance at Owen, who didn't meet her gaze.

"Becky Phillips."

Ava grinned, studying the picture. The girl *was* cute. "Looks like someone had a crush."

"She did that," Owen said. "Drew the heart around her picture."

"Oh, so the feeling was *mutual* then," Ava teased. She shifted her perch on the sofa, turning to face Owen, but stopped short when she caught sight of his expression. For the first time since she'd met him, Owen wasn't smiling.

"Yeah, you could say that," Owen said, finally bringing his gaze to meet Ava's. "She ended up becoming my fiancée."

Oh, crap. Ava felt a wave of heat sweep through her insides, her cheeks growing hot. "Oh, god. I'm so sorry—"

Owen flicked his hand, signaling for her to save the platitudes. He rested his head against the back of the sofa. "It's fine. I'm fine. It was a long time ago."

Ava thought for a beat. She knew she shouldn't press him,

but her curiosity was killing her. "Really? Can I ask what happened?"

"Sure, it's no big deal," Owen said, sitting up again and straightening his posture. He rested his huge hands on his knees. "We dated all through high school, all through college. Asked her to marry me our senior year. We were going to have the wedding after graduation, but about a month before, she bailed." He shrugged. "Simple as that."

Ava stared at him. "But—that's *awful*. Did she give a reason?"

Owen studied the ceiling. "She wanted to get out and explore life some more. Meet other people, see new places— get out of Shiloh."

"Mm." Ava didn't know what to say. Becky Phillips stared up at them from the page, a spirit Ava had inadvertently summoned. She had the sudden urge to cover Becky's face with her hand.

Owen cleared his throat. "Okay, let's get back to business. This murder won't solve itself." He tugged the yearbook from Ava's hands and began flipping back through the pages.

Phew. Bullet dodged. Ava let out a shaky breath, scooting closer on the sofa seat to see the pictures as Owen flipped. Faces flew by, grinning girls with glittery pompoms, trumpet players moving across a football field. Just then, something caught her eye.

"Wait," Ava said, holding up a hand to signal him to stop turning the pages. They'd reached the senior photos again. Ava traced her finger down the last page of senior photos and landed on one set slightly apart. She read aloud. "In loving memory of Tiffany Martinez. 1989 - 2007. Who's Tiffany Martinez? Was she...?"

"Oh my god," Owen breathed. His eyes widened. He brought the yearbook closer to his face to study the picture. "She's Juanita's daughter. *Was* Juanita's daughter. She died my junior year—her senior year. Car accident. Super tragic, really shook everyone up."

"Oh, poor Juanita," Ava murmured. The girl had been beautiful, with sparkling, clear eyes and shiny waist-length dark hair. "I didn't know she had a daughter."

"Yeah, it was pretty rough on her," Owen said, his eyes glazing over as if remembering. "I remember they had a whole special memorial for her at graduation. The valedictorians—Audrey included—all honored her in their speeches at the ceremony, and I don't think there was a dry eye in the house. God, it's crazy how things like that can just... fade out of your memory completely until you stumble across them again."

"Were they friends?" Ava asked. She didn't want to ask her real question yet. Not while Owen was still looking nostalgic. God knew she'd already done enough damage.

"Who? Tiffany and Audrey?"

"Yeah."

Owen shook his head. "Not really. Tiffany would've been in the more 'normal' crowd, and Audrey ran with the snooty academics. You know, the popular nerds."

Ava snorted. "No, I don't know. I was just a nerd."

"Well, we all have our shortcomings," Owen said, shooting her a grin. "But in all seriousness, I don't think this has anything to do with the writing on the photograph. It's definitely something that happened back then, but it was pretty far removed from Audrey."

"You're probably right," Ava agreed, nodding in resignation. What Owen said made sense, but something still nagged at her.

It seemed like too big of an occurrence to *not* be related. But if Audrey and Tiffany hadn't been friends, was there any connection? "What happened with the car crash, though?"

"Well, it wasn't a *crash*, per se. She was out walking late one night—I think after a party or something—and she didn't come home. Her parents called the cops, and they went out looking for her, and... they found her by the side of the road. Someone hit her and didn't even call the police, let alone stop to see if she was alive. And by then it was too late."

"That's awful!" Ava's stomach churned. "And they never found out who hit her or what happened?"

"As far as I know, no. Not a lot of traffic cams back then and for sure not in a small town like Shiloh." Owen grimaced. "It's been so long since I thought about it, I forgot it was that specific year that it happened..."

They sat in silence for a moment longer, the closed yearbook on their laps. In other circumstances, Ava would have liked to page through it further, pointing out the few people she recognized, sneaking peeks at a young, shy-looking Owen and the always sweet-looking Rose. Tonight, though, after the story she'd just heard, her heart felt heavy. She didn't know Juanita well, but she never would have guessed that beneath the woman's jovial, friendly nature was buried such horrific loss. What a heavy load that must have been—especially with never getting the closure that came with seeing the person responsible held accountable. Ava's heart ached for the kind, laughing woman she'd begun to know. *And Owen...* Ava swallowed hard. She should have never asked about Becky Phillips. It had become even more apparent that everyone was carrying their own pain, whether or not it was visible to the world.

"You know," Owen said, his voice breaking the silence. "For

what it's worth, I think you're doing a good job with everything."

Ava's eyebrows raised. This was unexpected. "What do you mean?"

"I mean," Owen said, shifting in his seat so he was facing her. "You mentioned dealing with tension in your own life, which I took to mean that you'd come through some rough stuff. You know now that I know a little of what that's like. And I just wanted to say that you ought to be really proud of yourself. Your cafe, your readings, moving somewhere on your own—that stuff's not easy, but you're pulling it off."

"Well, thanks," Ava conceded, offering him a grateful smile. Compliments had always made her uncomfortable, but she appreciated the sentiment. "I actually kind of feel like I'm hard-core floundering, but it's nice to hear it doesn't look like that from the outside."

Owen smiled, his eyes shining. "I think that floundering feeling is just sort of how it feels to be human."

"I guess so." Ava looked down at her hands. She was suddenly aware of how close they were sitting.

"Hey," Owen said, lifting Ava's chin up so her eyes met his. His fingers were cool and smooth on her skin. "It's okay. Things are going to come together."

He leaned forward, brushing his lips to hers. All thought gone, she let him kiss her, kissed him back even, relishing the softness of his lips. He smelled like soil, like earth and wind, and his kiss was gentle.

Suddenly, Ava stiffened. She jerked back, came crashing down into reality. What was she *doing*? Untangling her fingers from Owen's, she felt frantically for her purse on the sofa and got to her feet.

"Sorry," she stammered. "I can't do this. You're a great guy, but I'm—this isn't—"

"Isn't what?" Owen asked, standing up to face her.

"I don't *know* you!"

"What do you *mean* you don't know me?" Owen looked defeated. He ran a hand through his thatch of wavy hair. "How do you not get it? I've been trying to get to know you, let *you* know *me*—"

"What's it been, Owen? A week? You can't know someone in a week." Ava was exasperated, and the hurt look on Owen's face was only making it worse.

"You knew me well enough to call me last night. To come be with you." Owen held her gaze, his green eyes snapping.

"That's *different*," Ava protested.

"How's it different? You've been leading me on all week, and suddenly, you pull a complete one-eighty. It's fine if you want to take things slower, but don't say you don't know me. It's *mean*, Ava. You know that? It's *cold*. Cold-hearted."

Ava's eyes flashed with anger. "Don't you dare call me cold. That's completely unfair."

"Really? I actually think it's pretty accurate," Owen said, walking to the front door and opening it. "Anyway, it's getting late. I'm tired. I'll see you around, okay?" He held the door open, waiting.

"Fine," Ava snapped, slinging her bag over her shoulder. "You want to hurl accusations at me, kick me out? Fine by me."

Without so much as a glance backward, Ava stalked through the open door and down the sidewalk. Even when the screen door slammed shut behind her, she kept her back to the house, hopping on her bicycle and giving a ferocious whack of her heel to the kickstand. As she pedaled off toward home, the crunch of the pavement beneath her tires, her heart was still pounding, the anger still coursing through her bloodstream. But, she realized with a pang of something akin to helplessness, beneath it was the very feeling she had tried so hard for so many months to keep at bay: loss.

17

____

The house was dark when Ava arrived home, the sky behind it a hazy mass of turbulent gray clouds just visible in the moonlight. Ava leaned her bike against the splintered picket fence that encircled the lawn and pushed open the gate. The heaviness of the air was oppressive, covering the town like a dank, heavy blanket. Even the lights of Shiloh proper, usually visible down the long, dusty road leading to Ava's property, seemed smudged, barely aglow.

Ava heaved a sigh, fighting the sinking sense of loneliness that had settled in her chest. How could she have been so stupid? Of _course_ she had led Owen on, whether or not she'd meant to. She had seen what was happening, and she'd done nothing to stop it, had walked right into it and used it to her own advantage with no consideration for anyone's feelings but her own. Owen had been right when he echoed Riley's words. She was cold. And now she was alone, the shattered shards of a ruined friendship haunting her.

Ava trudged up the sidewalk. Aside from the rustle of the

heavy breeze in the grass and the faint murmur of crickets, the night was silent. Reaching the front stoop, she stopped. The screen door, which guarded the heavy wooden front door from the outside, was ajar, swaying slightly with the shuddery breeze. Ava stared. Had she done that? Forgotten to shut it all the way when she left for work that morning? She climbed the stairs, trying to think back. The door had come unlatched in the wind. That was all. And yet...

Ava swung the screen door open, letting it bang against her hip as she stood in the doorway and searched for her keys. Fitting the key into the lock of the front door, Ava twisted the key to the right. The knob turned with it. Unlocked? An alarm sounded in Ava's mind, and her fingers moved instinctively to her phone in her pocket. She'd call—

No. She shoved the phone back down into her pocket, angry with herself for even *thinking* the thought that had sprung to mind. No, she would *not* call Owen. And she never should have called him about the brick through the window at Arcana, either. It was that incident that had started this whole ordeal, wasn't it? This situation where he wanted more than she could give?

Stomping into the house, Ava set her bag on the counter and flipped on the kitchen light. The door *couldn't* have been unlocked. She'd simply forgotten to lock it. God knew she'd forgotten before, and she'd forget again. It happened to people all the time. She was finally home after a long day, even if she *had* managed to ruin a friendship with her partner in crime solving along the way. Things always seemed worse at night. She'd get into bed, have a much needed sleep, and sort things out in the morning when the sun came up and she could breathe again.

The kitchen was dim and bare, save for the checkered hand towels hanging from the oven handle and the stained-glass cardinal she'd hung in the kitchen window. Ava's father, along with her aunts and uncles, had insisted on moving most of Zaidy Mel's belongings out after he died, and she hadn't yet gotten around to decorating the place. She knew Zaidy Mel would have wanted her to make the place her own, but there was something about the sameness of it all that she couldn't bear to mar just yet. If she could have kept her grandfather's toast crumbs on the counter, his slippers on the rug, she would have.

Through the kitchen window, the night was black. The haziness of the rolling clouds, like the angry gurgling of water about to boil, completely obscured the stars she normally looked for above the treetops. But as she gazed, it was then that she saw it: the index card resting on the windowsill.

The sinking in Ava's stomach turned to a hammering in her chest. As she plucked the card off the sill with a shaking hand, she knew exactly what it was. This time, the female figure lay face up on the ground, ten jagged swords pierced right through her. She leaked blood, rich and scarlet, and her tongue hung out of her mouth, where it curled like black smoke. Where her eyes should have been, there was only black, like someone had carved out the eyeballs and left only dark, sunken pits.

And on the back of the card, a scrawled message:

Back off or you're next.

There could be no mistaking now who'd left the card or what their intentions were. Ava set the card face down and backed away. Her mind raced: the unlocked door, the card. Someone had been there. Could be here now! She tried to quiet her breathing, steady her racing heart, as she strained to hear any sounds. *Back off or you're next.* Whoever had killed Audrey and attacked Ricky lurked in the house, waiting to kill her. Her back to the wall, she pulled out her phone and dialed Owen's number. She bit back their argument—what else could she do? She couldn't endanger Rose and Ellie. And the police? What would they do? Take the card in for evidence and tell her to sleep with one eye open? At least if she called Owen, there was a chance he would put their argument aside and come spend the night on the couch, shotgun at the ready.

Owen's line rang. Once, twice. *Pick up.* She willed him to answer. A beep sounded after the fifth ring, and Owen's voice-mail played, echoing eerily into the darkness of the kitchen.

Hey, it's Owen. I can't take your call right now. Leave a message, and I'll get back to you soon!

Ava jabbed a finger at the screen, ending the call. She stood for another moment in the silence, listening to the tick of the clock above the kitchen sink. Even if the culprit had left, if they had broken in once, they could do it again. She'd pushed away the one person who might have come to her rescue—*had* come to her rescue—and now she had no one. She'd wanted to do it all on her own, and she was getting exactly what she asked for.

Grabbing a knife from the utensil drawer, Ava crept through to the living room and craned her neck beyond the doorway, searching for even the tiniest sign of movement. When none came, she gathered all her courage and began to stalk the entire house, flicking on lights as she went, ensuring that no intruder remained inside. Satisfied that she was indeed alone, she flipped the locks on the windows, bolted the door, and pushed the heavy kitchen table against it. With every light in the house still on, she wrapped a blanket around her shoulders and curled up in a ball on the living room sofa, her cheek resting on the musty couch cushions, staring at the knife lying on the ottoman next to her. It was a long time before sleep finally came.

18

Riley was busy helping customers when Ava parked her bicycle outside Arcana and strode coolly inside. Wanting to stop by the police station and alert Greathouse to the break-in the night before, as well as pick up the spare set of cafe keys she'd left with him, Ava had texted Riley at the crack of dawn, asking her to open the shop on her own. A bit surprisingly, the girl had already been awake and sent a thumbs up emoji almost instantly, to which Ava hadn't bothered to reply. If she wanted her little shop to stay afloat, she would need to buckle down, kick her butt in gear. Her focus needed to be laser sharp, and she didn't have time to waste sending emojis. A night of fitful sleep had made one thing clear: Ava was done playing detective. It was over. She was bowing out. What had happened to Audrey was horrible, but chasing down a killer was not what Ava had come to Shiloh to do. From now on, it would be best for everyone—her little cafe included—if she kept her nose strictly within her own business.

"Thanks for opening," Ava said to Riley, tying an apron

around her waist. The doorbell jingled as the customers who had been at the counter exited the shop.

"No problem," Riley said. She paused a moment, then turned a smirk toward Ava. "I guess you and Owen were out late last night."

"Excuse me." Ava held up a hand. "That's not appropriate for work."

Riley started, like Ava had slapped her. "Oh. Sorry…"

"For your information, I had to make a stop at the police station before I came in, and they only open at eight." Ava knew she was being stiff, but she couldn't help it. Getting caught up in the town's drama had only torn her down so far. She couldn't let Arcana fall, too—it was the last thing standing.

Riley's eyebrows raised. Ava could tell she was dying to ask why she'd stopped at the station. Like someone tiptoeing through a minefield, Riley spoke carefully. "Did something new happen with the murder case?"

"I'd rather not talk about it," Ava said, pouring herself a cup of coffee. "This case has caused me enough grief, and I'm done with it. I never should have gotten involved."

Riley looked skeptical. She had just opened her mouth to say something, but stopped when the doorbell jingled again and Rose came rushing in, Ellie bouncing on her hip.

"Ava!" Rose's dark eyes were round and glowing. There was a warm flush to her cheeks that Ava had missed seeing since Joel's arrest. She stopped at the counter, threw a look around the coffee shop to make sure she wasn't bothering any customers, and let out a giddy, breathless laugh. "He's out! Joel just called to say Greathouse let him go, all charges dropped!"

"Oh, thank *god*," Ava breathed, pressing a hand to her chest. Despite the heaviness of the last twelve hours, she felt her spirits rise, a tiny flutter of hope. "Now, that's a relief if I ever felt one."

"I know." Rose pressed her cheek to Ellie's, snuggling the baby. "I'm so grateful to you, Ava. I know you haven't figured out who killed Audrey yet, but letting Greathouse know about those horrible, creepy cards the killer kept leaving you was what tipped the scales."

"Cards—*plural*?" Riley asked, her eyes wide. She jerked her gaze from Rose to Ava. "You mean there was more than one? You didn't tell me that!"

"Because you didn't need to know," Ava said, shrugging. She took a sip of her coffee. "The killer's not after you, so there's nothing for you to worry about. Why don't you go see if the garbage in the back needs to be taken out?"

Riley stared at her. She looked crestfallen, like Ava had just torn up a college acceptance letter in front of her face. Then, without a word, she turned and did what she was told.

Rose's gaze followed her. "I thought you guys got along."

"We do," Ava said, shrugging. "I just don't think she needs to be involved in this whole thing. It's getting dangerous, and I'm out. Joel's name is cleared, he's back home with you and Ellie, and that's all I care about."

The doorbell jangled, and both Rose and Ava turned to see Juanita come strolling inside, her hands full of grocery bags. She beamed at Rose and Ava, her dark eyes disappearing in a wave of smile.

"Good morning, girls!" Juanita called, joining Rose at the counter and setting an armful of bags down with a huff. "I'm headed to the food pantry, but a cappuccino was calling my name." She beamed at the two women. Then, realizing who was standing next to her, she laid a gentle hand on Rose's arm. "Oh, honey. How's Joel?"

"Actually, he's great!" Rose offered the woman a broad grin, as though in reassurance that her cheeriness was okay. "All clear! Of course, we *knew* that, but what with these creepy cards Ava's been getting that Joel couldn't have had anything to do with, I guess Greathouse finally saw the light."

"Oh, that's *wonderful*," Juanita gushed, squeezing Rose's hand. She gave Ellie a playful pinch to the cheek. "I knew it was just a matter of time. These things have a way of working themselves out—good always prevails."

Does it, though? Ava remembered the memorial page in Owen's yearbook. Good hadn't prevailed for Tiffany Martinez in 2007, and from what Owen had said, justice still hadn't been served even now. Ava felt for the woman and admired her ability to persevere through hard times. Ava snapped a lid on the top of the finished cappuccino and slid it across the counter.

"But what's this about cards?" Juanita wrinkled her brow. She handed a crisp bill to Ava.

"Oh, someone's been trying to scare me off with these nasty hand drawn tarot cards," Ava said, waving a hand to dismiss the subject. "It's not a big deal."

Juanita's eyes grew wide. This was apparently the first she'd heard of the lovely little gifts Ava had been receiving. "Are you sure? That sounds pretty threatening."

"I'm sure," Ava said firmly. "Greathouse is on it, and with Joel's name cleared, I'm happy to sit on the sidelines. Whoever killed Audrey can rest assured there's at least one less person after them."

"Hmm." Juanita sipped her coffee and nodded, staring off into space. "Well, I guess law enforcement will handle it."

The look on Juanita's face suggested she had her doubts about whether Shiloh's law enforcement would indeed handle things, and Ava thought again of Tiffany. Law enforcement hadn't come through for Juanita fifteen years ago.

"Well, I've got to get going," Rose announced. "I told Joel I wouldn't stay downtown long."

"Me too," Juanita agreed. "Thanks for the good news, Rose. And Ava—I get it. One murder's enough, we don't need you putting yourself in harm's way, too. You take care of yourself, alright?"

"I will." Ava permitted herself to flash Juanita a small smile.

The older woman left the shop with Rose, just as Riley reentered the store from the back, having finished her errand. The coffee shop was empty now, with only the hum of the refrigerator and the rumble of cars from the street outside filling the silence.

"So that's it?" Riley came around back of the counter and crossed her arms over her chest. "We don't find out who killed Audrey?"

Ava shrugged. "We will if Greathouse comes through with something."

"But what about that Moon card?" Riley asked. "Did you ever figure out what that meant?"

"Nope," Ava said, shaking her head. She lifted each of the urns of coffee, judging whether she needed to brew more.

Riley let out an exasperated sigh. "Can I look at your cards?"

"Are your hands clean?"

"What am I—two?" Riley looked incredulous. "I'm taking that as a yes."

Without even waiting for a reply, Riley pulled Ava's bag out from under the counter and began rifling through it. Ava was about to protest, but Riley, having found what she needed, had already extracted the cards and shoved the purse back onto the shelf. She riffled through the deck for a moment, then slapped a card down in front of Ava.

"Here. The Moon." Riley's voice was brusque. "I'm going to go do the dishes. You mull that over, and I'll be back."

Riley strode down the back hallway. The supply room door shut with a thump. Ava looked down at the card Riley had set in front of her. What did Riley think was going to happen? She'd have some kind of epiphany and they'd magically know who had killed Audrey Wilson? Apparently, Riley didn't understand yet how the tarot worked.

Still, the card was intriguing in light of recent events. The Moon card, full of rich, shadowy imagery, represented hidden facets, things not brought to light. A young woman sat on the edge of a window, gazing out at a glimmering moon. Or at least —one side was glimmering. The other, the one not shown in the card, was shrouded in shadow. The dark side of the moon. Another facet. The other side.

From the other room, the sound of Riley's voice rose in a dull hum. Ava looked up, thinking at first that the girl was talking to her, but then realized by the abrupt pauses in between the girl's sharp bursts of speech that she must be on the phone. That was strange. Riley didn't normally take phone calls during work hours. Ava shrugged it off, brought her gaze back to the Moon card.

The other side. Something tugged at Ava's brain. Fishing her phone out of her apron pocket, she opened her maps app and navigated to the payphone across the street from the elementary school. According to Ricky and Jodi, there were no security cameras on the payphone box itself, and the ones at the elementary school weren't positioned to capture anything across the street. But there was something Marge Harding had said... The Catholic church, right next to the payphone box, had been the object of several burglaries in recent years. Hadn't Marge said that the church installed cameras after that chain of events?

There it was: the other side.

RILEY CAME out of the supply room, drying her wet hands on a dish towel. She glanced at the Moon card still on the counter, but said nothing, instead pouring herself a glass of water from the pitcher inside the refrigerator.

"Were you on the phone in there?" Ava asked, trying to keep her demeanor uninterested.

"Yeah, sorry," Riley said. "My mom called. I had to take it."

"Ah."

They were quiet a moment. Ava was over trying to push her way into other people's business, and Riley seemed reluctant to share any details of the conversation. But then the door of Arcana swung open, and a bottle blonde woman stalked in, making the bell atop the door jangle wildly.

"Riley Marie," the woman barked, ignoring Ava. Her voice seemed too raspy for how young she must have been. At the sight of her lined, tired brown eyes, faint recognition dawned in Ava.

"*Mom*," Riley hissed, coming out from around the counter

as though she hoped to push her mother back out the doorway. "Not here! I told you I'd talk to you when I get home."

The woman gave a harsh laugh. "No, we're going to talk about it now." She shot a sharp glance at Ava and moved to tug Riley outside. "Excuse us."

"Um," Ava said, stepping out from behind the counter. She was hesitant to interject herself into the conversation, but something in Riley's face looked desperate. "Riley's on the clock right now. Is everything all right?"

"Everything's fine," Riley's mom said curtly. "But speaking of her being on the clock, you'd better start looking for a new employee—because this one's going to be clocking out, whether she likes it or not."

"I'm not sure what you mean," Ava said, her voice a little firmer now. She didn't know what Riley's mom was talking about, but she didn't appreciate her tone. Riley's face had gone crimson, her arms limp.

"I guess she hasn't told you yet." Riley's mom cast an irritated glance at her daughter. "Since she refuses to get along with her stepdad, she'll be going to live with her grandmother in Norfolk."

"*Mom*," Riley repeated. This time, Ava thought she heard the girl choke back a sob. "I *said*, we'll talk about it when I get home. Ava doesn't need this at her store."

"I don't even know when you're *coming* home these days, Riley, which is half the problem."

Suddenly, something clicked into place. Riley's presence at the cafe so early in the mornings, her apprehension about whoever had thrown the brick coming back. Riley's rumpled clothes didn't just *look* like she'd slept in them—she had. Who knew how many nights the girl had spent on the sofa at Arcana, dreading what awaited her at home? Ava couldn't believe it hadn't dawned on her sooner.

"Wait," Ava cut in. She turned to Riley. "You're moving? Because of your stepdad?"

Riley looked at her pleadingly, clearly embarrassed. She glanced at her mom, then back to Ava. "No, I—"

"Oh, yes, you are," Riley's mom interrupted. "I'm not putting up with you in my house any longer."

"*Wait*," Ava said again. She cleared her throat, amazed at her boldness. She'd never even officially met Riley's mother, and here she was, demanding that she let her talk. "Let me get this straight. Riley's having issues with her stepfather, and you're kicking *her* out?"

The woman scoffed. "Well, that makes it sound like *I'm* at fault, which, I can assure you, is not the case. This is a larger problem that's gone on for some time, and frankly, doesn't concern you."

"Now, I don't know about that," Ava said. She looked dubiously from Riley to her mother, unsure where her nerve was coming from. Hadn't she vowed just this morning that she wouldn't bother getting mixed up in anyone else's business?

"It's fine, Ava," Riley said, pulling away from her mother. "Mom and I will talk it out tonight at home. But she's right. You'd probably better look for a replacement—I should've told you sooner."

As Ava's gaze moved between the two of them, from Riley's desperate, downcast eyes to her mother's lined, too-tense face, she saw herself suddenly as a doe-eyed eighteen-year-old, dragged along by her mother as a college tour group made its way across campus. A second later, and she saw herself being driven to the Kappa Kappa Gamma house, pulled inside by her perfectly coiffed mother. And then—a memory of her own high-ceilinged dining room, of setting the seder table with shaking hands. Her mother behind her, with her tinkly laugh and too-wide, red-lipped smile, carrying on with the Passover plans as though her daughter hadn't just found damning texts on her son-in-law's phone. Funny how that musical laugh held so much power, how it could transform itself into grating, authoritative commands. *You'll give him another chance if you know what's good for you, Ava. Don't do something you're going to regret.*

But she hadn't regretted it—had she? Walking away from Noah had meant, for the first time, walking toward *herself*. Placing her mother's wants on the sidelines had meant placing her own needs first. The change was glorious, empowering, and she'd been trying desperately since then to safeguard the small life she'd begun to carve out for herself. But what good was that when the very people she cared about—her gaze flicked to Riley—had *their* needs ignored while she stood by watching? She knew better than anyone the helplessness that came from letting others call the shots. Riley was young, sure, but Shiloh was her *home*. Was this what she'd moved to Shiloh for, to watch another young girl being steamrolled over?

Ava cleared her throat. "Riley can stay with me."

Both Riley and her mother stared. Their eyes narrowed, as though they weren't sure they could have possibly heard correctly.

"I'm sorry." Riley's mom was the first to speak. "Did you just say Riley can *live* with you?"

"Yeah, actually," Ava said, surprised at the strength in her voice. She looked at Riley's stricken face and nearly laughed. "If the problem is that she's not getting along with her stepdad and the natural other place for her to go is her grandmother's, which is miles away, I guess I'll throw my hat in the ring as a candidate, too."

"Don't be ridiculous," Riley's mom said, looking uncomfortable. The terrain had shifted. "Sending her to family is one thing. Pushing her on a stranger is another story entirely."

"Well, first off," Ava countered. "I'm not a stranger. Riley and I get along fine, and I think she's comfortable with me. Second, it's not *pushing* when I'm offering."

"Oh, Ava, you don't have to—"

Ava cut Riley off. "I know I don't have to, but I want to. It's an easy fix—and it's only temporary. This way, you get to stay in Shiloh, your mom gets to keep her daughter around, and I get to keep my employee. I'd say it's a win for everyone."

"Well," Riley's mom said. Her voice was terse. "I'll have to think about it."

"For sure," Ava agreed, chancing a glance at Riley. The girl didn't make eye contact, just continued to stare at the floor, her eyes wide with shock. "It's up to you and your family. Take as long as you need—just know that I'm serious."

"Fine." Riley's mom averted Ava's gaze, clearly not accustomed to being the recipient of such gestures of goodwill.

"You know," Ava continued, hoping to save Riley the awkwardness that would almost certainly ensue once her mom left the shop and Riley and Ava were alone together. "Riley, why don't you take the rest of the afternoon off to sort this out with your parents?"

Riley frowned. "Are you sure? You don't need me to...?"

Ava nodded, gesturing around at the empty store. "I'm sure. Business isn't exactly popping today, as you can see."

"Okay..." Riley looked skeptical, but she folded the dishtowel she held in her hand and set it on the counter. "You want me back in for closing?"

Ava shook her head, smiling. "Nope. I'm good. Get out of here! You guys have some important stuff to discuss."

Riley offered Ava a small grin, her dark eyes flashing beneath her shaggy bangs. Not having to be told three times, she scampered to the supply room to grab her backpack and, returning, tapped her mom on the shoulder. On their way out, Riley's mom shot Ava a dubious glance, as though she didn't yet trust what she'd just heard. Something in the air had shattered, though, some tension now released.

Now alone in the shop, Ava let out a shuddery breath, her whole body coursing with adrenaline. Where had that *come* from? Had she seriously just asked Riley's parents to let their daughter *live* with her? Ava laughed shakily to herself. She was thirty-three years old. Divorced. Barely back on her feet herself. Money was tight. What business did she have taking in a *teenager*? One by one, she plucked the thoughts from her mind and discarded them. They were only that: thoughts. She'd made the right decision. She knew it, and she hoped Riley's mother would come to realize it, too.

As she ground more beans for that afternoon's coffee, her mind strayed back to the Moon card Riley had plunked down before all hell had broken loose. *The other side. The other side of the street.* It had to be what she was missing... right? What if, unlike the elementary school, the cameras outside the Catholic church captured the payphone in their view? If she could just —*no*. Ava took a deep breath, shaking her head at herself. The killer's message had been clear: *Back off or you're next.* And anyway, she'd vowed not to get involved with other people anymore, to mind her own business. She'd already failed at that, obviously, by inviting Riley to live with her, but now was her chance to keep her distance. She'd stick to her own life...

...after checking out this one last thing. What if following through on this could help catch Audrey's killer? Bring some closure to the town this time? Ava's heart was hammering, still high on adrenaline. She pulled out her phone again, opened the maps app where the payphone was still in view, and zoomed in on the church. She clicked on it, scrolling through the entry for contact details. There was a phone number, but what would she even say?

Ava followed the entry to the linked website and scanned the church's contact details. *Aha!* An email address for the office. That was better. She'd at least have a chance to think how to word things so they'd be open to letting her check the footage—and Audrey's killer wouldn't have tabs on her email. It was worth a shot. She didn't have much else. Ava clicked the email address, and a new message appeared in her email app. How to start? *Hey Catholic church people, I think your security cameras may have caught a killer, and I'd like to see the footage?* They didn't know her. She wasn't even Catholic, for god's sake! She was Jewish *and* a tarot reader, which meant the Catholic church was probably going to be skeptical. Still—surely that wouldn't matter in circumstances like these? *It's not like I'm trying to get in on any sacraments.*

Hoping for the best, Ava began her email. She kept it short and sweet, simply introducing herself as a newcomer in town and summing up the idea she'd had about the payphone. She muttered a desperate prayer as she clicked send. Perhaps the dark side of the metaphorical moon was about to be revealed.

19

———

It was just after lunch, and Ava was still drumming her fingers on the counter, waiting for a reply from St. Patrick's. The front door swung open, and Tim Meyer meandered into the cafe, his hair windswept.

"Afternoon, Ava." The door clanged shut behind him, as though some invisible force had slammed it. Tim cast a fretful look outside. "It's getting awfully blustery out there."

"No kidding," Ava said, also casting a quick peek out the window. Tim was right; the boughs of the trees strained against the wind, and a mournful whistle swept through the crack beneath the door. "We might not be in Kansas anymore soon."

"Ha!" Tim let out a barking laugh, then shuddered. "Just so long as we don't end up in Iowa. Seriously, though, it's getting bad out there. You might want to think about closing up early today."

"It'll be fine." Ava waved a hand, but offered Tim a small smile. She knew he was looking out for her, but she didn't see any other shops rushing to close. Anyway, she wasn't afraid of a little wind. What she *was* afraid of was her email going to the St. Patrick's spam folder.

Tim shrugged. "Suit yourself. I heard on the radio they issued a tornado watch, so I guess just keep an eye out."

"Sure. Cappuccino?"

"You got it," Tim confirmed with a nod. As Ava set to work steaming a pitcher of milk, Tim gazed out the window. "I see Lucas Wilson is hard at work out there. Heard the city hired him to look after the flowerbeds—and I have to hand it to him, he may not be the world's nicest guy, but he's certainly diligent."

Ava followed Tim's gaze out across the street, to where Lucas was bent over the flower beds, setting up cloches over each cluster of sprouts. He'd been there all afternoon, and his sinewy shoulders were considerably pinker than when he'd started.

"I suppose," Ava replied, speaking over the hiss of the steaming wand. "I've only met him once."

Tim looked amused. "That bad, huh?"

"Well... Let's just say he wasn't exactly torn up about his sister's death." Ava stirred the freshly steamed milk into the espresso in the bottom of a takeout cup.

"I'm not surprised. It's sad, but that's just how things always were between them. I imagine he felt resentful, knowing his stepsister was the favorite, and that he—the flesh and blood kin—was seen as the failure."

Tim's explanation made logical sense, but Ava couldn't imagine it. She knew a bit about being seen as the failure of the family, but she would never rejoice if her brother, Aaron, died. She snapped a lid onto Tim's cappuccino, swiped his credit card, and handed him the receipt.

"Thank you much," Tim said, turning to go. He gave her a mock salute on his way out, stopping in the doorway. "Remember—keep an eye on that sky out there."

As Tim made his way down the sidewalk, Ava stood at the counter, watching Lucas as he crossed the street to tend the flowers next to Arcana. Interesting how the people of Shiloh seemed so ready to excuse his nastiness. Was this just how he'd always been, even as a child? In her mind, showing no remorse at the death of one's sibling seemed cause for suspicion. According to Greathouse, Lucas had been at a hotel in Omaha the night of Audrey's murder and busy doing landscaping work during Ricky's attack. Apparently, both stories checked out, but Ava still had her doubts. Sneaking out of a hotel while you were still checked in wasn't impossible.

Ava glanced down the street. Aside from Lucas and a few other stragglers, Main Street was nearly deserted. Lucas had straightened from his hunch over the flower beds and was now talking on the phone, his face drawn and tight. He seemed to be spitting his words. Just then, something skittered past the window, drawing Ava's gaze. Her easel! The sandwich board she used to display the daily roasts was skidding down the sidewalk, blown along by the wind. Apron still tied around her waist, Ava dove out the door and took off after it.

Luckily, the sandwich board only made it a block before it clattered against a lamp post and toppled over. Wrestling against the wind, Ava tucked the easel under one arm and trudged back toward her shop. When she reached the front door, she stopped, panting. Lucas stood with his back to her, still snarling into the phone, but his voice was hard to hear over the rattle of the wind in the leaves above her. He seemed not to have noticed Ava.

"God, you act like I *planned* it." Lucas's voice was sharp over the whipping wind. Ava's ears perked up. *Planned what?* "No—I can't deal with the courts right now. I'm trying to *fix it*. I don't know what else you want me to *do*."

There was a note of desperation in Lucas's voice that made Ava squirm. She knew she should go inside.

Lucas stabbed an angry finger at his phone screen, shoved the device into his pocket, and ran a hand through his hair. He gazed at the heavy sky, as though not sure what to do with himself. It was only as he brought his head back down that he turned around, his gaze falling on Ava. Their eyes locked for a split second.

"I'd stay in my lane if I were you," Lucas said, his voice eerily calm, eyes boring holes into Ava.

She managed a weak smile, looked away. "Just retrieving my sandwich board."

Lucas snorted. He looked up at the sky again. "Right. There's a storm coming in, and you're just out getting your sandwich board."

Ava held up her hands in a conciliatory gesture. She wasn't about to explain the situation further. She rose from her perch on the bench and went back inside. From behind the counter, she could see Lucas's eyes trained on her, even through the window. She wasn't sure what had just happened, but it had definitely been bizarre.

Ava pulled out her phone, navigated to the local weather channel on her browser. Sure enough, there was a yellow tornado watch banner at the top of the page. She glanced out the window again, glad to see that Lucas had moved on down the block, resuming his work in the flower beds. What *was* that conversation she'd just overheard? What had Lucas done despite not planning? And what was he trying to fix? Suddenly, she was desperate to tell Owen. He'd have a theory, no doubt—but she hadn't heard from him since the previous night. All morning long, her phone had been burning in her apron pocket, and she'd had to resist the urge to pull it out every five seconds to check if he'd returned her call from the night before. But every time she allowed herself a peek—nothing. Radio silence.

Before she could convince herself not to, Ava shot him off a text.

Hey. I'm really sorry about last night. Can we talk?

P.S. I just heard Lucas on a pretty tense phone call.

P.P.S. I think the Catholic church has security cameras.

She hated herself almost as soon as she hit send, but she couldn't help it. The stupidity of it all made her want to bang her head against the espresso machine in frustration. *You're weak, Ava. Weak.*

As expected, no return text came. Her phone remained painfully silent. To distract herself, Ava opened her email, crossing her fingers as she scrolled through her inbox. *Please, please, please let there be a reply.*

There was.

Her heart sped up. She was almost afraid to read the message—what if they said no? After all, someone making such a request might be a would-be burglar trying to get a lay of the land and camera angles ahead of time. Forcing herself to open the email, Ava scanned the text.

Dear Ms. Goldberg,

Thanks for reaching out to us. We are, of course, deeply saddened by the loss of Ms. Wilson.

As an upstanding member of our parish, she will be missed

greatly, and for this reason, we'd be happy to let you view our footage if there is a possibility it could lead to bringing her killer to justice. Would you be able to come around four o'clock this afternoon? No church activities are planned, and the office will be open. Please ask for Patricia.

Thank you,

Patricia MacDougal

St. Patrick's Church, Office Administrator

It was all Ava could do to keep from shrieking. This was it; she could feel it. She was *this* close to a break in Audrey's murder case. If she remembered correctly, the payphone box stood near the curb, while St. Patrick's was set further in from the street, meaning that any camera installed over the entrance pointing outward would also catch the payphone. Or so she hoped. She didn't want to think about the alternative.

Great! Ava typed. *I'll be over at four. Thank you for your help, and I look forward to meeting you.* She hit send, stuck her phone back in her pocket. Although the sky outside had taken on a hazy green shade, Ava's day was now looking brighter.

AT AROUND THREE THIRTY, the rain started up, drizzling at first and then coming in torrents of cold, rippling waves blown about by the wind. With the slick cobblestone streets outside empty, no customers had been in the shop for nearly two hours. It was only Ava, alone with the ticking of the clock on the wall and the violent pelt of rain against the windows. Ava scooped the change out of the cash register and began to count. Her hands were jittery; she couldn't tell if it was from too much coffee, from the turmoil outside that meant the storm was sure to be fierce, or from the anticipation of what she hoped to find at the church. Things were finally coming together. Not only was Joel cleared of charges, but she was finally on to something with the case—Owen's silence be damned. He still hadn't replied to her text.

Having already swept the store and loaded the dishwasher, it didn't take long for Ava to finish closing the shop. She gave the books on the coffee table one last stack for good measure, threw a drop cloth over the cash register and espresso bar, and zipped up her jacket, bracing herself for a torrent of brittle wind. Ava stepped out into the strange, warm rain. Only a few straggling people, whom Ava didn't recognize, braved Main Street, their jackets pulled tight around them, heads down to avoid the whip of the wind. The rest of the stores had already dimmed their lights, but the smell of pizza that wafted toward Ava as she made her way west down Main Street was a comforting presence. Something to add to the evening plan after she'd accomplished her mission.

Turning the corner, Ava headed north in the direction she and Owen had gone while tailing Jodi Laughlin. The uneven sidewalk was littered with puddles, and she dodged one after the other, hoping she might get lucky on the sock front and make it home with dry feet. Not only had she not had the sense to take the car that morning, but she'd also decided it would be the perfect morning for a little walk and had left her bicycle at home, too. *Ha. Talk about perfect timing.* There wasn't much of a walk left until she reached the church, so she'd just have to hope she didn't ooze dirty rainwater all over a hardwood floor. She was no Catholic, but ruining someone's hardwood floor was bound to be up there on the list of cardinal sins, she imagined.

The church was dark as it came into view, but the sun, still high in the west, made an appearance from behind the green, surly clouds, glittering across the stained-glass windows in an almost melancholy way. Ava stopped short for a moment, relishing the way the bits of fragmented crystal caught the light and sent it shimmering in all directions. It was almost like the story her grandfather had told from the Zohar, of the eternal Light of the Universe pouring itself into the Vessel, which could not contain it and shattered into trillions of fractals, which all the souls of all the ages were constantly attempting to put back together. Religions were all kind of the same when you stopped to think about it. She was glad her grandfather had taught her to see the light in all of them, the way she now admired the glorious sunset as it glistened though the church and was sent beaming outwards.

As Ava made her way up the sidewalk leading to the huge stone steps in front of the church, she groaned. Caught up in the rapture of the stained-glass windows, she'd missed sight of the gigantic puddle of mud standing between her and the steps. The sidewalk was sunken down into the earth, where the ground must have given way some time before, and the rainwater had come rushing down to fill the space. Ava glanced about for a way around the mud hole, wondering if she could detour onto the street and circle around to the steps from the other side. But no, the mud stretched all the way out in front of the stone steps, making a detour pointless. She'd have to cross over it no matter what direction she came from. There was no getting around it—except to jump and hope for the best. Creeping up to the edge of the puddle, Ava pounced, propelling herself forward in her attempt to clear the puddle and land on the bottom step. She had a brief second of relief as her soles hit the step, but then—*splat*. Her heels, still hanging off the edge of the step, slipped backwards and it was all she could do to clutch at the railing as her feet sloshed into the murky, slimy mud. Ava let out a sigh, then laughed aloud. Well—at least she'd saved her *whole* self from falling into the mud. And at least her sneakers were black, not white. Not that she *owned* anything white.

Doing her best to scrape the fresh mud off her shoes as she went, Ava traipsed up the stairs. A note was taped to the front door that read: *In west meeting room*. There was more than one meeting room? Ava wasn't one to know her directions, but she'd find it. She pulled the note down, stuffed it in her pocket, and tried the front door. It was open—very different from the temples she'd visited in recent years where security guards were posted, even on Shabbat. It worked in her favor now. The church was dim as she stepped inside, giving her feet one last scrape on the concrete steps, and pulling the immense door gently shut behind her. She hoped the note was recent, and that Patricia would still be here, what with the storm that was rolling in. She'd checked her email, and there'd been no update.

Inside, Ava stood in a stone foyer. A small fountain stood nearby, which she knew from her temple youth field trips held the holy water. It had been a long time since she'd been in a church, and she stopped for a moment to breathe in the silence. All was quiet. She could see the ever fading sunlight still glowing a glorious pink through the vast windows inside the sanctuary just ahead. Hoping she wasn't tracking in mud, Ava stepped across the foyer and into the sanctuary, enjoying the muffled thump of her footsteps on the stone.

Ava considered calling out to announce her presence, but

then thought better of it. She wasn't sure how Catholic prayer worked—might there be people praying somewhere or some kind of rule about making noise inside the building? The men in her mother's family all prayed three times a day, and she knew there were congregants in and out of the synagogue all day, but this seemed to be different. So far, the church seemed empty—except for Patricia, who was, allegedly, in the west meeting room. Ava reached a hand into her pocket to touch the note Patricia had left for her. Something nagged at her mind, but she couldn't think what it was.

Ava walked down the aisle, running a hand along the smooth backs of the pews and breathing in the fresh smell of polished wood mingled with the mustiness of the old building. It was exactly the right smell for a church if there was such a thing. Gazing around her, Ava's eyes traveled up to the high vaulted ceilings and the many paintings that lined the walls all the way around the sanctuary. The stations of the cross—or something like that. She remembered she'd learned it that time on the field trip, and it had struck her as interesting. The paintings led clockwise around the room, following the tragic journey of Jesus on his way to be executed, culminating in the somber, emaciated figure of the man himself, hanging off a large marble cross at the very front of the sanctuary. Ava shuddered. It wasn't the sight you wanted to see when you were alone in a strange building, coming to see someone about potential footage of a murderer.

Having reached the altar, Ava spun back around to survey the part of the church she'd just come from. There was no sign of anyone. No noise, no voices, no footsteps, no music. Perhaps Patricia had indeed gone home. But the church had been unlocked—were church buildings supposed to remain unlocked outside of church hours? There were two doors at the front of the church, one on either side of the sanctuary. Which way was west? Choosing as best she could, Ava veered to the left and opened the door to darkness. She was starting to get a strange feeling about being inside the building. Perhaps she should have called to confirm with Patricia, rather than just emailing.

"Hello?" Ava called softly, her voice jarring in the heavy silence of the church. With no answer, she tried again, this time louder. "Hello? Is anyone here?"

There was a slight echo as her words danced through the open door and hit against the tall, stone walls of the sanctuary. Other than the echo, however, there was no response. Where *was* she? Was this the west meeting room? Guided by the sliver of fading, eerie sunlight that shone through from the sanctuary behind her, Ava fumbled her hand along the wall and hit upon a light switch. The room flickered to life, but only dimly, as Ava stood in place and glanced around the room. On the far wall stood what looked to be an enormous wardrobe, beautifully ornate and made of heavy, polished wood. *Ah*, Ava thought, still recalling her field trip. *The confessional.* Although she doubted it was the room she was looking for, Ava found herself nagged by curiosity. Did one have to make an appointment for confession? Or was there always a priest around during certain hours —maybe *these* hours? As she stepped forward to get a better look at the confessional, she reasoned that perhaps Father Henley was around somewhere and might know how to get in touch with Patricia.

Suddenly, a heavy thud sounded behind her. The door she'd just come through had slammed shut. As Ava whipped around, wondering if Father Henley had come blustering through the door, she stopped short. The feeling that had been nagging at her flicked instantly into focus. Patricia's note on the door featured purple dots. She knew where she'd seen that paper before—the note the police had found in Audrey's pocket that was supposed to be from Joel. But what sense did that make?

Just then, someone stepped inside the door, alright, but that someone was *not* the Father.

20

"What—what are *you* doing here?" Ava demanded, backing toward the confessional. She felt herself shrink. Something was wrong. Very wrong. He was looking at her with pity, like a tom cat might look at a poor little mouse it's cornered before it goes in for the killing pounce.

Chris's smile was thin, cold. "I'm on the church board. Don't you remember?"

A wave of icy fear washed over her as her limbs froze. Chris's reply was straightforward, but there was something about his tone of voice that made her blood run cold.

"I... No, I don't remember," Ava stammered. But, of course, she did. He had mentioned it, hadn't he? That night at the committee dinner? The night before Audrey died? The night before he... "It was *you*."

Chris's lips parted from their snaky smile into a wide grin. His normally dazzling teeth now shone like fangs in the dim light of the confessional room. He stretched his arms out wide and shrugged his shoulders. "You got me—I confess."

The full realization of the words Chris had just uttered hit

Ava like a ton of bricks. And the irony of their standing in the confessional of the very congregation Chris was supposed to be serving was sickening. All this time...

"But—*why*?"

He was suddenly serious, all trace of irony or sinister glee gone.

"Hand over your phone," he demanded, taking a step closer. He reached out an open palm and snapped his fingers once. His tone was sharp. "Give it."

Ava's mind raced, thoughts flying in and swirling around faster than they ever had. Her phone was her only lifeline. If she gave it to Chris, there would be no contacting anyone, no stealthily calling Greathouse to come to her rescue, no alerting Owen. No alerting *anyone*.

"Goldberg," Chris said, drawing out her name as he took another step toward her, his other hand reaching behind him. With a click, he brought out that hand, which clenched a small pistol. "I'm warning you."

She had no choice. Ava slid her phone out of her jeans pocket and raised her other hand in the air where he could see it, carefully placing her iPhone on the floor instead of in his hand. No way was she going to move any closer to him—although the few feet of distance between them wouldn't make much difference if Chris decided to shoot her. Still keeping her gaze trained on Chris, she slid the phone along the paneled hardwood floor in his direction. He snatched it up, also keeping his eyes on her.

"That's better," he said, pocketing the phone. "Now, you want to know *why*. You realize if I tell you, it means you're not making it out of here alive?"

Ava seriously doubted she'd be making it out of St. Patrick's alive at all, regardless of whether he told her why he'd killed Audrey. But her mind was still working, still flicking through various scenarios, running through possible courses of action. Perhaps if she could buy time, stall him a little longer, keep him talking, she'd come up with a solution. She couldn't for the life of her think what the solution would be, what with him holding the gun and herself defenseless, but time had seemed to slow down, making her thoughts sharp and clear despite the panic in her chest.

"I gathered that, yes." Ava swallowed, her throat dry. She flicked her eyes around the room, trying to spot any potential escape routes without taking her eyes off Chris for longer than a second.

Chris laughed hoarsely, still pointing the gun at her. "I've gone to this church since I could walk, Goldberg. I know this place like the back of my hand. There's no way out but the door behind us."

"Okay," Ava said, raising her hands, as if in surrender. It was probably safer to just agree with him, make him think she'd given up the thought of escape. "Tell me why. Why Audrey? What'd she ever do to you?"

There was that throaty laugh again. Chris ran his free hand through his sweaty hair. "Oh, she's done *plenty*, don't you worry. She wasn't the standup woman this town thought she was." He stopped for a second, his eyes going distant. "But this time, it wasn't about what she *did*. It was about what she was *going* to do. I've got a family to provide for—you know that, Goldberg? And she..."

Ava wasn't sure what Chris was trying to say. Then a thought occurred to her. "Did you put that senior photo in Audrey's desk?"

Chris's face was hard, stony. "Oh, you found that, did you? Yes, it was a little reminder. Let her know that if she got any ideas about ratting me out, I could just as easily do the same."

"So you were blackmailing her…"

"I prefer to call it evening the playing field. Only it didn't work."

Ava's mind struggled to piece together the fragments of the story. There was something Audrey Wilson had discovered about Chris, something that Chris was so desperate to keep quiet that he'd resorted to blackmail and eventually murder to keep the secret safe. And there was something Audrey Wilson had done, perhaps years ago, that Chris knew about and had wanted to remind her of. Suddenly, something clicked, and a white-hot heat flooded Ava's stomach and limbs.

"Tiffany Martinez," she whispered, more to herself than to Chris.

Chris's thin lips turned up into a sneer. "You're not as loopy as this town thinks you are."

Ava ignored his comment. She knew it wasn't the smartest thing to do, egging on a killer, but she couldn't keep herself from barreling ahead. She *had* to know. "Tiffany Martinez died in 2007. Her senior year. *Your* senior year—and Audrey's. Audrey had something to do with it, and you knew. All these years."

Outside, the wind howled, sweeping through the walls of the old church with a groan. Ava wondered whether she'd prefer to be swept up inside a raging, twisting funnel cloud or killed here by Chris. With each minute she stood there, legs braced and barely daring to breathe, both possibilities seemed more and more plausible.

"You bet she had something to do with Tiffany's death. She killed her. Mowed her down in cold blood."

Chris's eyes were doing their distant thing again, and he took a step toward Ava. The gun was still clenched in his fist, the hammer still cocked. Ava did her best to hide her shudder. She had to keep him talking, make him feel like she understood what he'd done. It was her only chance at survival.

"What did she do, Chris?" Ava worked to keep her voice soft, her tone understanding. It was hard, though, with that gun still pointed at her.

Chris spoke through gritted teeth. "There was a party that night. At one of the senior's houses. Of course, I wasn't invited —never was—but I was out that night, too. I was biking home when it happened. They'd had a lot to drink—they always did —" Here, he scowled with disgust, shaking the gun. "I pulled up at the four-way stop just outside of town. I was on my bike going east, and there was a car coming down Main Street. Someone was walking through the crosswalk, and I wanted to let them pass. It looked like Tiffany, teetering around in her heels, but I wasn't sure. I figured the SUV would stop, too, but it didn't—it just kept barreling down Main Street, flew right through the four-way stop, and—" Chris's voice broke, and he paused for a moment, regaining composure over himself. "There was a crunch, and then cracking. It was Tiffany's bones breaking as the SUV slammed straight into her and then kept on driving. Tiffany's body was flipping under the SUV and the driver never even stopped. It was only after she'd passed me and I realized who the driver was that she finally slowed down. We made eye contact, and she knew that I knew."

Ava's eyes closed. Hearing Chris say the words was awful enough; she couldn't imagine what seeing it happen would've been like. What living with that secret for over a decade would've felt like. There really was a dark side to every moon.

"Why didn't you say anything?" Not wanting to provoke him, she tried to keep her voice steady and curious. Non-accusatory.

Chris gave a harsh laugh. "Accuse Shiloh's golden girl of drunk driving? Of *manslaughter*? As if they would've believed me. And her parents—they would've sued the hell out of mine for defamation, and we were already living in the trailer park. Yeah, right. And now? She just laughed at me. Said I had no evidence, it would just sound like a desperate effort to save myself." He shook his head, still with the same bitter smile on his stony face.

"Save yourself from what? What did Audrey have on you that was so bad you'd threaten to come out with such a damning secret?"

Chris looked somber, almost sorry. "She found out. I got myself in some trouble with some pretty powerful folks, and I needed to... borrow some money. From the firm. Audrey found out, and of *course* she had to be the golden girl again, felt it was her duty to *say* something."

"You were embezzling from the firm?" The words popped out of Ava's mouth before she realized it. She was still trying to make sense of what Chris was saying.

This time, Chris shook the gun, his face cracking. "I borrowed it—didn't you hear me? I *borrowed* it, and of *course* I had to sign those checks to do it. And Audrey had no right—"

His voice broke, but it was all Ava needed to hear. Things were sliding into place. She kept her eyes on Chris, her hands raised. Clearly, having to admit he'd stolen money from the firm was harder than admitting he'd murdered a woman, and

Ava didn't want to push him further. The anguish on his sweaty face already looked as though he might shatter into a blind rage at any moment—and then there was no telling what he might do. God knew he'd done it before.

"Okay," Ava said, taking two slow, almost imperceptible steps backward. Her mind was still racing, frantic. By the look on Chris's face, he'd nearly reached his limit. She was running out of time. Then, a thought struck her. "Where's Patricia? The woman from the office. Did you... hurt her?"

Chris barked a hoarse laugh. "Patricia was never going to be here. In fact, Patricia never read your email. *I* got your email, and *I* replied to it. It was almost too easy. I knew you were on to something, that I'd have to do something about it aside from those dumb cards, but I never dreamed you'd be so stupid as to walk *right* into my hands. You spun your own web, Goldberg."

"I don't... I don't understand..." She had to buy more time. Her back was to the confessional booth now, and Chris had taken two more menacing steps toward her. He was closing the distance between them.

"Oh, you *idiot*," Chris spat. "You think you're so smart, waltzing in here like you're some kind of private eye, screwing over everything I've worked for. If you paid attention to *anything*, you'd have remembered that I'm on the board at St. Patrick's, meaning I have access to the administration email. I guess you've never replied to an email and then hit delete. Nah, you're too good for that. Just like *her*, perfect little Audrey Wilson. But we all know you fools have got skeletons you're hiding." He laughed bitterly.

"Chris," Ava said, the panic rising in her chest as he took yet another step closer. "Please put the gun down. We can work something out. We can—"

"You think I'd ever believe you'd keep your trap shut?" Chris's eyes were narrow slits. "Ricky forced me to deal with him the hard way, going after that reward. I tried to do it the easy way with you—scare you off. Get you to mind your own business. You should've listened when you had the chance."

"Please," Ava said, her voice high. Panic clenched her throat. Her mind tumbled, shrieking. *Do something!* "I'd never breathe a word. We could just walk out of here. There's a storm coming. We could—"

"SHUT UP!" Chris roared, his eyes bulging from their sockets. His once placid face wrenched with anger, a mottled red crept up from his neck. "And speaking of the storm—when that storm hits, when they find the nice little Jewish girl dead from a falling branch or whatever I can find to place next to you after I whack your head in, the storm will be the culprit." He smiled an icy smile, all pleasantness gone.

Bile rose in Ava's throat along with the panic. She swallowed it back, searching her mind for any last-ditch ideas. Tearing her eyes from Chris's, daring to glance around once more in search of—what? A weapon? The only weapon there might be inside the church was already in Chris's hand.

As Chris stepped menacingly toward her, Ava's hands lowered, as if in resignation. Her luck had run out... And then she remembered. Her good luck charm. She heard the whisper:

Get him good.

The whisper entered her mind at the same time as the idea, flickering once before fading completely. And in their place, a glowing warmth remained—like an enveloping arm around her shoulder. The nape of her neck prickled. When Zaidy Mel had pressed the crystal into her palm, curling her fingers over it, he'd squeezed his own hand around hers. That same warmth. And now, as Ava inched her fingers toward her jeans pocket as imperceptibly as she could, she could almost see the crinkle of her grandfather's smiling eyes again.

"But..." She had to keep Chris talking, had to distract him from her hand's movement. A quaver warbled her voice—her one last plan terrified her, but it was her only option. "You framed Joel..." She forced her tone to hold a question, coax a response.

"Joel Robinson had life rolled out for him like a red carpet," Chris spat, disgusted by the very thought. "It was about time things took a turn for him. Let him know how the rest of us feel for a change. Audrey was always obsessed with him—everyone knew it. And given enough time, she would've won him over. All it took was a little planning. It's not like it's hard to discreetly slip a flashlight inside a closet while you're at the gym. I almost couldn't believe my good luck when they sent his stupid jacket home with *my* dry cleaning, and a handwritten grocery list in the pocket to boot. It's what got my wheels turning in the first place. Can you really blame me?" He barked out a laugh. Still holding the cocked gun at his side, Chris looked Ava full in the face.

Ava remained silent, closing her fingers around the crystal in her pocket, and met Chris's gaze with full ferocity, aware of the rush of energy that flooded through her. As Chris lunged at her with a roar, butt of the gun held high, she slid her fist lithely out of her pocket and, with an accuracy she'd never managed before in her life, hurled the crystal at Chris's face with all her strength. Chris's head jerked back in shock, and the gun went flying, landing with a clatter on the tile floor. Ava swept the skittering gun off the floor and bolted, hurling her body as fast as she could toward the door like a woman possessed. As she reached the doorknob, the door opened outwards, and she fell, landing against something—*someone*—solid who stood tall in the doorway.

Owen's sinewy arms gripped her shoulders, moved her deftly out of the way and shoved her through the door back toward the sanctuary. She turned, gasping for air and still clutching Chris's pistol in her shaking hands. She saw Owen take a step toward Chris. Cocked up at his shoulder, he had the muzzle of his shotgun trained on Chris.

"Hands in the air, Chris," Owen said, his voice steady over the howling of the wind outside. Owen's now hardened green eyes held Chris in place, his words fearless. "That's it. Where I can see 'em. You've done more damage to this little town than any storm ever could."

21

———

What happened next was a blur—so much so that as Ava sat at the police station that evening, a paper cup of weak coffee between her hands, she could hardly recall in what order things had happened, or whether they'd even happened at all. The storm had passed, the tornado skirting only the very southern edge of town, leaving in its wake a quiet, pure sort of calm. Chris's confession, Audrey's secret... the butt of the gun just feet from her face as she hurled that hunk of lapis lazuli and threw herself across the room. Owen's chest solid beneath her cheek. His hands gripping her shoulders. The howling of the wind. It all seemed like a faraway dream, but the images in her mind were sharp, impossible to forget. She shuddered.

A throat cleared near her. She looked up. Chief Greathouse stood over her, his mouth and eyebrows each drawn into a thin line across his face.

"You alright?" The chief sat down in the metal folding chair across from her. He spread his knees out, leaned back in the chair so it creaked. His gaze was fixed on her, concern in his dark eyes.

"I think so," Ava said weakly, forcing herself to take a sip of the horrible coffee. If only they had let her make a stop at Arcana to brew a mug of dark roast...

"You look like hell," the chief said, a smile toying at the edges of his somber mouth.

"I feel like it, too," Ava shot back, returning the smile.

"You're awfully lucky that youngest O'Kelly is sweet on you," the chief remarked, raising the line of his brow. "If he hadn't gone looking for you during the storm, seen those muddy tracks on the church steps..." Greathouse shook his head, like he didn't want to imagine what might have happened.

Ava felt her cheeks go red. She wasn't sure which was more embarrassing—the fact she'd somehow fancied herself as perfectly safe while walking right into a killer's trap, or that the chief of police had noticed Owen's more than friendly feelings for her. She ignored the latter. "I know. I was an idiot. I just—"

"—wanted to make sure a friend's name was cleared for good." Greathouse looked pointedly at her, and Ava thought she saw a hint of pride in his face. Approval? It was the look her father had given her when the principal sent her home from school for slapping the girl who'd been bullying the quiet girl in class.

"Yeah."

"Now, I expect this'll hit the news pretty quick," Greathouse remarked. "Have you talked to your folks yet? I know they don't live here."

Ava paused, then shook her head. "Not yet. I'll talk to them soon."

The chief was right. Regardless of how her parents felt about her recent life decisions, they deserved to hear about the whole ordeal before they saw it on Facebook. They were family, after all. And speaking of family—

"What about Katie?" Ava blurted out, the thought suddenly occurring to her. "Chris's wife, Katie. She's eight months pregnant—does she *know*?"

Greathouse winced, gave a gruff nod. "Not only does she know, but the shock sent her straight into labor. I expect we'll know more soon. That poor woman."

"That poor woman is right," Ava groaned. She didn't know Katie Mitchell well, in truth had only met her once, but she'd seemed lovely. Ava couldn't even imagine what feelings the woman must be grappling with—the downfall of her husband and the birth of her child at the same moment. She was going to need an incredible outpouring of support from the community, but Ava was sure the people of Shiloh would rise to the occasion. Just then, a thought entered her mind. "Is Chris even talking—now that he's in custody?"

Greathouse stroked his mustache, nodding. "He knows the jig is up. He came clean about everything—going after Ricky because he wanted him to quit trying for that reward, tampering with Audrey's phone. Which, by the way,"—he pointed a stern finger at Ava— "You be careful if you get one of them phones with that newfangled face recognition business. Turns out you can fool 'em with a picture."

"Got it, chief," Ava said, nodding back. She suppressed a smile. "And speaking of Ricky..."

"He's doing okay," Chief Greathouse said. "He's still recovering, but he's home now. Shocked to hear it was Chris Mitchell who tried to kill him—like the rest of us are."

Ava nodded. She still wasn't sure what to think of the gruff mechanic for whom most of the town seemed to have a soft spot, but she was relieved to hear he was on the mend. "And what about Lucas Wilson? I... Well, I overheard him on a weird phone call before I headed for the church..."

Chief Greathouse clucked his tongue. "You weren't going to give that up, were you? Well, I'll tell you—but it stays between us, alright? When Lucas came in for questioning, he told us the *real* reason he decided to start his own landscaping business in a place he feels stable. Apparently, he and his girlfriend had a kid about six months ago, but now that they're broken up, she's threatening to ask the courts for full custody. He's doing what he can to prove he can provide a stable home."

Ava's heart sank. *Poor Lucas.* She wouldn't have pegged him for a family man, but what did she know? If there was one thing she'd learned over the last week—hell, the last twenty-four hours—it was that everyone's lives are infinitely more faceted than what they show the world.

"Well, he's got an inheritance coming to him now," Greathouse said, thumping the desk in front of him as though that was that. "Lucas will be all right. But speaking of money..."

Ava looked at him questioningly, waited for him to continue. *Cafe Arcana's not going under yet, Chief, if that's what you're insinuating.*

"It just dawned on me that *you* have some reward money coming your way." Greathouse held Ava's gaze, his mustache quivering.

Ava was still. For a few seconds, she barely dared to breathe, afraid that even the smallest of movements would wake her from what *had* to be a dream. She'd forgotten all about the reward money that Audrey's family had offered. "Me?"

"Yes, you," Greathouse said, chuckling. "As stupid as you were to go to that church on your own."

Ava's heart surged with relief. That reward was $50,000. It would give her more than a little wiggle room as she worked to make Cafe Arcana into the thriving shop she knew it could be.

She waved away the chief's well-meaning jab with a flick of her hand, trying to keep her excitement under wraps. She didn't want him to think she'd gotten involved in the case only for personal gain. "Well—that's great."

Greathouse studied her for a minute, a smile playing below his waggling mustache. Then, leaning forward, he stuck out his hand for Ava to shake. "That it is. And by the way, Ava, contrary to what I may have said before—you've got a good head on your shoulders. I commend that. Your grandfather would be proud of you."

Zaidy. It was thanks to him she'd remembered the crystal. If it hadn't been for his voice in her head, as clear as day, she might never have felt the weight of the lapis lazuli in her jeans pocket. And Owen might have been too late. Knowing that if she spoke, her voice would break, Ava simply nodded. She and the chief sat together in silence for a moment, neither needing to say a word. Then Chief Greathouse chuckled and got to his feet.

"Well," he drawled. "I'll go see if they're about done in there with Owen. I'd say you two deserve some takeout and a night in."

"No," Ava all but barked. "I mean, he's not—we're not—I'll go home by myself."

The chief chuckled again, opening the door to the office. "Whatever you say. But couple or no, I recommend you take that man along the next time you embark on any late-night church field trips."

This time Ava laughed, swishing her hand toward the door as a signal for the chief to get on with his business. At this rate, he was just going to keep hounding her about whatever relationship he imagined between her and Owen. Greathouse shot Ava a knowing wink and disappeared into the office.

Owen appeared five minutes later. Ava heard his voice still conversing with Officer Harding as he opened the door a crack, telling him goodbye and stepping out into the lobby. His green eyes scanned the room before they fell on Ava, sitting on the folding chair and still holding the cup of wretched coffee in her trembling hands. She offered him a small smile and stood up to meet him.

"Hey," he said, his tone warm but worried. "Greathouse said you were okay, but god—Ava, you look like hell."

She grimaced, narrowing her eyes at him. "That seems to be the common consensus, yes."

At this, Owen's face broke into a grin. "Well, I see Chris didn't scare the sass out of you. That's a relief."

He looked at her a moment, his face awash with something she couldn't read, and then, without warning, wrapped his arms around her and drew her toward him, crushing her to his chest. They stayed like that for a moment, Ava barely daring to breathe, her arms still by her sides. He smelled good, like hardwood floors and fresh mown grass. Gingerly, she let herself draw in a shaky breath. Her hands crept up to rest on the small of his back, and she felt his chin rest gently on the top of her head. Her limbs felt light, like the heaviness of the night, that darkness that had threatened to close in, had lifted, leaving her buoyant and free. After a moment, Owen released her, drawing back and letting his hands slide down her arms. He grasped her wrists, gazing at her. His eyes were kind, green dappled with gold the way the sunlight streams through foliage in the golden hour.

"Thank you," Ava said, her voice quiet. What else was there to say? He'd saved her life.

"No need," Owen said, giving her hand a squeeze and shaking his tousled head. "Let's get you home."

Despite Rose's stern voice over the phone on the way home, insisting that she take a day off after what she'd "been through", Ava arrived at Arcana the following morning bright and early, the same time she always did. After Owen had driven her home and walked her to the front door (which, to her relief, was still locked), she'd barely managed to strip off her jeans and splash water across her frazzled face before tumbling into bed. Still, the pale pink morning sun lit up her bedroom window at the same time it always did, a peace offering after the torrential winds of the day before. A steaming shower and a cup of coffee later, Ava was on her bicycle and headed downtown. The chill of the morning air on her face made her happy to be alive. And rightly so—she was lucky *to* be.

Her shop was exactly the way she'd left it the evening before—no surprises. The books still in a neat little pile on the coffee table, the easel with the daily roasts written painstakingly across its front leaning near the door, ready to go. With Riley not having arrived yet, Ava set the first pots of coffee to brew and stepped across the creaking floor to stand by the bay windows. Main Street was all but deserted, the tiny town of

Shiloh still in a half-slumber. Soon, Tim Meyer would come striding down the sidewalk on his way to the gallery, checking his watch as he went, and the staff in the stationery store across the street would flick their overhead lights to life. It was in these moments, as the town was just opening its eyes for the day and stretching itself awake, when Ava saw the Shiloh she remembered. She could see it at its gentlest. And she was a part of it.

Ava set to work opening the cafe, straightening the chairs, counting the ones and fives in the cash register drawer. The rich aroma of fresh brewed coffee danced through the shop, and Ava relished the familiar gurgle of the coffee machines as they worked, dripping down their rich, earthy liquid. At a quarter past seven, the front door swung open and in rushed a disheveled, windswept Riley. Her cheeks were pink, and her eyes, though flustered, glowed with excitement.

"Sorry, sorry, sorry," Riley burst out in a single breath as she slammed the door behind her and tied an apron around her waist. "I slept through my alarm and—" She froze, looking wide-eyed at Ava as though she'd just realized something. "Oh my *god*, Ava. My mom heard from Mr. Whitlock, who I guess heard from Juanita, who heard from Marge that—"

"Slow down there, champ," Ava said with a half grin, pushing a mug of hot coffee into Riley's hands. "First off, you're fine. No harm done. Second—yes. Last night was a nightmare in every sense of the word, but I'm alive."

Riley still stared at her, barely taking her eyes off Ava as she took a sip of her coffee. She winced. "Holy crap, that's hot."

"It better be," Ava said, pouring a cup for herself as well.

"So what *happened*?" Riley's face was questioning, but behind it, Ava sensed something that almost looked like fear.

"Are you leaving Shiloh? My mom said there's no way you'll stick around after something like *that*."

That was when Ava realized: The fear she saw in Riley's face wasn't because of Chris—it was because she'd convinced herself Ava would leave. That not only would Riley's job be gone, but so would her only chance of staying in Shiloh. For Riley, more than a murder investigation had hung on the events of the previous night.

Ava shook her head. "Well, you can tell your mom she's wrong. It's going to take a lot more than a little showdown with Chris Mitchell to get rid of me."

Although her expression remained unflappable, Riley's eyes lit up. The girl spoke slowly, as though trying hard not to betray her excitement. "Well, if the offer still stands—you know, with you staying and all..."

"Your parents have decided you can stay with me?" Ava shot the girl a smile.

Riley grinned back. "Exactly. They said if you can handle something like a murderer, you might be able to handle me."

"Perfect," Ava said, giving Riley the tiniest of squeezes. Hugs had never been her forte, but she felt the moment called for it. "We can keep tabs on each other."

At eight o'clock on the dot, the doorbell tinkled, and the front door opened; Tim Meyer was right on time. He wore his usual cuffed jeans and t-shirt, looking every way the artist as he pushed his black-framed glasses up higher on his nose.

"Ava," Tim announced, giving her an incredulous look as he sauntered up to the counter. He placed both his palms on the countertop. "If ever there was a day to take a day off, this would've been it."

Riley was right. Word about her showdown with Chris at St.

Patrick's had already spread around town—no surprise there. Ava gave an apologetic smile and shrugged. "In all honesty, I'd rather be here today than sitting at home thinking."

"Ah," Tim said, as Ava gestured questioningly at the pot of medium roast coffee. His usual. He nodded. "Well, in that case, we're glad to have you, but..." His voice trailed off. It was clear he was dying of curiosity, but was unsure how much to ask.

Ava set the cup down on the counter and Tim took it from her, curling his hands around it. She smiled, a bit of a glint in her eye. "You want to know what happened?"

"Oh, thank *god*," Riley all but moaned. "I thought you'd never get around to telling us..."

Tim let out an emphatic breath. "Marge Harding called my wife last night as we were getting ready for bed, said she'd heard from Dan that you and Owen had been at the station. Told some story about Chris—Chris *Mitchell*—holding you at gunpoint, saying he killed Audrey and was going to kill you. Greathouse apparently confirmed the story but refused to give details."

Tim finished his monologue in what seemed like one long breath. Despite the gravity of the story she was about to have to recall, Ava nearly laughed. He was so in earnest.

"It's true," Ava admitted. Next to her, Riley sucked in her breath. "But honestly, I'm not sure how much I'm supposed to say. Even though we have a confession, it *is* innocent until proven guilty, after all."

"Right, right," Tim said, brushing away that fact as though it paled in comparison to the dramatic story he was after. "But— oh, I hope you don't mind if I ask—what about Joel Robinson? The note, the button—" he lowered his voice "—the *affair*..."

No sooner had the words left his mouth than Tim straightened, feigning an air of nonchalance. The door opened and there was Rose, cheeks flushed pink. She ran straight at Ava, throwing her arms around her friend's neck and letting out something close to a wail. Ava patted Rose's back awkwardly, trying not to make eye contact with Riley or Tim. She was glad she was alive, too, but she could have done without the theatrics.

Finally, Rose released her hold on Ava. "You should *never* have gone in that church alone."

A flicker of smile flashed on Ava's face. "Oh, you don't say? And here I was thinking it had gone quite well."

Rose rolled her eyes, then stepped back. "Well—*well* is debatable. I guess we have you to thank for Chris's confession, but I doubt he'd planned to give it to you alive."

Tim cleared his throat. He glanced from Ava to Rose, as though trying to decide whether to ask the question that was on the tip of his tongue. "Do you mind, uh, filling us in—"

"It was a set-up," Rose cut in, perhaps a little more forcefully than she'd meant to. She was no doubt steeling herself for the barrage of questions people around town were sure to ask.

"Joel was an easy target for Chris to pin Audrey's murder on," Ava said. "Actually, Greathouse released him *before* my run-in with Chris. That note was forged. Turns out Chris had been, um, practicing other people's signatures on certain important documents at the firm, and he put his skills to work in framing Joel."

Riley's eyes grew wide, realization dawning. She and Tim exchanged glances. "And the button?"

"Joel's jacket got mixed in with Chris's dry cleaning," Ava continued, shrugging. "Which is what gave Chris the idea to frame him in the first place. Like, he realized he might actually be able to pull it off."

Tim sipped his coffee, looking pensive. There was clearly something else he wanted to ask. Even though no other customers had entered the shop after Rose, he leaned forward, his voice still low. "But... why? Why did Chris kill Audrey? She found out about the forgeries?"

"Yeah," Rose put in, eyes narrowing. "He just—what? Needed to get rid of her?"

Ava nodded, wiping the steaming wand down with a towel. "Yes, although there's a bit more to it than that. Suffice it to say they had a history, and he had motive—but I'm not at liberty to say more."

Juanita's face flashed into her mind. Sweet, feisty Juanita, who had gotten so good at hiding her broken heart, Ava would never have guessed the tragic secrets she kept guarded inside. Everyone had their own dark side of the moon, and what had happened to Tiffany Martinez was not Ava's story to tell. Not now.

"Understood."

Ava's phone buzzed in her pocket. As Rose, Tim, and Riley continued their chattering, she extracted her phone and glanced at the screen. Her body tensed. It didn't matter that she'd deleted the number that now appeared on the screen— she'd recognize it on her death bed. The number belonged to Noah Shapiro. Noah Shapiro was calling her.

Ava stared at the still buzzing phone a moment, trying to regather herself. She'd called her mother last night following her conversation with Greathouse. It must have been Sara who'd alerted Noah to his ex-wife's brush with death, most likely as a last-ditch attempt at getting her daughter and her

Jewish, professionally successful, acclaimed former son-in-law back together. With trembling hands, Ava silenced the call. She wasn't about to let the sound of her ex-husband's voice shroud the day in pathetic, pining nostalgia. She'd deal with Noah later. Or... maybe not at all. That ship had sailed. Today, she was thankful to be alive and sailing under her own wind.

Tim grabbed a lid from the stack next to the cash register and fit it onto his cup. Sliding her phone back into her apron pocket, Ava willed her muscles to loosen, her face to relax.

"You're *sure* you're okay?" Tim regarded Ava skeptically. She could tell he'd glimpsed the unease that had no doubt darkened her face for a moment.

"I'm sure," Ava said.

"Well," Tim began, a glimmer of mischief lighting his eyes. "I guess you must be, having Owen O'Kelly rushing in to save your life."

Rose tittered, her blond lashes fluttering. Beside her, Riley shot Ava a small smile, her cheeks growing pink once more. It was obvious Riley was still flustered at any mention of Owen.

"Ha." Ava just laughed, shaking her head. What was it with these people and their obsession with her and Owen?

"Okay, okay," Tim said, holding his free hand up in innocence. "I'll get going."

Tim's departure was the opening of the floodgates. As Main Street filled up with the cars of shoppers making their way downtown for their morning errands, so did Cafe Arcana. Some of the more familiar folks shot strange glances her way, most likely having heard things around town already, but not enough for them to ask about. Rose stayed long enough to answer the most gossip-hungry customers' questions, leaving

Ava to go about her business, refilling coffee mugs for the folks who stayed to chat around the tables.

When the doorbell jingled just after lunch and a tight-lipped older woman stepped gingerly across the hardwood floors, Ava nearly dropped the pitcher of milk she was steaming. *Is that...?* Riley's gaze flashed to meet Ava's, her eyebrows raised. The look on the girl's face told Ava her suspicions were correct. They'd only met once, at a dinner that now seemed a lifetime ago, but the woman who'd just entered her shop was, no doubt about it, Donna Schroeder.

Ava straightened up, expertly pouring a layer of foam atop the cappuccino she was making. She flashed a small smile in Donna's direction. "Hi, welcome in. Can I get something started for you?"

Donna's face remained drawn, but she managed to pull up the corners of her pink lips in what could, Ava conceded, be taken as a smile. "A latte, please."

"Sure," Ava said, still smiling. She slid the finished cappuccino across the counter to the guest who'd ordered it. "For here or to go?"

"To go," Donna said firmly.

Well, Ava thought with a wry smile as she pulled a cup down from the stack. *It's a big enough deal that Donna Schroeder has even shown her face in my den of sin.* There was only so much she could expect from the woman on her first visit, after all. Baby steps, baby steps.

The pleasant hum of voices buzzed through the cafe, underscoring the hiss of steaming milk. Donna paused at the register, fiddling with her billfold. She cleared her throat. "I heard about your awful encounter with Chris Mitchell last night."

"I'm sure you did," Ava replied, a sheepish smile on her face. "Ninety percent of the town seems to know more about it than I do. Honestly, it's all kind of a blur."

"I just can't imagine," Donna said stiffly, which Ava supposed was true. She had a hard time picturing Donna imagining anything.

"I'll be alright." Ava poured the freshly steamed milk into the cup of espresso, stirring as she went. "The important thing is that no one else was hurt, and that Chris has been apprehended."

"Yes, I suppose your meddling was a boon in the end," Donna said, barely repressing a sigh. Her expression as Ava handed her the latte was one of pained acceptance.

"I guess it was," Ava agreed. She met Donna's drawn face with a knowing smile. "Anyway, I hope I see you around again. You take care, Donna."

"You as well," Donna replied with a firm nod of her permed head. Grasping her coffee, she lumbered out the door the way she'd come.

Ava turned back to the register and opened a fresh roll of quarters. The drawer was the fullest it had been since she opened the shop.

"Well, hey," Riley remarked as she moved to wipe the crumbs off a recently vacated table. "That seemed like progress. I'd say you're moving into queen of cups territory now."

"Gee, thanks." Ava suppressed an eye roll. She had to admit it was impressive how well Riley had remembered the card meanings. "Well, what about Donna? I'd hardly say she's giving off cups energy..."

"Oh, god, no." Riley frowned, thinking a moment. Then,

casting a mischievous glance at Ava, she announced: "Judgment. Donna's definitely Judgment."

"Girl, I have taught you *well*," Ava replied, giving Riley a clap on the back as they both erupted in laughter.

It was true Donna still exuded judgment, but she'd initiated a step toward peace, for which Ava was grateful. It was funny what could come of a person's intent to harm, she thought. Chris had meant to kill her, but in the end, he'd only made her more alive. Arcana was full for the first time, an unraveling relationship had been mended, and her walls had even come down an inch or two. She understood now that independence didn't need to be a cold feeling. Today she felt strong and independent, cared about and, yes, for the first time in, well, she didn't know when, she felt warm inside. The kind of warm that comes from a small, close-knit town. This was what she had needed from Shiloh: normalcy, simplicity, *community*.

22

———

The sun was high in the sky as Ava made her way toward the furthest side of the cemetery. She could barely make out the distant hum of carnival rides and the shrieks of gleeful children that echoed hazily upward from the town below, but she paused to take in the sounds. If her grandfather could hear them, wherever he was, Ava felt sure he was smiling. She hoped he knew that Shiloh Days had done well for her little cafe, making it one of the busiest spots on Main Street this weekend.

Ava stood, shielding her eyes from the sun, searching the span of lush green lawn for the exact location. There. Several yards away stood a beautifully polished wrought iron fence, a regal star of David sitting atop the gate. The Jewish section of the cemetery was small—a far cry from the cemeteries she'd visited with her mother's family in Chicago. Although she only came once a year on their *yahrzeits*, finding her grandparents' graves wasn't difficult, given that there were only a handful of graves in this section of the Shiloh Cemetery. Melvin and Ruth Goldberg's headstones were made of simple, gray stone, but even from his home two states away, Ava's father and his siblings made sure they stayed well kept, the grass around them trimmed and full.

She stood silently in the grass, gazing down at the Hebrew names etched into the stone. It was hard to believe it had been five whole years since Zaidy Mel had passed. Ava didn't remember her grandmother well as she'd died when Ava was small, but Zaidy—

Ava drew a deep breath. She wouldn't cry. She was scheduled at five to get a pie in the face, thanks to a partnered marketing effort initiated by herself and Owen. The day after Ava's run-in with Chris, Owen had shown up at the cafe with a boxful of *rugelach* that were so delectable Ava swore even her Jewish mother would have been impressed. Owen claimed he just hadn't been able to bear the idea of the town going hungry as they sipped their afternoon joe. The next day he'd shown up with another box, and by the weekend, he and Ava had decided to sit down and come up with a plan, factoring in how best to put Ava's reward money to use. It was too early to tell yet just how Owen's baked contributions would shape the future of Arcana, but the two were hopeful about their joint business venture. And really, there was nothing to cry about. She was safe. She was taken care of. And she was more whole than she'd felt in a long, long time. Zaidy Mel must have been right about Shiloh. It was a special place.

"Ava? Did you find it?"

Tearing herself from her thoughts, Ava turned from where she stood to see her mother traipsing daintily across the cut grass. Sara Goldberg clutched her handbag as she stepped through the gate, latched it behind her, and came to stand next to her daughter. Ava glanced down at her mother's strappy sandals, smothering a smile at the perfectly polished toenails that peeked out. Not even Shiloh Days could catch Sara Goldberg looking anything less than chic.

"Yeah," Ava said, her voice low. She wanted to preserve the air of reverence, the stillness of the vast blue skies above, that hung over the place.

Ava and her mother stood for a moment in silence, listening to the rustle of the cedar trees as the breeze sifted through them. Neither woman had spoken of the envelope addressed to *Mrs. Ava Shapiro*, or the award Noah had won for outstanding service. There had been no mention of Noah's phone call, which Ava had never returned. Neither mother nor daughter had even mentioned the precarious circumstances of Arcana's success, or the bated breath that Ava continued to live with day in and day out, crossing her fingers that her business would gain traction. And they certainly hadn't mentioned Owen, the friend and baker extraordinaire, who was handsome, polite— and decidedly *not* Jewish. Ava knew she wouldn't be able to skirt the issues forever; sooner or later, she'd have to pull herself together and say what needed to be said, no matter how hard it turned out to be. But for now, in the wake of Audrey's murder and her own brush with death, Ava was content to live a while longer in the tension. After all, disagreements be damned, her mother had come when she'd needed her, and that counted for something.

"The grass looks uneven," Sara Goldberg remarked, breaking the silence. She sighed. "Your father will have to have a talk with the gardener when he's here in September."

Ava started. She turned to her mother, eyes narrowed. "Come again?"

"The holidays, honey," Sara said, waving a manicured hand. "Your father and I decided it'd be fun to spend Rosh Hashanah here with you. You know, get out of the city, have a change of scenery. It'll be lovely!"

"Oh."

It was all Ava could do to hide the shock as it smacked her. Her parents? Were planning to spend Rosh Hashanah in Shiloh? With *her*—and Riley—at her *house*? Ava closed her eyes. It was a good thing Yom Kippur—the Day of Atonement —occurred ten days after the new year because she was bound to need some serious forgiveness after *this* was over. She inhaled, tried to push the thought from her mind. This was not a fight for today. She and her parents would sort their holiday plans out later. Just as she was working on letting go of the past, she also needed to relinquish her grip on the future.

Sara Goldberg glanced at her watch, sending a glare of sudden light dancing across the headstone in front of them.

"Twenty minutes until your pie-ing." Mrs. Goldberg turned to her daughter, a sly smile flashing across her red lips. "I'll go wait in the car, honey, okay?"

"Alright." Ava handed her mother the keys and watched her traipse back the way she had come. She knew she'd need to head back to Arcana soon to take the festivities over from Riley, but there was something she still needed to do.

Reaching a hand into her jeans pocket, Ava fingered the lapis lazuli she'd brought along, the same one she'd thrown at Chris's face inside St. Patrick's church. She'd gone back with Greathouse a few days after to walk him through the chain of events and had spotted it lying in the corner of the confessional room. It was cool to the touch when she picked it up, as though it had simply bounced off Chris, repelled his negative energy. It was cool now, too, despite being in her pocket. Pulling it out of her pocket, she held it in her palm and watched it catch the sunlight. Her grandfather had once held this stone in his cool, papery fingers. She remembered the day he gave it to her and wondered if he had known just how much she'd need it someday.

"Well," Ava said aloud, hoping her grandfather was listening somewhere. "We did it. *Yasher koach*, Zaidy."

Then, smiling to herself, she walked forward and placed the small blue stone on the gravestone. Making her way back across the cemetery, she stopped near the star-of-David-topped gate to look back, doing so once more just before she reached her car. Even there, from such a distance away, she could have sworn she saw a twinkle of blue, dancing in the light of the afternoon sun.

A NOTE FROM ALIZA

If you enjoyed *A Deck Stacked for Murder*, I'd love for you to let your friends know so they can follow Ava on her adventures, too! And if you leave a review for the book—whether that's on Amazon, Goodreads, or somewhere else—I'd love to read it. Email me the link at aliza@alizalevinebooks.com.

Want more Cafe Arcana? Keep reading for a sneak peek from Book 2, *Shofar, So Good*, where Ava's parents visit Shiloh for Rosh Hashanah and find themselves tangled up in a murder investigation!

Preorder *Shofar, So Good* at alizalevinebooks.com/preorder or scan this code with your phone:

SHOFAR, SO GOOD

SNEAK PEEK

Ava was jittery. She'd had entirely too much coffee, and now, on the way to the airport, her hands shook at the steering wheel. Her parents, on their way to spend Rosh Hashanah in Shiloh, were landing in an hour. With rush hour traffic well underway, that meant Ava would get to Eppley Airport just in time to meet Michael and Sara Goldberg as they got off the plane. And that was probably for the best—not being early meant there'd be less time to nervously down lattes at Scooters and flood her bloodstream with even more caffeine.

As Ava merged onto the I-80 on-ramp, the still brilliant sun flared orange in her rear-view mirror. She slid her sunglasses down off the top of her head. There was more than a month to go before they'd need to turn the clocks back, but the autumn days were getting shorter. Just the thought of crisp, dark nights and crackling bonfires surrounded by glowing pumpkins brought a chill of excitement to Ava's skin. Those days were coming. But she'd have to get through the holidays—and her parents' visit—first.

Ava rolled down the windows, feeling the cool September

air drift through the front seat of her car and tousle her chestnut hair. It was gloriously fall—and there was less than a week until October, the most glorious month in the Midwest. She cranked up the radio, grooving as she drove, not even minding the ads as they blared their discounts for haunted houses and apple picking tours. Now in the heart of downtown Omaha, Ava wound near what folks called the *new* baseball stadium, glimpsed the CHI Health Center Arena in the distance where the likes of Elton John and Paul McCartney were said to play, and bumped along the uneven pavement toward the airport. As she passed the *Welcome to Iowa* sign on her right, Ava snorted to herself. The states were so close that you had to pass through one to get to the airport of the other, yet all the Nebraskans she knew were adamant about not being mistaken for Iowans. She wondered if Iowans returned the sentiment.

Eppley Airport was surprisingly empty as Ava whipped her little car into a spot on the first floor of the parking garage. As she followed the passageway from the parking garage to the terminal, she was surprised to find herself nervous. Not only was it the first time since moving to Shiloh that *both* her parents would be visiting, but it was also the first time since her divorce that she'd be hosting them for a holiday. She could only pray that Riley, her teenaged employee who'd come to stay with her while she sorted out her family situation, would be on her best behavior.

Ava took the escalator up to the second floor and walked toward the airport's sole arrivals hall. As she leaned near the wall of a lonely gift shop, the clatter of dishes and the hiss of a steam wand from the nearby Scooters drifted toward her. She'd ended up with five minutes to spare and coffee *did* sound good, but remembering how her nervous self had splashed an espresso shot down her front an hour before told her it wasn't a good idea. No, what she needed was calm. She needed to be relaxed if she was going to field the barbed questions her mother would almost certainly have come armed with. Besides, they could stop at Cafe Arcana on the way back—her father had yet to see her shop in person.

A steady flow of passengers was beginning to trickle through the terminal exit, their luggage trailing along behind them. Tired dads with toddlers on the shoulders and Huskers caps pulled down low on their brows strode purposefully down the hall, accompanied by somehow still chipper moms who cooed and tugged at their baby's feet. There was also the occasional fresh-looking older woman who must have primped in the airplane lavatory before exiting the plane. Sara Goldberg would no doubt be one of these.

And there she was. There *they* were, Mike and Sara Goldberg, coming down the hallway toward her, each with a carry-on bag trailing the carpet behind them. Sara saw Ava first. Her darkly fringed eyes lit up as she waved a hand enthusiastically in the air. Ava almost smirked as she caught sight of her mother, noting how put together Sara Goldberg looked. *As expected.*

"Ava!" Sara called, elbowing her husband in the ribs. "Honey! Over here."

Ava grimaced, gestured to her mother to keep her voice down. They were in public, after all. As the pair neared her in the hallway, Mike cast one last look at his iPhone, then tucked it into the holster he wore at his belt. *Ever the dad.*

"How was the flight?" Ava asked, throwing an arm around

her mother's waist and standing on tiptoe to give her dad a peck on the cheek.

"Aside from the food—which, I can assure you, has gone downhill—not as bad as the last time I flew to see you." Sara Goldberg was searching for a cleansing wipe in her handbag. She ripped off the top of the package with perfectly manicured acrylic nails and set to work wiping the last of the plane germs from her fingers. She stretched a hand in front of her, bejeweled rings glistening in the fluorescent lights of the terminal.

"Can you believe it's only an hour?" Ava's father's eyes grew wide. Clearly, he could not.

Sara swatted her husband's arm. "Oh, Michael, really. You act like this is the first time you've ever flown into Omaha."

"Well, it's been *years*." Mike Goldberg ran long fingers through his wiry hair, repositioned the arms of his glasses atop his ears. "It was a pleasant surprise, that quick trip."

"Yeah? Must be nice," Ava put in, casting a teasing glance at her father. "It took me nine hours to make it here with my U-Haul."

Barreling ahead as always, Mrs. Goldberg cleared her throat. She glanced from her daughter to her husband, then back again. "Are you parked out front?"

"No, they don't allow waiting in the terminal loop. I'm afraid you're going to have to rough it in your heels, Mom." Ava flashed her mother a wicked grin but took the handle of the rolling suitcase from her grasp.

Mrs. Goldberg sighed. "I was afraid that's what you were going to say." She tugged the handle of her suitcase back from Ava and began plodding delicately down the carpeted hallway toward the escalator.

Mr. Goldberg followed his wife onto the escalator, leaning

backwards onto the railing. His salt and pepper hair was thick, effortlessly parted and pomaded to one side. He looked every bit the professor he was, which his father before him had been as well. Suddenly, his face lit up.

"Ava!" Mr. Goldberg hissed, jerking upwards off the escalator railing. Frantically, he began to dig into the front zipper pocket of his carry-on case. "I've got to show you something."

Mrs. Goldberg's eyes followed her husband. He stepped off the escalator at the bottom and pulled his luggage to the side, this time opening it completely to rifle through the pile of crisply folded button-down shirts and chinos layered inside. At this, his wife jumped forward.

"Not in the airport, Michael," Mrs. Goldberg barked. "No one wants to hear that."

"It'll only take a second," Mr. Goldberg said, dismissing her with a wave of his free hand. "Ava needs to hear it."

Hear it? As curious as she was, Ava had to admit she shared in her mother's wariness. There was no telling what kind of bee Michael Goldberg might get into his bonnet next, and she wasn't sure she wanted the whole of Eppley Airport witnessing whatever it was. Hearing whatever it was.

"Aha!" Mr. Goldberg said in triumph, extracting a small plastic sack from beneath his socks and underwear. "Behold."

"Oy vey," Mrs. Goldberg muttered under her breath, taking a few steps away from her husband. She turned her back.

As soon as she saw the outline of the sack's contents, Ava rushed forward to snatch the package from her father's hands. She knew what was inside. It was bad enough that she'd no doubt have to listen to it for three days straight, but there was no *way* she would let him blow that thing—

A piercing wail, something like a dying elephant, shattered

through the bustling sounds of the airport. Ava's hands shot to her ears, her face stricken with horror. But no sooner had her palms covered her ears than the dying elephant sound sputtered out, leaving her father with cheeks puffed out and blue in the face, gasping for air. He lowered the horn from his lips and looked giddily at Ava, his eyes gleeful.

"Did you hear it? I got it there—for a split second, I had it!" Mike Goldberg announced, pumping his fist in triumph.

"Uh," Ava said. From where her mother still stood at a distance, Ava could see Sara Goldberg chancing a glance around, as though to check if the coast was clear. Her shoulders were hunched. "Yeah. You're really on your way, Dad."

Thank *God* Owen hadn't come along. Ava was sure she would've died of embarrassment. Although, if her mother's preemptive reaction was any hint at how often this had been happening, Ava wasn't so sure Owen would escape the coming few days unscathed.

"I'm saving my chops for the ride home," Mr. Goldberg said, sliding the ram's horn back in the plastic sack.

Mrs. Goldberg approached her daughter and husband, catching wind of what Mr. Goldberg had just said. "If you try that in the car, Michael, I swear on all that is holy—"

"Jeez Louise, honey," Mr. Goldberg said, pushing his glasses up on the bridge of his nose and striding toward the exit. "I'm kidding! But really, I need to be practicing. I've only got two days to get my blasts down."

Ava pretended she didn't hear him. She still couldn't believe he'd actually pulled out a shofar inside the airport. Honestly, it was a wonder that security hadn't come rushing over to see what had happened. The sounding of the ceremonial ram's horn was a central part of the Rosh Hashanah synagogue service, and becoming truly skilled at blowing the horn was a difficult feat to achieve. Clearly, her dad wasn't there yet.

"Wait," Ava said, surveying the suitcases her parents wheeled behind them. "You guys didn't check any bags? And by that, I mean *Mom* managed to fit all her shoes in *that*?" She gestured to one of the small carry-on hard-shells.

"Don't be ridiculous, Ava," Mrs. Goldberg laughed. "We'll be in *Shiloh*. I'm not going to risk getting a Louboutin run over by a tractor."

Ava sighed, hardly managing not to roll her eyes. Instead, she led her parents out to the parking garage and settled into the driver's seat. As she wound her way out of the airport lot and headed back toward the interstate, Ava listened to her parents chatter: about the ever-dwindling amount of leg room on planes, how United's frequent flyer program wasn't all it was cracked up to be, and which neighbor's relatives were in town for the holiday. So far, the idle talk was harmless—pleasant even. She just hoped to god it'd stay that way.

ACKNOWLEDGMENTS

I wrote my first mystery novel in fourth grade, saved it on a floppy disk, and used the school printer to print the whole thing out. My mom read every page, just like she did for the early drafts of this book. I hope to G-d this one is better.

My parents always told me I'd be a writer, and I don't think they ever doubted it, even when I did. Thank you, Thomas and Gina, for believing in me for 30+ years and treating my future identity as an author as a given. Thank you for carting me constantly to the library and for still housing my childhood books. I love you both.

Thank you, Micah, for the many hours spent hashing out plot points and tying up loose ends. This mystery would not have come together without you as my sounding board. Nathan and Maggie, thank you for always being excited along with me and for reading my early drafts. You both made me feel like a real author.

Hope, thank you for being one of the earliest readers of this book. I've never told you this, but as I write, I write for you to read it. You are, quite literally, my target reader. So when you read the book and loved it, it was like—YES!

A million thanks also go to Dror and Michal for being so excited for me throughout this whole project, watching Adi while I worked on the launch, and providing valuable insights as publishers themselves; to my editor, Sandra, for being meticulous, yet always kind, and for helping me turn this story into a solid, polished book; to Tamar, Noam, and Shira for their input on the cover design and asking for launch plan updates each Shabbat; to Iris, for selling her company and giving me the perfect opportunity to finally finish this book (and encouraging me to do so); to Arik, who showed so much support the whole way through and provided endless marketing expertise; and to Mrs. Bundy, who not only put up with my weird, wordy "short" stories for four whole years, but actually encouraged them.

I also need to thank Nebraska for being the perfect place to spend a childhood. You may not be for everyone, but you certainly are the good life.

Adi, you can't read yet, but I am so happy that you'll grow up seeing Mama's books on our shelf. Thank you for being a good little sleeper and letting me get the rest I needed to finish this book.

And Ehud—what can I even say? I simply could not have written this book without you. You gave me time to write, even after our daughter was born and we found ourselves drowning in a sea of diapers and lone baby socks. You brought me coffee on the days I was so tired I couldn't think straight. You made dinner at night so I could keep editing, helped me with my website, talked through character arcs with me, and were even okay with me writing on our honeymoon. Thank you, from the bottom of my heart, for your constant support and belief in me. I love you.

ABOUT THE AUTHOR

Aliza Levine is a writer, tarot reader, and homegrown Nebraskan who lives for that first sip of coffee each morning. When she isn't writing, she's crocheting, running after her baby daughter, or watching ungodly amounts of *Murder She Wrote*. This is her first novel.